A SENSE OF LIES

By Paul Knight

"So we beat on, boats against the current,

borne back ceaselessly into the past."

F. Scott Fitzgerald

CHAPTER 1

MARCH 2018

The reaction to Helen's outburst during lunch the previous Autumn had created a split of opinion amongst the Elders. Until she had snapped in rage, Helen had kept up her alter ego of Martha, the woman the Community wanted to see, for years. It was clear the Elders had not made the progress they thought. She was even clinging onto the name she had taken in the outside world. For some it was evidence that she could not be retaught the lessons necessary for her to come fully back into the Community. Amongst those who agreed no more time should be wasted on her, there was no agreement over what to do.

An obvious solution would be to settle her into The Lodge; a building on the edge of the estate where the Community members who were too frail to contribute were housed. Most of the residents of The Lodge were simply old, with dementia creeping in for some of them. It had been used, too, for those who were weak in faith. So weak that if they were allowed to leave, they could become an active force against the Community from the outside world.

The Lodge, though, was unsuitable for Helen, given one of its current members. This option had only been suggested by the Elders who had not been around when Helen, then known as Martha, had escaped from the Community as a teenager. When the point was raised, the more senior of the Elders exchanged looks that quickly told everyone that it would not be pursued.

They could, of course, simply allow her to go. But no one believed she would leave without her son, or if she did, she would come back with lawyers or the police. They would have to move Ollie to another Community site. His grandparents, Elder Christopher and his wife, would resist that. There were just too many complications.

In the absence of an obvious solution, the thinking was pulled towards a renewed effort to bring her fully back to the faith. Daniel, one of the young men in the Community, had been given the task of correcting her, and he had spent the last few years working on this. Everyone accepted that he had made good progress. They could all see how Helen followed him around faithfully and that they spent a lot of time together talking. Daniel reported that she was indeed blessed with the true faith, and that they would soon be able to see the truth coming through her. Daniel was an excellent member of the Community and would surely be a future leader. His view could be trusted.

A concession was required, however. Something had to be done. So, it was resolved that a second level of support would be introduced. More subtly this time. They would find a young woman from the Community who could be trusted to spend time with Helen and report back on her state of mind. It was decided; she would be assigned a friend.

CHAPTER 2

Saric generally avoided shopping. Almost anything he needed could be bought online and delivered to his door without requiring him to spend time navigating crowds and dealing with over-friendly shop assistants.

One exception to this rule was shopping for books.

The logical part of Saric's mind knew that it would make more sense to download books to his tablet; they could be obtained immediately, at any time of the day or night, and would not take up space and create clutter in a house that was otherwise devoid of personal possessions that did not serve a purpose.

But shopping for books was different. Of course, the shop had to be the right one. Chain stores piled high only with bestsellers and staffed by people who had no interest in anything but what was on the cover would not work. But, in the right place, the ritual of buying books was a pleasure.

A small bell chimed as Saric walked through the door to *Downsview Books*. He had found the shop several years previously at the quiet end of the high street of a local town and was now a regular visitor. It was set in a three-storey property, which must have been residential when originally built. The walls had been knocked through to create a shop space, but as you walked across the ground floor, you could still see where the different rooms would have been located.

There was something about the air in a bookshop that made Saric relax. Perhaps it was the way the shelves lining every possible wall insulated the space from outside noise. Whatever it was, as Saric breathed deeply and exhaled slowly, he felt some of the tension of the last few weeks leave his body.

The ground floor was stocked with a selection of fiction and nonfiction, which had been carefully curated by the owner. The bestsellers were there, of course, but they were surrounded by the classics and stories from obscure authors from around the world.

As a child, Saric had read only nonfiction, predominantly concerning military history and the natural world, but over the last few years his tastes had broadened to include more fiction, and he was slowly working through some of the classics of science fiction, guided always by recommendations from the shop's owner, with the occasional suggestion from his friend, Rob.

Hannah Bond had grown up in the town and taken over the shop from her father three decades previously. Since taking it on she had built an excellent reputation for championing local authors and sourcing rare books. She had also continued to develop the shop's collection of books on local history, which was housed on the first floor.

In its past, the first floor must have been used for bedrooms, but these had since been transformed into more space for bookshelves. While the upstairs was open to anyone to browse, in Saric's experience, few patrons made it past the table of paperbacks at the front of the shop, so these rooms were usually empty. When the shop was quiet, this was where Hannah would spend her time.

The stairs to the first floor were at the back of the shop and had been built in a time when men as broad as Saric were even more unusual than today. Saric had to turn sideways to make his way up the narrow staircase, emerging slightly uncomfortably on the small landing at the top.

Hannah was standing with her back to him in the room at the far end of the corridor. She was taller than average and in her early 60s, although she looked several years younger. She was always well dressed in an unusual but not outrageous style. Today, she was wearing grey jeans with a tweed blazer, and her grey hair was pulled back in a messy bun.

Something in the way she was standing was not quite right, and as Saric straightened up he saw the man in the room in front of her. He did not break his stride, but as Hannah turned to look at him, he saw a look in her eyes that he could not remember seeing before.

The conversation between Hannah and the man ended abruptly, as soon as he realised they were no longer alone. He straightened, pulled his shoulders back and turned, expecting to fill the room with his own importance. For the briefest moment, his eyes met Saric's. Somewhere inside Saric frowned, but his face betrayed no emotion at all. The man's energy shifted, he immediately pulled his eyes away and bustled off. As he passed Saric in the small corridor, he ducked away from him and picked up his pace, breathing out only as he reached the stairs.

Saric was confused. The bookshop was a comfortable place; a place where he went to access another world – one of information and, in recent years, imagination. And Hannah, his friend, was his guide. He trusted her and enjoyed the time he spent in her company. Never once had he been in that shop and felt anything but a sense of calm. As he stood here now, looking at her after whatever exchange had just taken place, he saw the frailty of an everyday woman, not the extraordinary woman he knew. He tried to bring things back to normal.

"I finished *The Man in the High Castle*, and I know you said I should take a break from Philip K. Dick after that, but I don't think I want to stop now."

Hannah looked up at Saric. She took a brief moment before a broad smile lit up her face. "Now, young man, you asked me to show you this world; you have to have a little faith."

She did not mention the man who had just left and Saric saw no reason to ask her about it, but he did notice that the atmosphere was different as she tried to talk him into exploring a different genre.

"What about some crime fiction?" she suggested as they explored the shelves back on the ground floor. "We've just received copies of a new book by one of our local authors. She won an award for her last one and I think this is even better."

She trailed off when she saw the blank expression on Saric's face. The last thing he needed was another mystery. And anyway, the plots were always so transparent in those things.

"OK, then—" Hannah moved on, "—what about something historical?"

Saric spent a pleasant twenty minutes listening to Hannah describe the importance of historical fiction in keeping the past alive, and eventually consented to try a weighty hardback that covered the intrigue in the court of James I. Secretly, he still wanted to carry on with the science fiction bibliography that Hannah had created for him, but he had to admit that she was usually right when it came to literature.

She asked him how he had been. "I haven't seen you for a few weeks, I was actually starting to worry."

"I've been busy with work, it's like that sometimes, when we have a case."

He did not want to explain more. In fact, the last few weeks had been some of the hardest he had faced in years. Five years, in fact. While investigating a particularly heartless murder, he and his business partner Rob had got involved with a local criminal, Jim Callagher, who had used physical violence and intimidation to try and keep them away from his dodgy business affairs. While Saric thought that, on balance, they had come off better from the exchange, it had not been easy.

They had also found a new lead in the case of Rob's missing wife and child, which had opened up old wounds for his partner. The unexplained loss of his family had torn him apart so many times already, and Saric wasn't sure it was right to put him through that again.

13

He looked up to see Hannah staring at him thoughtfully. She raised an eyebrow ever so slightly. "Coffee?"

Five minutes later, Saric was at the heavy wooden table in the kitchen of the flat on the second floor, where Hannah lived with her wife Rose and their dog Griffin. Hannah had placed a large mug of steaming coffee in front of him. A 'Back in 15 minutes' sign had been put in the window of the door downstairs.

When Saric had first moved to Sussex it had been Hannah who had found him somewhere to live and connected him to the sort of people who could send work his way. She knew everyone and was a good person. More than that, though, she was thoughtful and considered, with a good eye to notice what people were thinking and anticipate what they might do. Saric valued her opinion. As he drained his coffee, he told her about the lead on Helen's case, and about Rob's reaction. "He's falling apart," he confessed. "He thinks this solicitor will have answers, but it's unlikely he will even remember Helen's grandmother, much less know anything about where Helen and her son might have gone. I don't know how to make it better for him."

Hannah sipped her tea slowly, replaced the cup in its saucer and looked at him. "Have you ever considered that perhaps he doesn't need you to make it better?"

14

He looked at her silently, waiting.

"Perhaps what he needs is you to just be there while you wait to meet this lawyer and he feels the hope and anticipation and goes through a thousand scenarios. And, if it doesn't work out, he's going to need you to be there for that, too."

Saric left the shop with three history books in a paper bag and walked the six miles back to Rob's house. As he left the village, a man in an expensive suit and shiny shoes stepped out of the café across the road.

CHAPTER 3

The weeks following his discovery that Saric had uncovered a new lead in the search for his wife and son were hard for Rob. They had a date to visit the lawyer who had written Helen's grandmother's will, and Saric had concluded that there was little point in doing too much more with the new information before that visit.

With their most recent case now closed, Rob had not been able to distract himself from his thoughts. He would allow a sense of hope to swell up inside; the memories of his wife taking turns to remind him of how she looked at him, or held him or whispered silly words of love and contentment as they sat together on the sofa. Memories of his son found a way back in, too. Normal memories. Not the dark and brutal ones of the last few days he'd spent with him, when he'd failed to see what was coming. These only came to torment him when he dropped his guard.

But hope would not find his wife and son, and he knew that. They needed facts. And this was where Sense Check came in.

Sense Check was a computer program that harnessed the information contained within all publicly available digital information –

along with some that was not publicly available – and used it to verify the validity of facts, and to form conclusions from those facts.

Saric had designed the program himself, with the assistance of a couple of specialist computer programmers, whom he had helped with a particularly tricky situation that had arisen when a foreign government objected to some of their activities.

Cashing in that service, Saric had almost unlimited access to two of the best programmers in the world.

The program had recently helped Rob and Saric to catch a murderer, by proving that certain parts of his alibi were impossible and spotting irregularities in financial records that the police had missed. It could not think, not really at least, but it was able to identify patterns, connections and errors in quantities of information that the human mind simply could not process.

In Sense Check, they probably had the most sophisticated piece of crime detection computing in the world, but even with the entire internet available as a resource and the ability to crunch almost endless logical sequences, it had to start somewhere. That initial spark was Rob and Saric's responsibility.

The name Julia Hawkins was in Helen's grandmother's will. They needed to find out where this lead could take the investigation. Saric had run the name through Sense Check. But a name in isolation was of little use. Rob had spent several futile hours adding speculative cross-checking information to try and come up with something, guessing at age, ethnicity, country of birth, and so on. It was pointless, though. Saric told Rob to pack it in, saying he would be better off with a clear head when they actually had some facts, rather than cramming a load of useless information into his head in advance. In fact, Saric just did not want Sense Check full of unnecessary searches. Its self-learning programs needed clear success parameters to allow it to refine its approach. But he thought Rob might prefer the clear head story. Rob knew exactly what Saric meant.

Rob did relent in the end. And he went back to his weights, which he always did when he needed to try and exhaust himself enough to slow his mind. It sort of worked, as it always did.

Saric was unsure of what to do for the best. He thought about telling Rob's dad there was a new lead and letting him take care of the emotional support. But Rob had been very clear that none of his family were to suffer the chance of dashed hopes. It had been hard for them, too, and he would not make that worse. So Saric decided to let the last few days pass without interfering. If he could get an angle on this case, he would give himself to it completely. And not just because it was the only case he had never come close to solving.

Saric let himself into Rob's house and placed two bags on the table. He could hear the shower running so spent the next few minutes tidying around the kitchen. It had been a long time since anything had been cooked in there, so it was clean enough, but he could not help but put the unopened mail and free newspapers into neat piles.

Ten minutes later, Rob arrived, his hair slightly damp and his skin flushed from the heat of the shower. He looked at his friend and smiled. "You know, normal people knock, or at least tell someone that they are coming."

Saric was pleased to see the smile, even if it was short lived. It was true, now he thought about it, that he had not called ahead, but he had wanted to see Rob this evening and had been fairly sure he would be home and not busy. "OK, OK, but normal is boring. I thought you might like some company." As he said this, Saric pulled a bottle of wine from one of the bags, opened it and started to pour two glasses. "I have food, too." He pointed to the second bag.

While Saric busied himself with preparing risotto, Rob watched, leaning against a corner of the kitchen worktop. Saric tried hard to make conversation, thinking of Hannah and what she had said. He told Rob

19

about his trip to the bookshop and the new books he had bought. He only complained for a few minutes about how Hannah had forced him to try something new.

Rob continued the conversation while they sat and ate; he was not sympathetic. "You should trust her; she knows what she is talking about. And you won't be well read by only choosing one type of book, will you? Surely it's better to have read widely across genres than deeply in one?"

"It can't be. How can you possibly have an opinion on something if you haven't established all the facts? And you can only do that by reading everything on that subject."

"But they aren't facts, are they? They're just stories. And wouldn't you be better informed by having covered a wide range of topics, not just one? Unless you think you can read all the books ever published? You're good, Saric, but not that good."

That's what Sense Check is for, Saric thought to himself.

Before he could formulate the next part of his argument, Rob changed the conversation. "Why didn't you tell me they had arrested her?"

Saric did not need to ask who Rob meant. Four weeks before, they had solved the murder of an accountant, Jane Evans. She had been killed by one of her clients, and Saric had passed the evidence of this to the police, who had arrested him. They had suspected that his girlfriend may have been more involved in the murder – and the fraud that led to it – than the suspect, Colin Edwards, had been willing to confess. Rob in particular suspected that he was protecting her. As part of obtaining the confession, Saric had led Colin to believe that they would keep his girlfriend's name away from the police.

While the murder itself had not made the headlines, Detective Stephens, or perhaps his PR team, had made sure that Colin's arrest had been well publicised. The news reports had focused more on Stephens's excellent detective work than the contribution Rob and Saric had made, but that was the nature of their relationship with the police, and something that both men had come to terms with. The PR team was obviously good because, when Rob caught the tail end of the lunchtime news earlier that day, it had mentioned the arrest of a second individual in connection with the murder.

"I didn't know they had," Saric said, truthfully.

"But you knew they would."

"If she was involved, she deserves to face the consequences."

21

"You promised Colin you would protect her."

"He is a murderer. If I had to lie to him to get a confession, then that had to happen."

Both men were dissatisfied at this explanation. Rob knew that he would never betray a promise like that, much less make one, knowing he would almost inevitably go back on it. He knew Saric was different, but he did not like it.

For Saric, the position was more complicated. He would have kept his promise to Colin if he could, but when he sent the evidence to Stephens, he could not find a way to keep Sarah out of the situation that did not also incriminate Jim Callagher. While Saric and Jim had clashed during the case, they had reached a compromise that might be useful to Saric in the future. There had been a cost benefit analysis performed. Jim won and Sarah was arrested. Not perfect, but he could live with it.

Again, Rob changed the subject as he picked up the empty bottle of wine. "Do you have another of these in that bag of yours?"

Saric would have liked nothing more than to say yes, and to reignite their debate on the merits of depth and breadth of knowledge, while they got gently drunk until the small hours of tomorrow morning. But that was not for tonight and instead he leaned behind him and flicked the switch on the kettle. "I think we should probably call it a night soon; we need to leave early tomorrow."

And with that, the two men's thoughts turned to the next day. With no more discussion than when he had arrived, Saric decided to sleep in the armchair in the lounge. Going home and leaving Rob alone was not an option tonight.

CHAPTER 4

MARCH 2018

After her outburst disrupted her alter ego of the meek and compliant Martha, Helen was concerned she would have to rebuild her progress with Daniel, but it quickly became clear that her influence over him had withstood the incident. Only a modest reframing of the situation had been required.

Whilst it was important for the Community to see Helen's Martha persona, it was just as important that she continued to present herself to Daniel as the Great Mother, a leading spiritual figure for their religion. As the Great Mother, Helen had been building control over Daniel for years.

"You understand, Daniel, that I needed to do that so we could find out which of the Elders have true faith," she said.

"Er, yes, I see." He clearly did not understand what she meant.

"Those with the true faith must follow. The Elders will discuss me. You must observe those who want me to leave the Community. They will be the ones we may need to leave behind. We cannot tolerate such weak and changeable minds."

"Oh, I see." This time he did seem to follow.

Helen had taught Daniel to accept her instruction. She was the Great Mother, brought back to the world to renew the faith, and her authority could not be denied. It was not his place to question her word.

In the days that followed, Helen was kept in her room as the Elders contemplated their next steps. Daniel kept her informed on the discussions. The conclusion was that she would stay in the Community, with little change to her routine, and only the inconvenience of a friend being allocated to spy on her. It was a satisfactory outcome and Helen saw it as nothing more than an inconvenience. She was perfectly capable of feeding the right lines to whomever this friend was going to be. Hopefully, she wouldn't have to do any more than that. She knew the potential damage she could be doing to Daniel and had more or less reconciled herself to it being necessary. She did not want to have to ruin another mind to get her son out of this prison and go home.

One morning, Jessica appeared in Helen's prayer group. No explanation was given for this, or for the reason she had been moved from her previous group. Changes in the groups were not unusual. The Elders liked to make sure that the participants were well matched to be a good influence on each other, but they were usually announced with some ceremony, seen as they were as another chance for the Elders to impress upon the Community their insight into the wishes of the Great Lord.

Jessica was small, with dull brown hair and eyes that were almost grey, giving Helen the impression that at any point she might just fade away to nothing. She had approached Helen nervously and asked if she would help her to understand something that the group leader had said during the session.

"The Elder from my last group has told me how deeply you understand this, and how serious you are about your studies, so I thought you might be able to help me understand," she had said hopefully.

Helen had to suppress a laugh. This was hardly subtle, and not very clever. No Elder in the Community would have recommended that anyone consult her for guidance. She was a threat, to be contained and managed, not a role model. But she was pleased that they were underestimating her. Even without the information from Daniel, she would have seen through this plan. Helen consented and spent an hour discussing the passage from the day's meeting. Jessica was friendly and seemingly genuinely keen to learn, but she did not appear to have a single original thought in her mind. Everything she said was simply a repeat of something that had been said by their group leader that morning.

Jessica was the daughter of a friend of Helen's father. She wasn't sure that her parents truly had friends, not in the way the outside world would understand, as the Community did not allow such relationships, but Jessica's parents were the closest they had to them. They were trusted.

A few years younger than Helen, Jessica had lived in the Community all her life. She had a nervous smile and a pleasant face, although she could not be described as pretty. Importantly, to both the Elders and to Helen, she was compliant and naïve, and very keen to please those around her.

After that first prayer meeting, Jessica had found many excuses to spend time with Helen, asking for guidance or offering to help her with her chores. As they got more acquainted whilst taking inventory in the food stores, Helen started to explore how much Jessica knew about her assignment.

"Do you remember when we used to play together as children?" Helen asked. It was a perfectly innocent question, which she felt confident would not cause alarm even if Jessica did report it back.

"Not really," Jessica replied quietly. "I thought I remembered playing by the river with you and a girl with curly blonde hair, but my mother told me that can't be true because we weren't friends. I was very young when you went away."

That's true, Helen thought. She had been sixteen when she had escaped, which meant Jessica could have been no more than eleven or twelve. She wondered what Jessica's parents had told her about where she had been for the fourteen years prior to her arrival back at the Community. She suspected that whatever it was, it did not involve any of the facts of her escape, or her reasons for leaving.

Could she risk another question? She had to balance her need for information with what Jessica might report back to the Elders.

She needn't have worried. Jessica continued without prompting. "You are so lucky to have been able to experience the Great Lord's work overseas. The Great Mother must truly favour you to have led you to that calling, and at such a young age." Her pale eyes were wide now, as she looked at the older woman. "Did you not miss your parents while you were away for such a long time?"

So, that is what they had told her. She had been in another Community doing the Lord's work. She wanted to tell her what nonsense this was. She wanted to tell her about her escape from the Community and her journey to the UK. About taking on another girl's identity and living as her for fourteen years. In fact, the girl with the beautiful curls, whom Jessica remembered playing with by the river, was taken from them because the Community refused to get her the medicine she needed.

She was angry now. She wanted to tell Jessica about a world of opportunity, experience and love. But she could not do that. She had to stick to the plan. So, she summoned all her resolve, moved her face into what she hoped was the right expression and replied. "I missed them every day, but we must follow the Great Mother's plan, and her plan for me was to learn from others so that I could return to the Community and share that learning with you."

Jessica looked serious. "Sorry about your first husband."

Helen knew that to account for her son, a husband would have to be written into any fictitious past. She didn't want another lie to keep track of. "It was the Great Lord's will. I can't talk about it," she said, confident that would cover any story Jessica had been told.

"Oh, Martha. Well done."

Jessica was in awe of her, that was clear. For one moment, Helen almost felt sorry for her.

CHAPTER 5

Rob and Saric's appointment with the retired lawyer who had written Helen's grandmother's will was at 2.30 pm.

Saric had run the legal firm through Sense Check. The results were tedious. They could at least conclude that the firm was reputable. The office was in Birmingham, which is also where the lawyer was based.

Mr Sable had worked for the same legal firm for thirty-five years. For the last ten of those, he hadn't needed the money, but his almost complete lack of imagination had left him unable to find a better option for his life. He had been retired now for fifteen years and had filled his time with five grandchildren, a tidy garden and, more recently, two mild heart attacks. His mind had held up well, though. "I'm alright as long as I keep my marbles," he would tell people, but he sometimes wondered if the gentle drift into a lost mind might be preferable, at least for him, to the endless worry of when 'the big one' was going to finish him off.

It was a welcome distraction when Saric contacted him. Although he had an excellent memory for clients and cases, the length of his career and the repetitive nature of the work would have made it impossible for him to add much to the vast majority of the wills he worked up for people. This case, however, was sufficiently odd in its backstory that he had no trouble remembering the client. She had a sadness in her eyes that troubled him, and the story she told of losing a daughter and gaining a granddaughter had a rare touch of drama that left him hanging on every word. It was a story he had never repeated to anyone. He had let Saric know he had information to share but knew as he said it that the amount disclosed would depend entirely on what he thought of this curious visitor. He would be quite happy to waste their journey entirely if he took a dislike to them. Why should he care?

The journey to Birmingham was almost three hours. Rob let Saric drive. He was agitated, as Saric knew he would be, of course. In the weeks running up to this interview, Saric had tried to talk to Rob. He'd suggested they review some old cases, but Rob could do no more than go through the motions. Saric then tried talking to him about the latest novel he had read; although he was quite certain it was brilliant, he was not entirely sure he really understood it. Normally, this could keep them chatting for hours. Rob tried, but the conversation felt heavy in the air and crushed the enthusiasm out of them both. Saric even tried putting a film on for them to watch, but this was such an unnatural thing for the two of them to do that it immediately felt awkward, and Saric faked an important call to put an end to it.

When he had first met Rob, Saric had not really noticed his pain. It was different now he was his friend. He felt ill-equipped to help him cope. He knew only one way to help: find his wife and son.

For the first hour of the drive, they simply sat in silence. Then Rob spoke. "What are the odds of this meeting producing anything useful?" he asked.

Fifty per cent at best, Saric thought. *Probably much lower.* "We'll make everything we can out of whatever we get," he said.

Rob did not press it. "If we find them, do you think he will recognise me?"

"Yes." Saric's tone left no room for debate.

"Do you think they want to be found?"

"Do you want the truth?"

"Yes."

"I'm less interested in what they want than I am in what you want. If she left you on purpose, leaving no message and knowing what that would do to you, then you have a right to know that, and to have her explain things to your face. If they have been taken from you, you have a right to get them back, and—"

"And what?"

"And someone is going to pay a price for what they have done."

Rob looked at Saric, who kept his eyes on the road, and let a small shot of hope through. If anyone was going to help him bring some resolution to this most personal case, it was this most unusual man.

CHAPTER 6

Mr Sable's house was a detached property that looked like it had been built in the middle of the last century. It was situated in a quiet, leafy road and had a large drive with space for three or more cars. It was similar in every respect to each of the large, detached houses on that road, which must all be owned by retired lawyers or accountants. It was just that sort of road.

There was a large car parked on the drive that must have been at least twenty years old. Leaves that had fallen from the surrounding hedges were strewn across the roof and caught at the bottom of the windscreen. It had obviously not been driven in some time.

Saric parked their car on the road outside and they walked a short distance to the door. It was answered quickly by a small woman, perhaps in her early twenties, wearing a dark grey uniform. *A carer*, Rob thought.

"Can I help you?" She had an Eastern European accent that Rob could not quite place.

"Hello, we have an appointment with Mr Sable, he should be expecting us."

"Wait here. I will check."

She retreated down the hallway and turned right through a door. A minute later, she returned. "Please come in," she said with the sort of forced smile common among people who have just had another job added to their to-do list by their employer. "Can I get you some tea or coffee?"

They accepted tea and stepped into the room on the right. It was large and bright but stuffed with more furniture than it could possibly hold. Large rugs covered a heavy, patterned carpet, and every surface was covered with ornaments, photographs and other objects. The photos were the usual family snaps, depicting individuals over several decades.

In the corner, sitting in a tall armchair that did not match the rest of the furniture, was Mr Sable. He was older than Rob had expected and dressed ready for a business meeting in the way that older retired people seem to do, even when they have not, in fact, attended such meetings for years.

"Good afternoon, gentlemen," he said with a smile. "Please come in and take a seat. You'll have to excuse the fact I'm not standing to shake your hand, but I find it rather difficult to get up and down these days."

"That's quite alright, Mr Sable, thank you for seeing us. I am Saric and this is my colleague, Rob."

"I have to say, I was rather surprised to receive your call, it has been a long time since I was in practice."

"As I said when we spoke, we are looking for information regarding Alice Hawkins and the beneficiaries of her will."

As Saric started to ask his question, the carer returned carrying a tray with a tea pot, three cups and saucers and a small jug of milk. She placed the tray on a small coffee table between the old man and Rob and was making to leave when Mr Sable interrupted.

"Please pour for us, Sofija."

Sofija gave him a dry look, seemingly wishing that she could tell him that was not part of her job, but nevertheless, she poured the tea. Saric thanked her in a language that Rob couldn't identify, and she beamed with pleasure at him as she left the room. Mr Sable studied Saric closely, as if trying to decode him.

Rob briefly wondered if Mr Sable would remember the topic of conversation, but his worries were soon dispelled.

"You understand, gentleman, that my work is covered by confidentiality agreements, which continue to apply even when the client is deceased?"

"We do, Mr Sable," Saric replied, "but this is very important. It relates to a missing person case we are investigating."

From the other side of the coffee table, he felt the tension in Rob's body.

He went on. "We are not asking you to break any confidences, but simply to give us some background on Mrs Johnson. I understand the conditions of her will were . . . unusual?"

The man sitting across the table hesitated slightly, weighing up the morality of breaking confidentiality against his obvious interest in the case. His curiosity won, at least in part. He took a sip of tea, breathed out heavily and began. "Mrs Johnson was a client of mine, first in the late eighties and then again in the early part of this century. I drafted her will for her. She had a small estate, primarily the family home, but also a small amount of cash and other investments. When we first drafted the will, her entire estate was to be left to her daughter, Julia, barring a few small items of jewellery that were to be left to her granddaughter."

Saric and Rob waited. Mr Sable was enjoying having an audience.

"Some years later, Mrs Johnson returned to me to amend her will. Now, the majority of the estate was to be left to her granddaughter, Helen, but she left a clause requiring that we retain funds to pass to the daughter in certain circumstances, namely if she returns to the UK to collect it."

"Did you ask why?" Rob struggled to contain his frustration.

"I did. She was under no obligation to tell me, of course, what a person chooses to do with their estate is their own business, but she did explain the reasons for her change of heart. In short, Julia had left the UK some years previously with her daughter – Mrs Johnson's granddaughter. She did not elaborate on the details, but I believe there was a man involved." Mr Sable had a disapproving look in his eyes as he said this. "I believe Julia had become involved with this man and he had persuaded her to leave her home and move overseas to live with him. Mrs Johnson disapproved and lost all contact with her daughter. She probably should have changed her will then, but she was still young, and I suppose she never got round to it. That happens more often than you would think."

He stopped to sip his tea and looked at the two men closely before continuing. "It would really help if you would tell me why you want to know this. I am under certain obligations, and I really don't know who you are or what you will do with this information."

Looking around, Rob could see that this man had been successful in his career. Despite its tired appearance, this was the home of a wealthy man. He was shrewd and he was asking for a deal. His information for theirs.

"We need this as part of a case we're working on," Saric stated, as if this was a sufficient explanation.

But this was not what the man wanted. He wanted details. Something to brighten up a lonely day in a series of lonely days spent sitting in that room, dreaming of the man he used to be.

It was up to Rob now to give him what he wanted. He breathed deeply, blinked slowly and sat tall in his chair. "Mr Sable, five years ago, my wife and young son disappeared during a trip to our local park. I believe they were abducted. I have not seen or heard from either of them since they left the house that morning. The police and investigators have found nothing that explains what has happened to them, and I have spent every moment since then trying to find them."

He paused and took another breath. "I know very little about my wife's past. Her parents died when she was young and she was brought up by her grandmother, Alice. I suppose Julia must have been her aunt, though she never mentioned her. But what I do have is Alice's will, which mentions Julia, and if she is alive and we can find her she might know something that could help me find out what happened to my wife. She is the only woman I have ever loved, and I don't even know if she is alive or dead. Being apart from her and my son is the worst thing that could ever happen to me, and all I want is to know the truth."

He hesitated and looked Mr Sable in the eye. Tried to read him. The old man must have been an excellent lawyer, his face gave nothing away.

"I don't know where Julia is. I don't even know if she is still alive, it has been a long time. But I want to help you. What I know is that she went to the US, somewhere in the Midwest. This man, I forget his name, was something to do with the church and got her involved in all sorts of strange customs. They had to test their faith by spending time in the wilderness, that sort of thing. That's why Alice hated him so much. She thought he was exploiting her, and when Julia took Helen too it was all too much for her."

Rob knew he was staring but could not find the words. Thankfully, Saric was there. "I'm sorry, Mr Sable, I think you must be mistaken. Helen was the other beneficiary of the will. She lived with Alice, her grandmother. She wasn't in the US."

"By 2003, when we redrafted the will, she was in the UK, yes. Prior to that, she was in the US with her mother, Julia."

Rob's mind went racing for the evidence that Helen's parents had died when she was young; a piece of knowledge he had never questioned before. She had shown him pictures of her parents from when she was little. He wondered if he still had them. They would prove nothing, though. She never said they had anything to do with the church. And she had never been to the US.

"I think, Mr Sable, that we are mixing up two different people," he said. "It was a long time ago, after all."

"Was your wife called Helen Johnson?"

"Yes."

"And did she claim the inheritance under the will of her grandmother, Alice?"

"Yes."

"Then we have the same person."

"OK, well, in that case, your memory must be playing tricks on you," said Rob.

41

Mr Sable raised an eyebrow. He could have taken offence, but he could see the confusion on Rob's face so let it go.

Saric cut in. "We just need the data here, Rob. We can do the thinking later. Mr Sable, is there anything more you can tell us about Julia Hawkins and her daughter? Did you meet them?"

"No, I did not meet them, I'm afraid. I've told you all I know."

"And would you have records in the office?" Saric asked.

"No. This is too old. And quite rudimentary in legal terms." Mr Sable was starting to look a little tired.

"Thank you, I think that's all," said Saric.

"Yes, thank you, Mr Sable," added Rob, although his mind was elsewhere.

"Good luck, gentlemen," the old man called out as Sofija showed them to the door.

As they walked to the car, Saric answered the question Rob had not yet asked. "Well, it's something, which is better than nothing."

Rob nodded and slumped back in the passenger seat.

"I don't think I can prove him wrong, Saric," said Rob. "If you asked me to actually prove it with some evidence, that is. You know, she didn't really talk about her past. She told me not to ask, so I didn't. But she would have told me if she had been brought up in the US. Why wouldn't she just tell me?"

Saric knew that question was not for him to answer. In any case, his mind was a long way away from 'why'. For the first time in years, he had some material facts to work with, at least if he was to assume the lawyer had been both truthful and accurate in his memories. All he wanted now was to sit down with Sense Check and focus. He accelerated hard up the road and resolved to drive home fast to get started.

CHAPTER 7

A short time later, Saric was sitting behind his heavy wooden desk contemplating how to approach this next phase of work. The wood that had been used to construct the desk had been salvaged from a ship that had fought at the Battle of Trafalgar, and it helped Saric at times like these to remember all that this wood had seen, and all that it was destined to see in the future. It gave him a sense of perspective, which he sorely needed. He had new data, which meant new possibilities, but to be assured of getting the right answers, it was important to get the questions right.

Rob sat at his own desk, in the opposite corner of the room, staring at a blank screen. They had journeyed home in silence, each man preoccupied with his own thoughts and wondering what to do next.

The next step was obvious for Saric, which is why he now sat in front of his computer.

The interview with Mr Sable contained points of information that could be checked, corroborated, refuted or cross-referenced. They knew that Helen's mother was called Julia Hawkins and that she lived, or had lived, in the US. They knew that she had been there for more than twenty years and that it was likely she had been in the Midwest for at least part of that time. They also knew that she had been involved with a man, who in turn had been involved with some kind of religious group.

This was all interesting information, but the thing that gave Saric hope that it could also be useful was Sense Check. The program would enable him to run in hours the kinds of checks that would take the police months. As it was able to interpret speech, Saric's first task was to upload the recording of their interview with Mr Sable. He had not mentioned that he was recording the interview at the time, and he suspected that the old lawyer would have had something to say about his rights if he had known, but one of the benefits of not being a law enforcement official was his ability to bend the rules from time to time.

He asked Sense Check to consider the likely whereabouts of Julia Hawkins using the information available. If she was in the US, this could be a problem. Of course, Sense Check was able to utilise anything available on the internet worldwide, but it also had access to other, less public UK databases, thanks to certain people Saric had helped over the years. If the US angle looked likely, he would have to consider how to gain access to the equivalent databases there. He was sure he would know someone who could help, and he was willing to call in any favours owed to get this done.

After he had issued Sense Check with its basic instructions, and he did keep them basic to avoid prejudicing any conclusions, he had to wait. There was a lot of information out there, and it all had to be considered before Sense Check could interpret it. Over the years, he had made the program more efficient, and it now operated at least seven times faster than it had at the start, but the simple fact was that he couldn't improve Sense Check's efficiency as fast as new data was created.

Saric was just contemplating whether to make another cup of coffee when his phone rang. He glanced at the screen; it was Hannah from the bookshop. She often called him when she found something she thought would interest him.

Saric took the phone from the desk and walked out of the room, starting down the stairs towards the kitchen. "If you're calling to check how I'm getting on with the novel, you'll have to wait a bit longer," he said with a cheery tone that surprised him given the situation he found himself in.

"Saric—"

The voice at the other end of the line was quiet, shaken. He knew instantly that something was wrong. "Hannah, what's happened?"

"I'm sorry, Saric, I didn't know who else to call. There has been a break in, at the shop."

"What happened? Are you OK? Where's Rose?"

"She's fine, Griffin scared them off."

Saric thought of Hannah's large crossbreed dog. He was the kindest dog Saric had ever met and liked nothing more than sitting at Saric's feet while he shared a cup of tea with his owners. But he was a large dog and must be terrifying in full attack mode. Saric did not blame an intruder for thinking twice when they saw him.

"Saric, they're not going to leave it there. The police have been here, but they just told us to lock the doors. I can't tell them what's going on. It's too complicated. Please, Saric. I need help."

CHAPTER 8

February 2019

Helen's plan was now fully formed. She would try and get help to come to her, and if that didn't work, she had a backup scheme to escape. Daniel would play his part, although he didn't know it yet. Jessica had proved to be a bonus. She was easy to appease and her reports to the Elders were so banal that they were starting to lose interest in them altogether. But the process of gently accumulating sufficient trust to implement the next step was taking time.

However, time was working against Daniel. He had standing in the Community. His close relationship with Helen was clear, and there was growing anticipation that they would soon take the next step. It had been over four years; marriage was expected.

Helen had put off any conversation of marriage for a long time. The Elders expected her to demonstrate her full reconversion to the true faith before any such idea could be entertained. She had drawn that out for as long as she could, but other factors were working against any further delay.

It would be easy enough to simply go through with it. She felt sure she could control the physical side of things; that did not concern her. But even as she thought about it, she was completely repelled. They would make Ollie call Daniel 'Dad'. She would never allow that. When she got him out, she would find Rob; Ollie would have his father back and she would have her husband. She would not betray him, even in pretence.

When he was with Martha, Daniel felt comfortable with how things were. They made sense. They had more important things to do than focus on themselves. And in any case, they were connected at a spiritual level, far beyond that which earthly bonds could achieve. But when he was with the Elders, he could not entirely hold back the confusion.

"Daniel, we are all concerned that a young man of your standing has not found the fullness of marriage." There were knowing nods and sincere looks all around him. "We have come to the conclusion that Martha will not be fully back with us until she is committed to you." Again, there were noises of agreement. Not finished yet, the Elder that was speaking looked straight into Daniel's eyes. "You know, there has never been an Elder in the Community that has been unmarried."

Daniel did know. *This is important*, he thought. He was fond of Martha; she made him happy and he thought perhaps that was what love felt like. Yes, he was sure this feeling must be love. Martha would make a good wife and by being a good wife, she would enable him to become an Elder. That was his rightful path.

He arranged to meet her for a walk in the grounds. That was the correct way to do things. He had spoken to her father, and he had given his permission for the marriage to go ahead. Now, he just had to give Martha the good news.

When he arrived at her living quarters, he stopped outside. She was with her friend, Jessica. Jessica was sitting on a small chair by Martha's desk, while Martha perched on the edge of the bed. He knew that he should not eavesdrop, but he was tempted. Perhaps they would be talking about him. He would like to hear Martha speak of her love for him with her friend.

Daniel and Jessica were the same age and had been in class together in school. In the Community, boys and girls were educated together when they were young. It was not until they reached fourteen or fifteen that they went through the Emergence. After the ceremony, they re-entered the Community as young adults, after which time it would not be right for them to be educated together. Daniel and Jessica had barely spoken since sharing a classroom. It was his destiny to become an Elder, and her path was to become a wife and mother. He wondered for a moment if Jessica was jealous of Martha. Perhaps she wished that it was her who had been chosen to become his wife.

But they were not talking about him. Martha was talking to Jessica about the landscape. She described the open spaces and the expansive feeling of power as she stepped into the wilderness. Martha often spoke like this, and it was her direct connection to the true message that made her so powerful.

He stepped quietly into the room. Helen turned away from Jessica and smiled at him, just enough to look happy to see him but not too much that she would appear too enthusiastic. She thought she had got it right.

"My love, it is so good to see you today. We are truly blessed," Daniel said.

Helen had noticed that Daniel had a strange way of speaking to her at important moments. It was almost as if he thought he was being watched. This strange language put her on edge. She moved her face to expand her smile. "Indeed, we are, my love." It was good to mirror his language. "I am blessed to see you today."

"Are you ready for our walk? I thought we could head to the lake by The Lodge."

It was a nice day and Helen thought this might be a good opportunity to spend time alone with Daniel and continue with her plan. He seemed happy, and he was easier to work with when he was cheerful. But there was something odd in the way he stood. They said their goodbyes to Jessica and stepped out into the bright morning.

The lake was really too small to be called a lake, it was more like a large pond. It was manmade and held the water that ran off the mountains when the snow thawed. Helen supposed it must have been created to supply water to the property back in the days when it was a hotel; before the Founder established the Community. Their water was supplied differently these days, but the lake remained. It was a nice spot to sit and reflect, but, more importantly, it was a natural barrier that distanced the main Community from The Lodge.

While it had originally been a hunting lodge, where holidaymakers would meet before a day in the mountains and gather afterwards to tell stories of their kills, The Lodge was now the building in the Community that made Helen feel the most uncomfortable. It was functional rather than beautiful and it was surrounded by a large garden used to supply much of the Community's vegetables, as well as a sturdy fence.

It was solely inhabited by women who were too old to bear children and too frail to work. In short, it was the place the Community sent those who could no longer serve their purpose, or who might cause trouble for the Elders.

The strange thing about The Lodge was that while everyone knew it was there, and might refer to it when discussing the grounds, no one ever mentioned what happened there. These women just disappeared and were never spoken of again.

As they arrived at the lake, Helen's mind turned to Daniel. She had re-established with him her role as Mary, The Great Mother, and the next stage was to develop the idea that the Great Lord had chosen her to start a new Community with those of the strongest faith. She thought that if she could convince Daniel of this then she could persuade him to help her with her mission to test the faith. If she achieved this, she was sure she could engineer a scenario where she could take Ollie and use Daniel to aid their escape.

She turned to him to suggest that they sit under a leafy tree that gave some shade to the lakeside. But as she looked at him, she saw a terrible smile on his face. She felt ice flow through her entire body.

"Martha, I have the most joyful news. The Great Lord has made it clear to the Elders that we should carry out his work together. Your father has given his blessing. We are to be married."

He was beaming. Truly beaming. Helen wondered what on earth he could be so pleased about. Daniel did not love her; she was sure of that. Rob loved her, and she could feel that when she was with him. She knew it completely and without doubt. She did not believe in souls, but if she did, she would have spoken about a connection between them.

This was not the case with Daniel. But he looked truly happy, as if he believed himself to love her. Maybe he really did believe it. After all, he had never known anything different.

Suddenly, Helen was aware that she needed to respond. She hoped her face had not shown the thoughts in her mind. But how to reply? She could not marry him. She would not do that, but she did need him as part of her plan.

She smiled gently. "My love, that is indeed excellent news. We are truly blessed to know such love."

Daniel moved to embrace her.

"But is this the correct path?" she continued, keen to stop his advancing arms. "I am still learning the true way and you are teaching me. I must consult with the Great Mother to see if this is the true path. You do want to please her, don't you?"

"But Martha, the Lord wishes it. He wishes us to live together and for you to be my wife."

"I want that, too," she lied, "but the time must be right."

Daniel hesitated. The conflict was plain. He had his instructions and could not disappoint the Elders, but he was also scared to disappoint the Great Mother.

I've got him, Helen thought. She was sure she had done enough to buy some time.

CHAPTER 9

It was late by the time Saric arrived at the bookshop. Rob had argued that he should have stayed at the office and waited for Sense Check to complete its investigation, but the reality was it would take hours, and there was no benefit to be had from sitting and watching it work. It had been hard to tell Rob that, though, and even harder to leave him sitting there waiting.

Saric had been alone when he arrived in Sussex a decade ago. When he left the military, he had spent some time travelling the world and solving problems for people. Some of them were good people, others less so, but they had collectively left him with enough assets to mean he no longer needed to worry about money. He had been a nomad, traveling from place to place, and he had enjoyed that. Eventually, though, he had grown tired of living in hotels and eating only in restaurants. He wanted something else. Some peace.

There was no real reason why he had ended up in the UK, other than the fact he happened to be there when he decided to stop moving. Though it was not his first language, he spoke English as fluently as any Brit, so there was no problem there.

Sussex seemed a logical place to settle. It was close enough to London to give ready access to the benefits of the capital, while allowing him to be in the true deep countryside when he needed that. It was near Gatwick Airport and ports at Newhaven and Portsmouth, making international travel practical. He had found a large house well set back from a quiet road and engaged contractors to fit it out to his specifications.

It proved a good decision, but he had been lonely. Although he did not require the company of others, he missed it. As a child, he had always been with his father, and then in the military, he had rarely been by himself. He enjoyed his new sense of peace, but he lacked the stimulation of interesting and challenging conversation.

One day, he visited the bookshop and met Hannah. She had filled that gap in his life. She was intelligent and articulate, and he enjoyed spending time with her and her wife, Rose. He had spent long evenings at their kitchen table eating dinner and had joined them on long walks on the Downs. He had started to learn something of how to live a normal life.

Hannah had also been helpful in other ways. She was born and raised in the area and had introduced him to people who were useful. It was Hannah who had helped him to start the business in its current form,

57

and she had also been a sounding board for the initial concept of Sense Check. She had encouraged him to develop the idea and contributed to some of the underlying rules for how it operated.

All this meant that when Hannah called and said she needed him, he had to help. At this moment, there was probably no one else in the world who could pull him away from Rob, but he owed her, and for Saric this was a powerful reason.

The front door to the shop was open when he arrived. It had been kicked in. This had not been a subtle break in. The police had evidently left already. He knocked to warn of his approach but stepped into the shop without waiting for a response.

"Hannah? Its Saric."

There was no answer, but he continued through the shop up to the second floor anyway. It was never a tidy place; there were always too many books and not enough space for them, but he had never seen it as it looked now. It seemed like every item had been pulled from the shelves and strewn across the floor. Shelves had been smashed off the walls, and bookcases tipped over.

He knocked again as he stepped into the flat. In the small sitting room, he found Hannah curled up in her armchair. She looked up at him and, in that moment, she barely resembled the confident woman he knew.

"What happened? Where's Rose?"

"She's fine. She has gone to her brother's house. I need to wait here for a locksmith. I couldn't leave the place unlocked like this. You saw what they did to the door."

"What happened?" Saric repeated.

She looked at him and took a deep breath. "Take a seat, there's a lot I need to tell you."

Before he sat down, Saric prepared a pot of tea and poured a cup for Hannah. She took it from him and sipped at it while he took a seat at the other side of the coffee table. They were silent for a minute or so and Saric felt no need to fill the emptiness. Hannah would tell him when she was ready.

Eventually, she began. "I have lived in this town for a long time, Saric. In this shop for thirty years and before that just down the road. I was christened in St Mary's, at the other end of the high street. Did you know that?"

He did not, and he was not sure how it was relevant. He let her continue.

"I love this place. I know it's not exciting; Rose is always telling me that there are other places where there is more to do, better places to eat and drink and museums and shops and theatres, but it's my home. I have tried hard to use the shop to celebrate the village. I keep copies of as many local history books as I can.

"What I mean to say is that this place is important to me. I know that time can't stand still, but I believe that the past is worth protecting if we can."

Saric started to wonder whether he should be recording this conversation. There was a lot of content and Sense Check might prove useful at some point in the future, but he was talking to a friend. He had to draw a line somewhere.

"A few weeks ago, Rose and I were walking the dog through the Downs. We took the bridleway north from the crossroads and noticed signs for a new housing development, just where the path crosses the old road near Woodmancote. I didn't think much of it at the time, the land borders the Leith Estate and I know they have been looking to sell off some of it for a while, so it wasn't really a surprise. It's a shame that they must ruin the countryside around here, but there's such a demand for houses and they have to be built somewhere.

"I remember being a bit surprised that I hadn't seen any planning applications for it. They looked ready to start building, but these sorts of projects usually cause a bit of a stir in the village far before they get to that stage.

"Anyway, it was such a lovely weekend that we walked all the way down to the coast and had lunch on the seafront. I think we must have covered twenty miles that day, so I didn't really think anything about it until the following Monday. Something started bothering me. I couldn't work out what it was all day, but eventually I remembered. As you know, I have a lot of books about the history of the area, and some of them are rare. I don't often make a sale – there isn't really a lot of demand – but I like to keep them because I think it's important that someone looks after them.

"I can't say that I have read every word, but I have covered most of them and there was something in one about that particular area. I dug the book out and it hit me. It was the location of a large number of Neolithic flint mines."

Saric looked at her blankly. Flint mines? What on earth did that have to do with anything? And should he know when the Neolithic era had been? He didn't want to confess his ignorance; he could always check later.

"What was the relevance of the mines?" Saric kept the question broad enough that Hannah, hopefully, wouldn't realise he was out of his depth.

"Well, it seemed strange to me that it would be a suitable site for housing. The mines left a network of tunnels under that part of the land, so I didn't think it could be safe. I checked the records in the book I had on the first floor and confirmed that it was the same area. I didn't want anyone getting hurt so I called the planning department at the council. I just wanted to check that they were aware of the situation. I suppose they have to conduct ground surveys, or whatever they call them, to check these things, but better safe than sorry.

"I spoke to a lovely, helpful man and told him about the mines and the book that references them. He was a history buff, so he wanted to know all about it. He even asked for the name of the book. I gave it to him but told him it's not the sort of thing he'll find on Amazon; these old local books are rare. I'd be surprised if there are more than a handful of copies still in existence, and most of those will be stuffed in people's attics.

"The man I spoke to said he was sure it was all in order, but just to be sure he would run it past the planning officer responsible for the site. He even offered to give me a call back to confirm when he had done that, to put my mind at rest."

Hannah stopped and took another sip of her tea. So far, there was very little in this for Saric, but he waited for her to start again.

"To be honest, I didn't think anything more of it. I'd done my civic duty. But then earlier this week, this man arrived at the shop. I was there on my own because Wednesdays are usually quiet. It was odd because he didn't stop to browse at all. People always have a look around, it's just what they do.

"He marched straight up to me and asked if I had a copy of Turnbull's *History of Sussex*. I thought it odd because it's such an obscure title.

"Of course, I do have a copy, although I wasn't really sure I wanted to sell it to him. There was something not right about him, so to stall him, I offered to have a look on the first floor. He followed me up there, and when I got to the room where I store the history stock, he demanded I found him the book. I looked around for a bit and then I told him I must have sold it. I don't know why I said that, but I didn't think he deserved such a rare title.

63

"That's when he changed. Until then, he had been polite enough, but then he said he knew I had it and that I would regret it if I didn't sell it to him. I told him that he couldn't threaten me and that he should leave, but he just stood there daring me to challenge him. As if there was anything I could do to stop him if he decided to rip all the stock from the shelves. He was half my age and twice my size. Thankfully, that was just the moment that you walked in, Saric."

Saric thought back to the large man in the expensive suit who had left the shop in such a hurry when he had arrived earlier in the week. "Why didn't you tell me what was going on when I came in on Monday? I could have stopped him. He would not have bothered you again."

Saric was already thinking of the ways he could have stopped the man, and what he might do if he saw him now. A quiet word might have worked, but Saric thought he might have settled on something less subtle.

"It was nothing, really. I have lots of strange customers, you'd be surprised. If it hadn't been for the title of the book, I would have thought nothing of it."

"But it was the same book you had mentioned to the planning department?"

Saric knew the answer already, but he should still confirm the fact.

"Yes, it was the same title. This was all connected."

"What happened this evening?"

"Rose and I were watching a film in bed. She has had a hard week at work, so all we wanted to do was relax. I'm pretty sure we had both nodded off, but suddenly Griffin started barking. I've never seen anything like it from him. He was growling and then launched himself at the door.

"I didn't know what to do. We hadn't heard anything, but Griffin was certain there was something wrong. I managed to shut him in the kitchen and opened the door to the stairs down to the shop. I could hear someone down there – they weren't trying to be quiet by this point. They must have heard the dog, and it would have worried them. I'm not sure what Griffin would have done if I had let him out of the kitchen; normally, the worst the old boy would manage would be to knock someone over by jumping up to greet them over enthusiastically, but it was like he was possessed. I suppose it's his instinct to protect us after all.

"Whoever it was left pretty quickly, and we didn't see them, although, to be honest, I was too scared to try and look. Rose called the police and we waited in the shop for them to arrive. There is a terrible mess on the first floor, so the burglars must have been looking for the book. And they knew where to look."

"But they didn't find it?"

Hannah shook her head slightly "It wasn't there. After the man in the suit arrived, I moved it somewhere safe. I'm not exactly sure what's going on, but I felt it was important to protect it."

"Did you tell the police about the book?"

Hannah looked at him resolutely. "No, I didn't."

"Why not?"

"Because of what these men will do if the truth comes out."

CHAPTER 10

Sense Check had completed its analysis of the content from the meeting with the lawyer. Saric had set the basic tasks that would move them forward in searching for Julia Hawkins. The program would run three primary processes. Firstly, the transcript of the meeting was checked for logical consistency within itself. Secondly, Sense Check would take purported statements of fact and test them against the information available to it from its own databases and the internet. Finally, once it had determined statements that were more likely than not to be true, Saric would use them to refine the areas where the target, Julia Hawkins, could possibly be and then direct Sense Check to try and find her.

On the first point, Sense Check had, as always, highlighted significant chunks of the discussion that were irrelevant. This was meaningless small talk that Saric liked to cut out of his analysis altogether. Other than that, though, the lawyer's statements were not inconsistent or logically incapable of being true. Saric had weighted Sense Check's programming to carry out this task first, as he had come to learn that lying was harder than it looked. The changing of the slightest fact would precipitate a sequence of other alterations in a story. The typical liar would generally seek to bring the story back to the truth, or risk losing control of the narrative altogether. Only the most accomplished fibber could pull this off without allowing for some small inconsistency to cover over the cracks. In a normal human interaction, this realignment could be easily missed. But the cold hard analytics of Sense Check would almost always unpick such an attempt. So, to be confident that the lawyer wasn't a liar was an excellent start, allowing the program to calculate how much reliability it should place on the statements he had claimed as facts.

Every asserted fact was then checked for validity.

"My work is covered by confidentiality agreements," the lawyer had said. Sense Check cross-referenced various sources and concluded that no such agreement would have been made. In fact, the obligation to maintain confidentiality was written into the legal code of ethics and would only form part of a separate agreement where there was a specific need to do so.

"Those continue to apply even when the client is deceased," he had gone on.

This was correct.

Saric found it strangely calming to wade through the obscure differences between how people articulated their points and the actual underlying facts. *Almost nothing anyone ever says is actually right*, he thought.

On the basis that the lawyer was not lying, and assuming his memory was accurate, there were a few key facts that Saric focused in on.

Alice Johnson had written a will in the 1980s. Julia Hawkins was her daughter and the only beneficiary. In 2003, Alice rewrote her will, leaving most of her estate to Helen Johnson, her granddaughter. At some point, Julia Hawkins went to the US, and she was also involved with a man.

"It doesn't make any sense," said Rob. "Are you saying Helen's mother left her behind and went off to the States never to be heard of again? And Helen simply forgot all about her and never mentioned her to me?"

"According to the lawyer, Julia Hawkins took her daughter with her to the US."

"Oh yes. So, you're saying Helen spent a chunk of her childhood in America?"

"The lawyer is saying that, yes."

"She had no hint of an accent," Rob said, more to himself than to Saric.

In their earlier investigations, Saric had discovered that Helen was born and raised in the Midlands. She said she remembered nothing of her father and only glimpses of her mother; both of her parents had died when she was young. Saric had understood that, like most people, Helen had led a simple enough life. Whilst Sense Check had not been able to verify much of her background, the overall account had not been inconsistent, so Saric had not spent much time on it. Maybe that had been a mistake.

"Rob, I think we need to try and move away from what we thought was the truth and deal with these assertions as presented. If it turns out there are things you did not know about your wife, let's assume she had a good reason for keeping secrets. Sometimes people need to put aside their past in order to move on in life."

"Yes, OK, I know. Let's get on with it."

"So," said Saric, "let's start drawing out some inferences. Julia Hawkins was probably born Johnson. And her daughter had the same name. So, we can have a working assumption that she changed her name after Helen was born. Most likely upon marriage. If Julia had married Helen's father, Helen would probably have taken his name, wouldn't she? So, perhaps she got Hawkins from a subsequent remarriage. We are told it was a romantic relationship with a man that took her to America. This man could be our Mr Hawkins." Saric did not look convinced.

"Seems like a bit of a leap," cut in Rob. "Maybe Helen just took her grandmother's name when she lost touch with her mother." Rob did not like the way it felt to talk about his wife in such a detached way.

Saric stared out the window for a moment. "OK, let's forget the names for a minute." He paused again. "We have no reason to believe that Julia Hawkins is dead." The comment did not seem to add much.

"When did Sable say Julia left the UK?" asked Rob.

"He didn't. Just somewhere between the first will in the late eighties and the new one in 2003. She went to the Midwest of the US."

"Fine, so we have a twenty-year window to find a Julia Hawkins, or Johnson, leaving the UK for the American Midwest with a man who could be called Hawkins, or not." Rob could not hide the disappointment in his voice. It felt like they had got more than that.

"We are coming at it from the wrong angle," said Saric. "The question is, why did they leave? And Sable gave us that. The unnamed man was—

71

" Saric read from the transcript, "—'something to do with the church.' And not just any church. A church that meant Julia would have to go through a 'cleansing rebirth in the wilderness'. Have you ever heard of a ritual like that?"

Rob, who had never had much exposure to religion, shook his head. It was the same for Saric, who had always distrusted the sort of certainty that seemed to come with the profoundly religious.

"Well, let's see what Sense Check can make of that. And meanwhile, we should go and ask someone who knows more about this stuff than us."

He opened his list of favours owed. Unusually, that did not help. No priests or vicars, no one connected to any church.

"We need a priest, right?" said Rob.

"Or perhaps a religious historian."

"I think a priest might be a bit easier to find," Rob said, lifting an eyebrow. A few seconds later and the internet had taken him to the UK Catholic Directory and a phone number for his local church. Rob navigated the puzzled but rather intrigued fussy sounding woman who picked up the phone. He was then passed onto Father Rupert.

"Hello . . . Father," he said tentatively.

Father Rupert ignored the social awkwardness of a non-Catholic addressing a priest, and after a brief discussion in which Rob explained they needed his help, he agreed they could pop by the presbytery for a cup of tea at 4 pm, although he would only have half an hour, which he hoped would be enough.

"Thank you very much, Father," Rob said, more comfortably this time. The brief exchange left him feeling strangely calm.

CHAPTER 11

The presbytery was an imposing, three-story building with external beams and cream walls to the front, with brick to the sides. It stood next to the church, although it was not obvious which building came first. In fact, this was one of the longest-running Catholic churches in the country, with a rich history that in different circumstances both men would have enjoyed learning about.

The arched wooden door had a heavy ornate door knocker in the middle of it, but the back plate was missing and the knocker had been crudely nailed down. A 'Please use the doorbell' sign had been handwritten, carefully laminated and stapled into the door. Saric pressed a poorly fitted doorbell to the side of the notice and heard the chime go off inside.

A heavy latch was lifted and Father Rupert opened the door to them. Saric gave little consideration to the way people reacted to him. Objectively, he knew he could appear imposing, and men would often shrink a little before him. So, he noticed how Father Rupert accepted him openly and without the slightest moderation of his body language. Rob noticed it, too, of course.

Rob wondered if he was expected to shake the man's hand. That would be the normal thing to do upon meeting someone for the first time. The priest made no move to offer his hand, so Rob chose not to and as a result felt awkward and off balance.

"Thank you very much for agreeing to meet us," he said, as he caught the priest's eye.

"Well," said Father Rupert, "if I can help you, young man, I will be glad to have done so." He did not add, "you look like you need it", but they knew that was what he meant.

Father Rupert led them into a small room that seemed to be part library, part study and part storeroom. A well preserved but ancient computer printer sat on a deep sideboard. A similarly aged monitor was positioned on the desk next to it, and a desktop computer hummed on the floor. Piles of small, white cardboard boxes had been stacked in one corner, and Saric could not help but wonder what was in them. A huge radiator ran across one wall, with a cheap electric heater sitting in front of it.

Father Rupert offered Rob and Saric chairs at a side table and pulled his swivel chair over to join them. As they sat, the gentle face of a small, round, late middle-aged woman with a severe hairstyle appeared at the door. Tea was offered and accepted, and she disappeared off to organise it.

"We have a long story, and no time to tell it," began Rob, "but in summary, my wife and son are missing and we are trying to find them. We believe the person who could lead us to them belonged to a church, which operated somewhere in the American Midwest. I appreciate this does not help much, but we also know that they have a ritual where new joiners go through a cleansing in the wilderness. How would you go about trying to find a religious organisation like that?"

Father Rupert looked both sad and intrigued. "I'm sorry that you have lost touch with your wife and son. And for the circumstances in which you lost touch. Can I ask, though, are you sure they want to be found?"

Rob looked him straight in the eye. "Yes, Father, they want to be found." He thought how he could get used to calling the priest Father. He found it comforting.

Father Rupert looked at Rob for a long moment and made some sort of mental calculation. "How unusual," he said. "I wonder if we are looking for a religious group at all. I cannot think of any branch of official Christianity that would require a joining ritual. Sadly, there are many groups that claim Christian beliefs, or a whole mix of beliefs, that have fallen away from the true Church of Jesus Christ. They may well call themselves a church, but it is not the true one. Do you know anything more about this group?"

"The only other point of interest is that they may well have had a program for seeking members in the UK, at least in the 1980s or '90s," Saric said.

Father Rupert seemed to notice Saric for the first time. He stared out of the window. "Interesting," he said. His eyes moved around without looking, and Rob knew he was scanning his memories. "Do you remember Waco? David Koresh? It was a great tragedy."

"Yes, I remember it," Saric replied.

"It was a sorry story, and it opened the eyes of many to the peril of masquerading as a real church. The Catholic church comes straight from Jesus. It gives us a way to be with Him. It presents a simple truth."

Instinctively, Father Rupert held the crucifix that hung from his neck. "Over the centuries, many branches of Christianity have been formed, often with perfectly virtuous intent. But the further one drifts from the source, the harder it is to keep Jesus at the centre of all that you do. The Waco tragedy highlighted the danger to us all. But they were not the worst. Some groups are far more cynical and corrupt than they were.

77

"I never worried about the long-term effects of the one-off cult leaders. These groups only last for as long as the leader has the energy to pull it all together. Yes, we should reach out to help those injured by these people, but it would never reflect on our work.

"But the organised groups, the ones that call themselves a church and live on with an idea even after the founders are long gone, these are the groups that dilute the message of Jesus."

"Did you come across an organisation like the one we are looking for?" Rob cut in.

Father Rupert looked at Rob with sad eyes. "Maybe." He stood up slowly and went to one of the many bookshelves. He pulled out several books and pushed them back in, stood with his hands on his hips for a moment and then found the one he was looking for. He leafed through it, still with his back to his guests. He turned around. "There was a 'church' we came across that claimed the path to the truth required a cleansing. It had centres in Australia, Germany and America. And here," he said, pointing at the book, "is the man at the centre of it. Andrew Peace." He held up a picture of an odd, intense-looking man with a bald head and sloping shoulders.

"Is that all it says?" asked Saric.

"That's it. Does that help?"

Rob looked dazed. He took the book from Father Rupert's hand and stared at the picture. *I want to kill this man*, he thought.

Saric used his phone to take a photo of the picture and the associated brief text, which said nothing more than Father Rupert had told them.

As he put his phone away, Saric studied Father Rupert's face. There was more to this than he was saying. "If you know something more, anything, it would really help us," he said.

"I have told you what I know. The rest I have no evidence for," he replied.

"Even so, we would be grateful for anything you can tell us."

"As I said, I have seen these so-called churches come and go. Most of them give me no cause for concern. When they do, it's usually because of what they might do to the reputation of the real church. And for the poor souls who are taken in by them. In the end, though, they are of little consequence.

"This group gave me concern for a different reason. This man, Peace, was dangerous. Like I said, nothing was ever proven, but he was a threat, and he was well connected. He knew people and knew how to get what he wanted. If you do come across him, please be careful."

Finding themselves on their feet and seemingly at the end of their discussion, they all recognised the meeting was over.

"Thank you, Father," said Rob.

"Good luck with your search," Father Rupert replied. "You know, sometimes when you search for one thing, you find more than you were looking for. Take this."

He picked up one of the white cardboard boxes and pressed it into Rob's hands.

"Thank you, Father," Rob repeated.

"Time to get on," said Saric. And they left.

CHAPTER 12

June 2019

The children of the Community were generally well behaved. This was especially true of those who had been brought up there. A lot of effort went into educating the children brought in from the outside to understand the importance of adhering to the principles of the faith, which included obedience. But they were still children, and the instinct to explore could not be eradicated fully. It required a certain maturity of mind to understand the danger of new things.

Ollie found it easy to break the rules. "You are who you are, not who they say you are," his mother would whisper to him when she could. She wanted him to keep resisting, but also to keep his head down. "You can pretend you agree with them, but we will know." She would give him a deep, warm smile and look at him in a way that no one else in the Community did. It made him feel safe.

Ollie's favourite rule to break was not leaving the boundaries of the compound. The old metal link fence that ran around the whole area was put in when the site was a hotel, to keep the wildlife away from the holidaymakers. If anyone reported a major problem with it, the

Community would fix it. But it had been a long time since they had seen anything come in that would bother them. So, it was easy for Ollie and his friends to pull a section back from the ground to create a gap big enough to squeeze through, yet small enough to cover with loose vegetation.

The children had found that a good way to buy themselves a couple of hours was to run errands to The Lodge, sneak off for some adventuring and then return to the main building with stories of how they had got talking to the old ladies or helped in the garden. The children knew these ladies had almost nothing to do with the main house anymore, and even if they were asked, they would not be expected to have a proper memory of their presence.

Although he was bold, Ollie was still only seven years old. He would not brave a trip into the wilderness without his best friends, Mark and Carly. Mark knew things, and Carly was almost ten.

"Let's go to the dolphin, I bet I can break my record today."

Despite being the youngest, Ollie held the record for the most consecutive direct hits throwing stones into the valley beneath, at a rock that looked to them all like a dolphin leaping out of the water.

"OK," said Mark, who liked to adopt the role of leader, provided Carly did not have a better idea. The three children strode out, keeping their eyes open for any good stones to pocket for their record attempt.

As an unspoken rule, they stayed close together. Instinctively, they knew there was danger here.

"Look at that!" said Ollie. He had spotted a whole pile of loose stones. They were just out of reach. He started scrambling up to get them, leaving the other two below him. As he was concentrating on getting a good foothold, Carly screamed at him, and a whole load of things seemed to happen at once.

"Ollie, wait. No, come back down. No, stay still."

There was a hiss, like nothing he had ever heard before. It was a resonating noise that seemed to come straight out of the rock behind him. Ollie saw that it was some kind of wild cat. He froze with terror. It was too close.

"Don't move!" ordered Mark. He grabbed a stone from his pocket and swung his arm back ready to throw. This caught the cat's attention and it stared at the two children below him. Its body was taut and its back arched, as if ready to launch an attack.

83

"Run!" Carly screamed. The world stood still for a moment. Carly grabbed Mark's arm and pulled him to join her. Mark let out a strange noise. He dropped the stone and the two children sprinted back the way they had come. Ollie could not move a muscle, not even to scream. The cat made up half the ground to the children in what seemed like one bound. Ollie wanted his mum. He could not even open his mouth to scream.

The wildcat is going to take them both, he thought.

Carly and Mark did not look back, but fast and nimble as they were, there was nothing they could do. Ollie did not want to look, but he could not turn away. Just as the thought that it was too late ran through his mind, a great blur of grey appeared from round the corner, kicking up clouds of dust as it moved. It seemed to be coming straight at his friends from in front of them. They had no time to dodge, but they did not need to. The grey thing shot between their legs and stopped in a skid that kicked up more dust. It roared. No, Ollie realised at last, it barked. A ferocious bark, which rattled all the way through its body. Its lips were curled back to reveal its strong white teeth.

The children disappeared round some rocks. The wildcat paused, bristled and considered its options. It leaped out of the dog's reach. The dog sprinted to where Ollie was still clinging to the side of a rock and stood between him and where the wildcat had just run off. Ollie still could not move, but the dog's company allowed him to breathe again.

"Hello, dog," he said.

Texas did not reply, other than to tilt her head, which she thought might put the boy at ease. A few moments later, they both heard a whistle. Texas replied with a "here I am" bark, which was an entirely different noise to the one Ollie had heard earlier.

"There you are. What are you doing up here? Oh, I see. Well, well."

Ollie looked at the man before him and knew for certain that he was now safe.

CHAPTER 13

Saric and Rob had both found their meeting with Father Rupert rather strange. Saric was incredibly confused by the priest. He was obviously an intelligent man, capable of clear thought and careful contemplation of information. On the other hand, he believed in God, which seemed to Saric to be an utterly irrational conclusion. He found it difficult to hold these two truths together in his mind.

Rob was surprised that while he was no closer to seeing his wife and son again, he could feel the edge of something he had not felt for many years. Something close to peace. It wasn't fully there for him, but it was like he had suddenly remembered that such a state existed. He felt he had known that all along, but until now he had not been conscious of it.

Saric wasted no time uploading the new data to Sense Check. Rob offered to make lunch while he worked. This was the first time Saric remembered his friend thinking about anything as mundane as eating since they uncovered the will; it was a relief for him, even if he was a little worried about the mess Rob might be creating in his otherwise pristine kitchen.

Sense Check had already drawn some preliminary conclusions based on the data they had provided from their interview with Mr Sable. Saric glanced at this but chose to ignore it. Every conclusion included a list of assumptions and caveats that made them largely worthless, and he wanted to avoid clouding his judgment or getting distracted from the task at hand.

They ate lunch on the deck at the back of Saric's kitchen. It was still warm, although the evenings were getting shorter as autumn approached. They talked about the priest, and religion. Rob seemed sad when he remembered how disappointed his parents had been when Helen refused to have Ollie christened. They weren't a religious family, but it was apparently expected in middle-class Sussex. Saric was pleased that Rob felt able to speak about Ollie. It had been a long time since he had done so.

As they finished their meal, Saric's phone buzzed. It was the Sense Check alert; the program had reached its conclusions. Saric could have viewed the results on the app, but it was much easier to read on his large desktop screen, so they made their way upstairs to his office. As they climbed the stairs, Saric could feel a slight tension across his chest as the apprehension triggered an adrenaline release; the ancient part of his brain was preparing to deal with the unexpected that might lay ahead.

Saric knew that calmness was what was needed now, so he took a deep breath to reset that response before entering the office.

They sat together behind the large oak desk and Saric moved the mouse to bring the screen to life. The jumble of inferences had been simplified and there were fewer caveats and conclusions. This was promising.

The first conclusions related to Andrew Peace. He was easy to find on the internet, due to the fact he had been imprisoned in Australia fifteen years previously. He had apparently conned hundreds of people out of their life savings, and the resultant court case had made the news across the world. Saric did not remember the case, but when he looked at the dates he remembered being in Dubai at the time, in a situation where he had not had easy access to the media. Sense Check could not find out anything about Peace leaving prison, although it seemed likely he must have by now. He seemed to have just disappeared. There was nothing in the reports about Father Rupert's suggestions of violence or intimidation. Perhaps the priest had misremembered, but Saric thought not. He reflected on the suggestion of Peace's connections. Had they protected him from more serious charges?

Following Sense Check's logic, they looked at earlier information on Peace. As Father Rupert had told them, he had caused a small stir in the late '80s, when he had set up a series of communities, telling potential recruits that membership was the only way to demonstrate something he described as the 'true faith'. He had been quite successful, and at the time of his arrest, he had already established eight communities in numerous different countries.

Sense Check was also able to corroborate that Peace had been on a recruiting mission in the UK around the time that Julia Hawkins and her daughter had left for the US. The local papers had been in uproar about the events, in which he took interested parties into the woods for twenty-four hours, to replicate a small part of the ceremony that all new Community recruits went through.

The facts seemed to fit so far. But what if Julia had met Peace? What happened next?

Sense Check had found the website for Peace's Community. It had, apparently, not been affected by the disgrace cast upon its founder and proudly proclaimed that Community members were the holders of the One Truth and were destined for eternal happiness. On the other hand, outsiders would be forever condemned. The 'About Us' page spoke of the cleansing and strengthening benefits of The Emergence, a ritual involving new recruits spending four days in the wilderness to cast off their old lives and emerge as full members of the Community and trusted holders of The Truth.

"This is it, Saric! It has to be. We've found her."

Saric took a moment to respond. "No, Rob, not yet. We have found something, but it's not her yet. Please remember that."

Not knowing what else to say, Saric scrolled to the next item on Sense Check's list, which detailed the possible locations for Julia Hawkins. The Community now had twelve centres. Four of these were in the US. Mr Sable thought that Julia had travelled to the Midwest, so Sense Check had eliminated the ones in Georgia and Pennsylvania. This left two Communities highlighted on a map of the US; one was in Readbury, Wisconsin and the other in Grandcast River, Nebraska. Neither of these names meant anything to Saric and nor did they to Sense Check. At this point, the program had been unable to draw any further conclusions and had simply listed other areas where further data might enable it to do so. It suggested locating the contemporaneous flight records and travel histories for the parties involved. Saric thought it unlikely they would find any of this information from the '90s. While computer records probably did exist, anything created before the cloud was harder to find. Still, they had two fairly solid possibilities for the location of Julia Hawkins.

Saric turned to Rob, whose face was ghostly white. "What is it?" He'd hardly dared ask, not knowing what the response might be.

"We've found her, Saric. I know where Julia Hawkins is, and I know she is connected to the disappearance."

Rob seized the mouse from Saric and began frantically clicking through the files to the data gathered at the time of Helen's disappearance. They had meticulously scanned images of anything of Helen's that might prove relevant, and a lot that appeared completely irrelevant.

In a file entitled 'H memory box', he found what he was looking for. Among images of school and graduation certificates and old cinema tickets was one of a postcard. On the front of it was a photo of an old hotel framed by a backdrop of beautiful mountains, while at the bottom was the line "Greetings from the Lakeview Hotel, Grandcast River, Nebraska."

CHAPTER 14

Saric asked Rob to go back to his house and find the postcard that had been scanned into Sense Check. If Helen had nothing to do with Peace's Community, it seemed a ridiculous coincidence for her to have kept a memento from one of the areas he operated in. But Saric needed to rule out any doubt. He at least wanted to see the actual postcard.

Whilst Rob was gone, Saric turned his attention to the situation of his friend, Hannah. Initially, she had seemed reluctant to tell him about the hold the people that broke into her shop had over her. She had told no one else, not even Rose. But once she had opened up to Saric, her relief was obvious.

As he did with all his clients, Saric listened to Hannah's account with no change in his expression at all. He gave nothing away.

"This is my home, Saric, you know that," Hannah had explained. "I have lived here for years. When I first took the bookshop over, I had no money, so my parents left their names on the lease – it's all long leases down this street; some lord of the manor owns the land. Once I got on my feet, I took to overpaying for it, but it was never officially my property. It was just a commercial space in those days, some small office

92

rooms and storage. We fixed the place up and turned the top floor into a little flat. You know me, Saric, I just never got round to sorting out the paperwork. All that lease stuff and planning regulations is so boring. The whole thing is a muddle.

"The man who came to see me before called me no more than fifteen minutes after the break in. He told me they knew I didn't have the right to live here anymore, and that I would have to pay to put everything back the way it was before I moved in and then leave. He said if I didn't give them the book, they would let the relevant people know. I don't want to lose all this, Saric, but I also don't want that man to get what he wants. And I don't want ancient history to be wiped out for houses."

She stopped talking, sighed and sank into her chair, looking at Saric.

"OK, Hannah," Saric had said. "I take it this man gave you a phone number to get hold of him on. Can I have that, please?"

Something in Saric's stillness had sent a flash of dark thoughts through Hannah's mind. "I don't want your help if the solution is violence," she said.

"It's an option," he replied, talking half to himself. "But if you don't want that, that's fine."

In practice, it wasn't normally the most effective response anyway, so he wasn't concerned about ruling it out. In any case, if needed, he could do that in secret, without Hannah ever finding out.

Saric looked at what Sense Check had done, drawing connections between local planning applications, concerned parties, land ownership and, of course, the phone number he had been given. It was not hard for Sense Check to give a pretty clear picture of the potential source of Hannah's problems.

Gary Lambert's website called him a Property Development Manager. It had been easy to find the website via the mobile number Hannah had given him, and Saric recognised the smug, shiny face displayed on the homepage. He was the same man he'd encountered in the shop on his last visit before the break in. In Saric's opinion, Gary looked rather too pleased with himself.

From the website, Saric found the name of Gary's company and from there it was easy to search for its financial records. Within an hour he had built up a good base of knowledge on the man and what he might be worried about.

Gary seemed to make a living by finding landowners who wanted to make money from property development without the hassle of having to do anything for themselves. He would identify sites and then arrange for planning permission to be obtained and for properties to be built and sold. In return, and based on the most recent company accounts, he received a healthy portion of the profits. As Saric saw it, he got a share of the benefits without any of the risk involved with actually funding the project.

The South Downs development was not on the website yet, but there were examples of similar projects Gary's company had been involved in across the south of England. Internet reviews of Gary's developments were not altogether positive. It appeared he sold the idea of luxury living but left a trail of issues, often landing purchasers with expensive repair bills.

Saric then turned his attention to the development Hannah had seen. Sense Check had found the planning application, which had been approved nine months previously. It set out plans for eighty new houses on the site. The application was in the name of Gary's company, but the underlying landowner wasn't disclosed.

Saric asked Sense Check to go through the land registry for that information. He then turned his attention to what Gary might want and, more importantly, how he could be persuaded to move on.

The 'what' seemed fairly obvious. If there were ancient mines on the site that meant tunnels. And tunnels meant it would not be a good option for housing. Saric was no expert on geology or construction, but he assumed that at best the mines would mean costly remediations and at worst make the land worthless. He made a note to find a surveyor who could provide more detail on these assumptions.

It wasn't clear to Saric how the tunnels would have escaped the attention of the planning department, but if Gary was willing to blackmail Hannah, it was also reasonable to assume he had ways to ensure his applications went through. That would also explain how Gary found out about Hannah, who had told him the only people she confided in about her concerns were Rose and the planning department. If he ruled out Rose as the leak, it made sense that a corrupt member of the planning team could push through a dodgy application, as well as letting him know when people were poking around on the matter.

Gary knew that Hannah had evidence of the tunnels and wanted to stop her making that information public. All that was left for Saric was to work out how to stop him while keeping Hannah in her home.

CHAPTER 15

February 2020

When Helen had first been abducted and brought back to the Community, she had looked for ways to get a message out, but without success. In the five years she had now been there, she had not once seen a phone. Her early attempt to walk out of the Community to get to help had shown her how impossible that was, too. She trusted no one there to pass a letter to. She had gently tested Daniel, using her influence over him to get him to bring her a phone, but it transpired he had no access to one. He explained that only the Elders were equipped to manage the outside world. Daniel seldom left the Community grounds. Giving him a letter to post would be an enormous risk; he would have to find an excuse to be taken to the local town, get some time on his own, get hold of a stamp and do it all secretly without her around to keep him on track. No, she needed to get into the town herself.

Jessica had become the key to this. Harmless, simple Jessica was trusted by the Elders. Nothing much was expected from her, but whilst they waited for the Great Lord to bless her with children, she did her bit for the Community in other ways. Being one of the most reliable Community members made her an ideal addition to the shopping group.

Every month, a small group from the Community would drive out to the local town to carry out a number of errands. It was a small town, and the Community was a significant part of its population. The Elders had formed an understanding with the town leaders. Every year the Community made a support payment to the town. The terms of this payment had never been formalised. They called it a thank you, but it definitely bought something more, and what exactly that was depended on who in the town you asked.

The Community placed their grocery order with what passed for the town's supermarket, which stored the goods for collection. The shopping group then took two large vans into town to be loaded up. Whilst there, they would disperse into the various smaller shops for bespoke or last-minute requests. As another gesture of their support for local business, the Community ensured it bought something from nearly all the shops. During these monthly trips, the supervising Elder would have an appointment with the town leaders. No one in the shopping group knew what those discussions were about, and it did not occur to them to be interested.

Jessica had been part of the shopping group for several years. She took no joy from it. Leaving the Community grounds worried her. Evil was out there. And she could see it all around her whenever she left home. Rough men looked at her and sometimes made comments to each other and sniggered.

It had taken Helen some time to persuade Jessica to include her in the group. "You won't like it, Martha," she protested. "It's not safe; you should stay here. Perhaps you could help the cooks or the cleaners instead. They are important roles and more suited to you."

"But I want to see the town," Helen said. "I feel it is what the Great Lord wishes, and anyway, we will have fun together."

A knot tightened in Helen's stomach as she said this. Manipulating Daniel was one thing, he was part of the Community leadership structure so she could convince herself that he deserved it. Jessica was different. She was innocent. In many ways, Helen often reflected, she was more of a victim than she was.

Jessica had given in, as Helen had known she would, and asked the Elder's wife responsible for organising the women's work to allocate her to the shopping group.

Two evenings later, as Helen read quietly in one of the shared living areas, Daniel visited to tell her she was to be allowed to assist Jessica.

"You must be blessed," he had said, as he sat down next to her, a little closer than she would have liked. "Elder Christopher fought hard against allowing you to go, but eventually all the Elders resolved to permit it."

Daniel always referred to her father as 'Elder Christopher', never 'your father'. She thought this strange in a way that she could not quite describe. There was nothing wrong with it really; it wasn't like she was close to her parents, but it still said something about Daniel's role in all of this. In Daniel's mind, this man was his boss, not his future father-in-law.

Helen had said all the right things about how grateful she was and that it was surely the right path for her, as the Great Lord would wish.

She hoped Daniel would leave after he had given her this message, but he stayed. She had chosen this room because it was quiet. Most of the rest of the Community chose to sit together in one of the other communal rooms, and now she wished she were there, too. Under the Community's rules, unmarried men and women were not permitted to be alone together. Helen both resented this rule on principle and wished that it was being enforced here, but she suspected that even if the Elders saw them together, they would turn a blind eye. Daniel was the golden child, after all, and he obviously believed that he operated outside of the rules that applied to others.

He told her about his day, which appeared to involve nothing more than thinking of ways to ingratiate himself with the Elders. Helen did her best to sound impressed with this nonsense, but in a short time she was dreaming about what it would be like to spend an evening having conversations about things that really mattered, with people she loved, and who loved her back.

She must have drifted a little too far because she suddenly became aware that Daniel was looking at her expectantly. What had she missed? His eager smile was frozen on his face.

"My love, please explain that to me again?" She hoped this would work and, of course, it did, as it proved to Daniel how much cleverer he was.

"I have reflected on what you said by the lake, and I have prayed on it every day. Of course, you are right, we cannot be married yet."

Helen's heart jumped as she struggled to contain her relief. It was short lived, however. There must be more to it.

"I know how worried you have been about your faith and about becoming strong enough to fulfil your destiny with me."

When he spoke to her like this, he had the same expression as the ancient Elder who led her prayer group sometimes. It was like he was explaining something impossibly complicated to a small child.

"And as I prayed, I realised that you will not be sure of your faith until it has been tested and you have triumphed against the darkness."

He was beaming now. She was sure he was supposed to avoid pride, but he seemed to be bathing in it.

"And so, I have spoken with the Elders, and they have agreed with me that this is right. Next month, you will start preparations to go through The Emergence ceremony again, to enable you to step back into full membership of the Community. Only once you have done this will you be ready to marry me."

He reached out and put his hand firmly on hers. Then he hesitated, as if waiting to see how she would respond. It was the first time he had touched her, maybe the first time he had touched any woman; after all, it was against the rules. Clearly, after his hesitation the last time they were alone together he had resolved that she was his now, so the rules should no longer apply to them.

Internally, Helen recoiled from his touch, but she knew she must not show this. Ceremony preparations took six months; she had time, but she also now had a deadline. She would not be coerced into marrying this man and betraying Rob. She smiled at him and squeezed his hand gently. It was time to start the next phase.

CHAPTER 16

Saric watched Rob pull in and park in his driveway. It was obvious even from a distance that he was on edge. He let himself in, which, given Saric was watching him on his screen, Sense Check needlessly alerted him to. Since Saric had gone live with 'the complete home protection solution', the program knew exactly who had been in Saric's house, in which room and for how long. He decided he better get a new code written to allow Rob a key. He had never anticipated anyone else needing one.

"I've got it," Rob announced as soon as he came into the study. He placed the postcard carefully on Saric's desk.

Saric picked it up and examined the front, which had been scanned into Sense Check. He turned it over. "All fine here", the message read. Saric knew where he could get the handwriting tested, but the curly, fluent lettering seemed obviously female to him. He would double check.

"Any idea who wrote this?" he asked.

"No."

Rob didn't seem to think it mattered. "It can't be a coincidence. Someone in this middle-of-nowhere town in the US sent a message to Helen. And this church thing is out there. And it looks like this Julia Hawkins might be out there. And she might be connected to Helen; for all we know, she might even be her mother. We need to speak to her, now."

Rob saw hesitation in Saric. "What?" he said, his frustration growing.

"Nothing we have seen up to now makes me think that this is the sort of place where you can just call and speak to a resident."

Rob laughed. "These aren't hardened criminals, Saric. It's a religious community. Of course she'll take my call."

Seeing that Rob would not be dissuaded, Saric gave a small nod towards his phone. "Go on, then, give it a try."

Rob located the Community's website on his phone's browser and clicked the button to dial. A foreign dial tone rang twice before it was answered in a language that Rob thought sounded like German.

After being knocked off beat for a couple of seconds, he introduced himself awkwardly. "Hello, do you speak English?"

The voice at the other end responded immediately, with only the slightest hint of an accent. "Yes, of course, sir. Good evening, thank you for calling the Peace Community International Outreach Line, how may I help you today?"

"I'm very sorry, I thought this was the number for the Community in Nebraska."

"You have the right number, sir, we deal with all incoming communications for our communities around the world. How may I help you today?"

"Ah, OK, I see, I was hoping to speak to one of your—" Rob struggled to find the right word, "—members, please."

"I'm sorry, sir, our brothers and sisters live a life of quiet reflection and do not take incoming calls."

"I see, but these are unusual circumstances, perhaps I could—" Rob didn't get the chance to finish his explanation.

"I'm very sorry, sir, but our brothers and sisters do not take incoming calls. Is there anything else I can help you with today?"

Frustrated and with growing rage, Rob told the operator that there was nothing else, hung up and slammed his phone on the desk. He knew

Saric had heard the exchange. "We have got to go out there. You can see that, right? That place isn't right. If she's there, we aren't going to find her from here."

"Yes, OK," Saric agreed. He seemed to process some deep thoughts. "You are right, Rob. We've definitely got enough to justify going out there." Again, he processed his thoughts. "I'm owed nothing out there, though, understand? No connections, no debts owed. Even Sense Check will be learning a lot from scratch; it's not set up for a US mode of thought."

Rob would normally have picked up on that; how does a mode of thought impact a computer program? But he missed it completely. "Good. I'll look at flights."

"There is one thing, though."

"Yes?" said Rob, clearly impatient. He had not sat down yet.

"We're not ready." Saric looked at Rob intently. In the US, it was going to be just them. "We need a couple of days to process this. We need to consider a few options. We don't know the laws out there. The geography. We don't even know what to pack. Is it hot or cold? Where can we stay without being noticed? This is the most important case of your life, and if I'm honest, of mine, too. We need to get out there quickly, but more importantly, correctly."

Rob took this in. A delay. He screwed his face up. Surely, they needed to act. Get out there and sort it out later.

"I don't think I can wait, Saric," said Rob.

"It's not just the practical stuff," said Saric. "You need to process this, too. We don't know what happened with Helen. If she ran away, or was killed, what would you do? You need to know. If she is being held against her will, what are you going to do then? I can tell you. You are going to destroy. I've seen the pain, the immediate pain, the long, drawn-out simmering pain, and now the pain of hope. If there is something out there for us to find, I don't want to go there just to watch you destroy everything you see, and yourself along with it. You need to get a handle on this hope."

Rob sat in his chair. He let out a deep breath, as if he had been holding it for days. "I don't know if time will make any difference," he admitted.

"Maybe not. But we need to prep properly anyway. So, unless you want to go out by yourself, we need a couple of days. I have another little concern we can distract ourselves with, too, if you want to help?"

"Oh, I see, that's it, is it? You have another client you don't want to let down, so Helen can wait."

Saric looked at Rob. Rob held his gaze. "You will have to decide for yourself if you think that's true."

Rob decided. He felt the heat rising inside him; he was stepping towards an edge he wasn't sure he wanted to cross. As he started to speak again, it was as if the voice coming out of his mouth belonged to someone else. He was angry, but also in pain, and the pain held back the fury. "You owe me this, Saric. Don't all the years I've been working for you here mean you owe me like all those other people in your book? This is where I'm supposed to be able to call that in, and all you can do is sign up another client. I thought this meant more to you than business."

This hurt Saric. Why couldn't Rob see that it was exactly because it mattered that they needed to wait. He was being irrational, and he wasn't listening to Saric's reasoning.

"Rob, I promise you, when the time is right, we will go, but it's not right now. You need to trust me here. If this lead is what we think it is, we have one chance to get it right. We need to get the background information and make a plan."

Saric explained to Rob the steps he had already taken to start the preparations; the work Sense Check was doing and the conversations he was having with anyone who had ever owed him a favour, and who might have some insight into the US.

"But Rob, I need you to play your part. I can find the place, but I need you there with me. You understand Helen, that will be important."

Rob let out a small laugh in response. "Do I, Saric? Do I understand her? Did I ever know her, or was it all lies? You're right, for all I know she left because she wanted to. Maybe it was all planned. You read about things like this happening."

"Maybe that's true, and if it is, wouldn't it be better to know than to live the rest of your life in the dark?"

Rob looked up, his eyes wide, and stared at Saric.

"But I don't think that's what this is. I want you to be prepared, but I also believe that Helen and Ollie were taken, and that we will find them."

Rob sighed and half fell back into his chair. "OK, we can do this your way, but we haven't got long. If I think you are trying to delay me, even for a minute, and without good reason, I will go straight to the airport and get on the first plane to Nebraska.

"OK," said Saric, "here is what I need you to do."

CHAPTER 17

Saric made coffee and sat with Rob at the kitchen table. It was unusual for them to work here but nothing was normal anymore and Saric thought a change of location might remove thoughts of the bookshop problem being just another job. He had no intention of charging Hannah for his help, in cash or in favours. Her friendship was more important to him than any possible favour owed.

Rob listened quietly, saving his questions for the end, as was his usual manner. He took a minute to gather his thoughts before responding. "Is there a way that the details of the mines could have been released outside of Hannah?"

"I thought about that, but I think Gary will assume she is responsible, even if the source appears unconnected, and I wouldn't be surprised if he came after her anyway. He is like a spoiled child; he's angry that he's not getting his own way, and, in my experience, this is likely to end with him losing his temper with someone."

"Why don't we get in ahead of him, then? We could pay him a visit and persuade him to rethink his approach."

Saric noticed Rob's hand tense around the handle of his mug as he spoke. Even if this was the right strategy, he didn't think he would let Rob anywhere near Gary right now. His friend needed an outlet for his anger, and even Gary didn't deserve to be on the receiving end of it.

"Same answer. We might scare him off, but I don't think fear of us would outweigh his desire for profit. The risk of him retaliating at Hannah's expense is too high."

"Well, what then?" There was frustration in Rob's voice again.

"If we can't solve Gary then maybe we can solve the lease. Gary is just the middleman, the face of it, but he doesn't own the land and he's not party to the lease. Both the land and the lease are owned by the family at the big estate in town. I think we should try and agree something with them."

"And how do you propose we do that? When it comes to making money and keeping it, the landed gentry are just as bad as property developers. What's the plan? Just go and knock on the door and ask them to overlook the fact that Hannah has no right to live in their property? You won't get past the entrance gates!"

"We won't," agreed Saric. "We need some help."

"We better look at the list of favours, then," said Rob.

"Well, we won't actually need to do that for this one."

Saric looked a little awkward.

"Because?"

"I mentioned the situation to Grace when I was mulling it over. She's offered to help out."

"You mentioned it to Grace? In passing? You never told me you had stayed in touch with Grace."

Just for a moment, Rob's instinct to gently mock his friend came through in his expression.

"We have stayed in touch, yes—" he realised more was expected, "— she's very nice."

"Is she?" Rob smiled. His mood softened. "Well, I need to hear all about that."

Saric offered nothing more. Rob would have to draw that out of him at a more appropriate time. "Did she have an idea as to what she would do to get to these people?"

"She said it shouldn't be too hard. I gave her the Sense Check output on the landowners, and she trawled through their various interests. Much of what they do is focused on maintaining their cash, and they're also keen on preserving their history. They represent various good causes, mostly in the arts. Grace reckons money is not the best way in. Wealth is assumed, so, I guess she will be focused on something else. Anyway, she said she would have it figured out by the time she got here. Which is tonight."

"Tonight, eh?" said Rob, "it will be nice to see her again."

"She only said she would help because it needs doing quickly. We agreed not to work together again. She needs someone in her life that just wants to be with her for . . . er, to be, well, a friend."

"Oh," said Rob. "I hope that's not a problem."

"She wants to help. It will be fine." Saric really hoped that was true.

Saric had met Grace several years ago when he had helped her out of a tricky professional situation. She had come back into his life when he asked her to consult on the case of the accountant's murder.

This was how business worked for Saric; he had made all the money he could reasonably expect to need on a big case in Dubai years ago.

Since then, he had only asked for payment in kind; he would spend time helping his clients and in return they would owe him time doing whatever it was they did. Sometimes that was practical things, like gardening or electrics. In fact, Saric hadn't paid a tradesperson in years. More often, it was consulting on a case. With Grace, he had asked her to use her financial knowledge to help him catch the person who had murdered an accountant. Without her, Saric was sure it would have taken them much longer to resolve that one.

Saric still wasn't quite sure how it had happened – although Rob had engineered it somehow, he was sure of it – but one evening, he had found himself sitting at a table for two in a nice restaurant enjoying good food and excellent wine in the company of someone who had made him look at the world differently. She was beautiful, he had noticed that the first time they met, but, as he sat there, he realised that what he enjoyed even more than that was the way her brain worked. She looked at the world differently to most people, and differently even to him, as if she were looking at a slightly different reality to everyone else; the same but also different. She had challenged him and teased him, and then she had made him smile.

Since then, Grace and Saric had spent several evenings together. He had even visited her house last weekend, where he had cooked for her in an incredibly expensive kitchen that appeared never to have been used.

"I just don't have time to cook," she had said when he commented on the absence of anything other than wine, olives and chocolate in her fridge.

If anyone deserved that excuse, it was Grace. While Saric understood a little of what was involved in her work from their past encounters, they had resolved early on not to spend time talking about work and he was still not sure he had seen the extent of her role. What Saric did know is that it involved sorting out the messes made by the rich and powerful. She was always on call, often taking calls in the middle of the night to deal with the demands of oligarchs and celebrities with identities unknown to Saric. She was formidable when she was in work mode, fixing problems and healing rifts with an assurance that didn't somehow match her petite frame.

It suited Saric not to talk about work and he was grateful to have someone in his life who wasn't impressed by his skills and wealth but enjoyed him for who he was. He thought she might feel the same way about him.

Saric wasn't sure why he hadn't mentioned his meetings with Grace to Rob. Meetings? Should he call them dates? That didn't seem quite

117

right, either. He told himself it was because there wasn't much to tell; a few dinners and a couple of films were hardly worth mentioning. But perhaps, if he allowed himself to listen to the smaller voice in his head, it was because Grace made him happy, and he didn't think he could bear to tell his friend that, when the two people who had made him happy were still lost to him.

CHAPTER 18

February 2020

"You shouldn't have to do these menial trips." Daniel was agitated. "I won't have it when you are my wife."

Helen couldn't tell whether he would forbid her to join the shopping team, or if he would tackle the Elders about it. Either way, it didn't matter. She was going to have to make her escape before planning got underway for this ridiculous marriage.

If she couldn't get a message out, she would use Daniel to help her and Ollie escape. It was a more dangerous plan, and she hoped it wouldn't be needed. It wasn't just the risk of it not working out, it was also the damage it would do to Daniel. She would have to take him to the edge. She had created her Mary, the Great Mother, to gain control of him, turning all her years of study into the human mind to meet her own needs. She had only ever helped people before, and she knew that even if her plans got her home and free, she might never forgive herself for the harm she had done. At first, she thought she could get Daniel out with her, and then help undo the impact of the years of manipulation she had applied. She knew now this wasn't feasible. She and Ollie would need to get as much distance as possible between them and the Community, immediately call for help and hold out long enough for support to arrive. Having Daniel hanging around was a complication too far. Also, it would take months, maybe years, to de-program him. And there was no way she was going to hang around in the US for a minute longer than she needed to. In the end, she would simply walk away from Daniel, leaving him lost, confused and no doubt unable to take the place in the Community he was destined for.

She had used her version of Mary to direct Daniel to keeping her safe through profound spiritual guidance, which she had created. He knew that their time was coming, and that he and Mary would lead the Community with the truly faithful. Outside of this fantasy, she had tried not to impact Daniel's character too much. She needed him to remain a trusted part of the inner group of Elders. That meant she had to tolerate some of Daniel's natural self.

This had become significantly more difficult since the marriage had been approved. Before then, Daniel had been respectful, perhaps even slightly scared of her. It helped that her parents were senior Elders and that Daniel deferred to them, but she was also older than him and had experienced the world. As far as Helen knew, Daniel had hardly ever gone further than the Community's front gate. She thought it unlikely that he had tried to sneak out through any of the gaps in the fence, as she and her friends had done as children. When their parents thought they were doing chores, the girls used to enjoy mornings spent wandering in the hills. For Daniel, rules were there to be followed not broken.

Since their betrothal had been approved by the Elders, Daniel had changed. He now appeared to believe that he had some control over Helen; an ability to determine what she should and should not do. This was inconvenient in terms of her escape plan, a further factor to be managed.

However, Daniel did not have control over Helen's actions yet. Until they were married, she was the responsibility of the Elders, and they had determined that she should join the shopping team on their trip to the town for supplies.

Helen and Jessica sat together in a large truck with two other members of the Community. Helen had not met them before. They were in their early sixties, she thought, and they had that easy familiarity that suggested they were married. The women's responsibility was to undertake the shopping tasks and they were not permitted to drive. Therefore, each truck included a man behind the wheel. The Elder was in a separate vehicle.

As they drove out of the gate, the older lady said with a motherly smile, "It's scary, isn't it? But don't worry, the Lord will look after us."

"I trust that he will," Helen replied cautiously. It was important that these people grew to like and trust her; she must build a friendship with them. In this situation, Martha would be scared, and so Helen appeared that way. "There is so much wrongdoing out there, I am sure I will miss the safety of the Community."

"You will, but our task is important, and we must each play our part. We will look after you. Don and I have been making these trips for over twenty years. We know how to stay safe and away from the town's evils."

Helen wondered whether the Community had heard of online shopping. Surely, it was impossible for them not to have done. She considered why they chose to continue these journeys when other options were available. No doubt it was to perpetuate the fear of the outside. The safety of the Community was boosted by the terror of elsewhere.

The town, if it could be called a town, was barely more than a single street of shops. This made Helen smile. It was far from terrifying. In fact, it appeared very middle class and well kept. Flowers grew in pots outside every shop and statues lined the centre of the road. She wondered what Jessica would think if she ever saw a truly rundown city. But it was unlikely that she ever would, and that thought was not helpful to her now.

Her objective for this visit was twofold. Most importantly, she would be polite and helpful and ensure that she was able to take part in future visits, but if an opportunity arose, she would also gather information. She needed to find a way out. She wasn't sure what this would be yet — an opportunity to make a phone call or send a letter, perhaps — and first she needed to know where she was. She had thought about going to the cops, even a small town like this must have some sort of police presence, but she was cautious; she would have to be sure she would be taken seriously.

"This way," said Jessica, interrupting her thoughts. "Our first trip is to the pharmacy."

CHAPTER 19

February 2020

The shopping trip had been a success for Helen. At least to the extent that nothing had gone wrong. Strangers had looked at her, and she had followed Jessica's lead. She looked away when the town's people stared. She sunk into herself a little so they could see nothing of her female form. And for the whole time, her contented expression never altered.

What Helen wanted was some time to herself, to maybe find a local with whom she could strike up a conversation. The end game was simple – a phone. And, critically, some time before she was missed. But that was not going to happen in one trip. Like everything she had done to get home, this was going to take time.

When she got back, Daniel was straight over to check on her. "You seem fine. I wasn't sure you would be alright out there. The outside world has done quite enough to you already."

"Yes, I am fine. I told you not to worry."

"I wasn't worried. I just know it's not right. You should be spending your time here preparing for The Emergence. You are going to be my wife soon. Should I not get a say in what you do? Anyway, you are home now—" his expression changed, "—we should have a bit of quality time."

"That sounds nice, but I need to see Ollie now. I told him I would visit him as soon as I was back."

"No, you don't need to see Ollie now. You need to spend time with me."

Helen looked up. She breathed in deep and controlled her emotions. She started to formulate what the Mary she had constructed would do to get Daniel under control.

"Don't talk. Just walk with me. And I will explain a few things that you need to know."

Don't talk. This could be a problem, thought Helen.

"It's important to talk, Daniel," she said, "especially now." The 'especially now' meant nothing, she just knew it might give strength to her statement.

"I said, don't talk. I just want to be alone with you and quiet. I'm always thinking when I'm with you. This isn't right. Sometimes, we should just be together." He reached out and took hold of her hand. It was not a romantic gesture, and he did not try to entwine their fingers. He just put his large hand around hers.

This was all wrong. Only one man should hold her in this way, and that was her husband. This hand felt wrong. It was too big. The fingers too long. And the skin wasn't right, either. She could not articulate why, but she knew. Every part of her rejected it.

"We will be able to walk hand in hand in front of everyone soon. That will be a joy for us both." He squeezed her hand in his to make the point, but it was too hard, and she winced. He did not notice.

"This isn't allowed," Helen said, trying hard to keep her voice level. He made no move to let go.

"I know your false husband would have touched you. You have a child. I understand this." Daniel stopped walking and stepped in front of her. He was too close to her now, the gap between them was too intimate. Helen opened her mouth to say something. She had to get Mary back into his consciousness. But as she opened her mouth, he put a big finger over it and pressed it against her lips. The touch was too much. She could feel everything about him through his skin. Her instinct was to bite. To fight. But she had invested so much in this relationship, and she needed it to get her son home.

Daniel took his finger away and placed his hands on her shoulders. He tried to look deep into her eyes.

He wants to kiss me, Helen thought.

"Yes, he did. He touched me. He thought he loved me, but he did not know love. No one can know love unless it is through the Great Lord."

"Yes, I know, and the Great Lord is in me!" Daniel beamed. She was his betrothed. He had waited so long. So many dreams had been sent to challenge his commitment. But here it was, so close.

Think, Helen. There is danger here. Think.

At home, Helen knew how to deal with situations like these. Like every woman, since her early teens she had faced her fair share of unwanted attention. Lonely classmates whom she had thought of as a friend, only to discover they wanted something more and figured they were entitled to it because they had let her share a bottle of cider in the park; men in bars showing off in front of their mates; even one of her tutors at university. Most of it was well meaning, some of it less so, but she had usually been able to deal with it by talking her way out of it; making a joke and being clear that their attempts would get them nowhere.

127

This was more complicated. She couldn't tell Daniel the feeling of repulsion she felt when his hand touched hers; she couldn't be honest and say he stood no chance with her, because he had to believe that he did. She had to give him just enough.

She gently touched his cheek and then took his hand from her shoulder and held it in both of hers. She pulled it close to her chest, hoping he wouldn't feel her heart racing but figuring he would think it was passion if he did. "My love, what we have is special, more special than you know. The Great Mother has spoken to me and told me of our destiny. She shared this with me because it is important for us to know and to understand.

"We must trust her, even when this feels strange to us. She told me our destiny is to lead the Community away from its incorrect beliefs and towards the truth. But – and this is where it will be hard, my love – she told me that we must prove our worthiness. We must be tested."

She paused, there was a lot for Daniel to take in and she could see his confusion. He must be confused, this was part of the plan, but he must also feel part of the decision. She was patient with him, waiting for him to take her thoughts on board.

Slowly, she saw the understanding grow within him. He looked down at his hand in hers and spoke. "My dearest, the Great Mother has a plan for us, and we are to be special within this Community. We must face our tests and demonstrate our strengths. We should not be together as man and wife until we are married; we must pass this test."

Helen held back a smile; it was working. She pulled his hand to her lips and softly kissed the back of it. "You are so wise, my love. This will be a difficult test, but through your strength we will prove to the Great Mother that we are worthy."

CHAPTER 20

Saric and Rob were deep into preparations for a visit to the US. Rob's only experience of America was going to Disney World in Florida as a teenager. He had fond memories of that trip, but apart from the heat, it could have been anywhere. Saric was well travelled, especially across Europe, Asia and the Middle East. But his work had never taken him to the US, and he had never been on a holiday, at least not in the traditional sense. Rob was unconcerned, but Saric insisted they understand the terrain they would be operating in, including the heat and humidity, the governance structure of the local town and the main routes in and out.

Saric's computer alerted him to someone turning into his drive. It was a taxi with Grace in the back seat. She passed some cash to the driver and got out carrying an overnight bag. Instinctively, Rob got up to let her in; it was his job to answer the door to their guests. Saric stood up at the same time. They looked at each other.

"Don't you think I should let her in?" Saric said, mostly to himself. "Yes, I think I should," he concluded.

"Are we talking up here or in the lounge?" asked Rob.

"She might be hungry?" said Saric, as he left the room. "She forgets to eat when she works."

Rob followed him down the stairs.

Grace didn't bother to press the doorbell; she knew Saric would have seen her coming. She was ending a call as he opened the door. "We'll finish this off tomorrow . . . no, it can definitely wait until tomorrow. Yes, that's right, yes, OK." She put her hand on Saric's arm and smiled at him. Then into her phone, she said, "Yes, OK, goodnight."

Saric put his big hand over hers. "Thank you for coming."

The ease of their interaction caught Rob off guard. There was a softness in Saric's eyes that he had not seen before.

"That's no problem at all." Grace smiled at Saric and at the same time noticed Rob, who was hovering on the final step of the stairs.

"Rob, how are you?" There was genuine pleasure in her eyes; it was a look Rob hadn't seen from her before. She put her bag on the small desk by the door and squeezed past Saric to give Rob a brief hug.

"I'm well, thanks, Grace," he lied. "How are you?"

"Not bad, it's been a busy day, but that's over now. I hear you and Saric have been getting involved in more trouble?"

"This one's all him, I don't think we should be anywhere near it." His voice sounded harsher than he had anticipated. Grace twisted her head slightly, as if assessing him.

"Oh," was all she said. "Shall we get a drink. It's a bit odd to stand at the foot of the stairs all evening."

Saric led her through to the kitchen while Rob followed behind slightly. While Grace sat at one of the stools, Saric made for the fridge and started to collect wine glasses and a corkscrew. There was an interesting air of familiarity between them, Rob thought, as he settled himself standing in a corner, forming a triangle between them.

Once they had their drinks, Saric started to cook. As he did so, he started talking about Hannah, the development and Gary Lambert.

When he mentioned the developer, Grace nodded. "Yes, I have asked around about him. He thinks a lot of himself. He's been doing the rounds promising landowners astronomical returns on investments. None of it works financially, of course, but he sells a vision that they like. Half of them are too stupid to understand that the numbers don't add up, and the other half fancy themselves returning to some kind of lord of the manor status by putting these properties at the edge of their land."

"The thing is, he's got Hannah trapped," Saric explained. "She can't tell anyone about the mines because then he will have her evicted, but she can't stand by and watch these properties being built if they are going to put the people who end up living in them in danger."

Grace nodded. "And you can't use any of your normal strategies to deal with this because they all risk him going to the landlord?"

"Exactly, either through anger or embarrassment – with him, both are possible. I just can't risk it."

"And what do you have to say about all of this?"

Suddenly, Rob, who had been occupying himself by pulling at the label on his beer bottle, became aware that Grace was addressing him. He looked up and shrugged slightly. "I just don't see what it's got to do with us. We have our own problems."

"You think you should be on a plane to Nebraska, you mean?"

Rob wasn't surprised that Saric had told Grace about the new lead, but he still felt his temper rise. This was his case, Saric shouldn't be

133

discussing it without him. Even before he had finished the thought, he knew he was being unreasonable. "Maybe," was all he could manage.

"Well, you shouldn't. You need to get this right, not rush into the unknown. I know that isn't what you want to hear, but it's true." The anger kept rising. Of course she would take his side. "But Rob, I also know that he won't have told you that the reason he is making you take your time is because he loves you, and because this case matters nearly as much to him as it does to you."

Now it was Saric's turn to object.

"Rob, you must understand that Saric is doing what he is doing because he thinks it's the best strategy, and Saric, you need to understand that Rob isn't going to get that until all this is over. So, both of you need to trust me and tell me what you need so that I can help Hannah."

A silence ran between them for what seemed like a long moment.

"Alright," Rob eventually said. He looked at Grace with wide eyes. "You're right. I do trust Saric. And you. And my brother. And my dad. And that's it, really. All I've got. He reached out and held Grace's hand. "Do I trust you because I need to, or because I should?"

Grace absorbed his look and squeezed his hand. "Are you asking me or Saric?"

Rob answered her by looking across at his friend. His expression did not change, but a tear started to roll down his cheek.

With her free hand, Grace reached out to Saric, and he accepted it. The two big men looked at each other. Grace nodded at Saric. The sauce popping as it boiled on the stove was the only sound to interrupt the silence. The men moved at the same time, reaching out to each other. Grace smiled to herself as she watched them avoid holding hands. Even in this moment, that was too much. Each put their hand on the other's shoulder and the three of them stood there. Another tear dropped from Rob's face and hit the floor.

"Please help me," Rob managed.

"Yes," said Saric. Pop, pop, pop went the sauce.

"You said there was tuna," said Grace, and they all let go of each other.

Over a dinner of tuna steak in a tomato and garlic sauce, with steamed green beans and fresh bread, the three of them talked about Hannah's dilemma.

Grace had a plan, which they all agreed should work. Some years ago, she put in some time on the board of an enterprise promoting social responsibility in small business. Lord Chandlerton, the owner of the land where the development was now taking place, had been on a panel the organisation had facilitated to discuss the role of the private landlord in modern society. He had presented himself as a socially responsible landlord that genuinely cared for his community. Grace had been at the event but found all the panellists uninteresting and assumed they were mostly lying. She had left early to meet her sister at the Albert Hall and watch a showy but indisputably impressive version of *Swan Lake*. Grace was confident she could leverage their brief meeting to get access.

"You don't need me for this interview," Rob noted.

"It would be good to have you there," said Saric, "you might pick up something we don't."

"Yes, perhaps, but you don't really need me there. I could follow up another lead. Speed things up a bit."

Saric made a mental calculation. "OK, why don't you go and see this planning official Hannah spoke to? Check him out." Saric considered it highly unlikely that this individual would be in the loop. And even if he was, he wouldn't be a significant part of the housing scheme. He was probably more of a paid-off official. In any case, at most he was a bit player. It did not matter if Rob got this interview right or not.

Rob looked unconvinced.

"It needs ticking off, Rob. It will speed us up." Saric thought that was probably true.

"Fine. I will check the guy out."

CHAPTER 21

The next morning, Rob organised an urgent appointment with Mr Russell to discuss a recent approval that had been given by the department, but which was a cause for concern to Scotland Yard due to a possible connection to a terrorist organisation. He emphasised that a quick discussion should be sufficient to rule out any requirement for a comprehensive police investigation into the approval process.

"He will be able to disprove that with one phone call," said Saric.

"True, but that's one phone call he would rather not make. He will see me first."

"We should go now," Grace told Saric. Saric was in a suit, which fitted him perfectly, but seemed to restrict him in some way.

"Come back here when you're done. We'll come straight back, too." Saric added.

"Will do," said Rob.

If putting some pressure on this pathetic middle manager is going to wrap this thing up, I'm going to tear him apart, he thought.

•

It was only a short drive to Lord Chandlerton's house. Saric was grateful for this. As Grace had arrived by taxi the previous evening, they were in his car. He felt strangely uncomfortable, unsure of whether he should behave differently now that they were in a professional context, even though they were still alone.

Grace was quiet beside him, staring out of the window and watching the countryside pass. He left her with her thoughts.

Grace had called Lord Chandlerton before breakfast. Saric had assumed he would have staff to take calls for him, but Grace had his direct number and he had answered himself. From what Grace had told Saric previously, she and the lord had barely met beyond the panel discussion, but she had clearly made a positive impression, and he had agreed to meet them that morning.

Franklin House was an impressive stone property positioned at the end of a long, winding drive.

Hannah would no doubt compare it to something from an Austen novel, thought Saric, as they parked next to an array of cars outside the front door.

"He said we should meet him in the stud office," Grace said, as she stepped out of the car and straightened her jacket. Saric wondered what a stud office might be, but he nodded his assent and followed Grace along the side of the property and through a large wooden gate. They followed the path through a brick arch with a clock above it and into a stable yard, where wooden stables lined three sides of a brick-paved square.

Saric knew very little about horses, but he sensed that these were impressive animals. Nine stables were occupied, and the horses poked their heads out over the stable doors, keen to see who had just walked through the gate. One stable door was open, with the box empty.

On the final side of the square was a single-storey timber building with a sign that read 'Office'. Grace walked part way through the open door and found the room empty. As she did so, one of the staff emerged from the empty stable. She pushed a wheelbarrow full of straw in front of her.

"Good morning," she said with a confidence that surprised Saric; she was young, perhaps in her late teens. "You must be looking for Ralph. He said he was expecting visitors."

"Yes, we are a little early," Grace said with a smile. Saric thought that odd; they were exactly on time.

"Not a problem, he's running late. You'll find him in the arena just around that corner." The groom indicated the space between the office and the end of the stables.

"That's very helpful, thank you."

Saric followed Grace, who stepped confidently towards the arena. She looked at home here; while her outfit was incredibly smart, her tailored jacket, skinny black jeans and leather boots blended perfectly with the rural surroundings. As they turned the corner, Saric understood what the groom had meant by the arena. Lord Chandlerton was standing in the centre of a large, fenced area. A horse was attached to a long rope and was trotting in circles around him. The animal was beautiful. Its deep brown coat shone, and its muscles rippled as it moved.

It took a few moments for the man to notice them. Saric knew from his research that he was in his early seventies, but he looked at least a decade younger. He wasn't tall, but he looked strong. Saric assumed that keeping hold of horses as large as this one would necessitate strength. He was dressed exactly as Saric would have expected from a country gentleman, with a tweed coat over a checked shirt.

He smiled as he saw Grace and indicated that he would be a couple of minutes. He then made a small noise, and the horse instantaneously dropped his pace. He let the animal walk for a couple of minutes before taking hold of its head, giving it a scratch behind its left ear, and leading it out of the arena.

"Grace, it's lovely to see you," he said warmly. "Sorry I'm running a bit late; the old boy was a bit livelier than I was expecting this morning." He gave the horse an affectionate pat. "Why don't you and your colleague make yourselves at home in the office, there is coffee in the pot. I'll just put this one away and I'll meet you in there."

Behind a messy desk covered in paperwork, Grace and Saric found a comfortable seating area. Grace took Lord Chandlerton at his word and poured them both a coffee, before settling in a worn armchair and turning the pages of an old copy of *Horse and Hound*. Saric, feeling incredibly overdressed in his suit, moved a pile of bridles and other pieces of leather from a seat opposite Grace and sat down uncomfortably. The office was smart but well used, with photos from several decades showing various horses and riders. A selection of heavy trophies was on display around the room. Lord Chandlerton had obviously been successful. The more recent photos showed a number of different children on a range of ponies. These must be his grandchildren.

Lord Chandlerton joined them and apologised again for being late. He and Grace exchanged pleasantries, catching up on the exploits of mutual contacts and trading information. It was subtle, but Saric recognised a power game when he saw one.

"I saw that you are developing the site at Woodmancote," Grace said casually. "That is your land, isn't it?"

"It is," Ralph replied with a slight smile. "As you know, I don't usually sell to developers, our strategy for the estate is to keep it intact and find other ways to make it pay its way, but this is an interesting opportunity. The land stays in my ownership and the properties will be made available to local people."

Saric thought it sounded like a return to feudalism. He could see why the lord might like that, but he didn't think it sounded like anything other than an opportunity to increase his wealth and power.

"How did the opportunity come to you?"

"It's being organised by a consultant, who brought the idea to me. I believe he heard me speak about the importance of local communities in planning management."

"Is that Gary Lambert?"

"Yes. Do you know him?" There was a slight note of tension in his voice now.

Grace shrugged. "I know the name, but I have never met him."

"Look, its lovely to see you, Grace, but what is this about? I know you are far too busy to spend your mornings chatting about small-scale property deals."

Grace smiled but Saric interrupted. "I think we have a mutual contact, too. Is Hannah Bond one of your tenants?"

For the briefest moment he looked blank but picked up almost immediately. "She is. Hannah has the bookshop in the high street. She has been there longer than I can remember; built the shop from scratch. Did you know that? How do you know her?" He appeared genuinely interested now.

"I met her through the shop, and we became friends. She mentioned that she was a tenant, so it's nice to put a face to a name."

"But I really must ask, why are you here?"

Grace looked at Saric. They had agreed that she would make the decision regarding how far to push the meeting. This was what she did, after all.

Saric gave her an almost imperceptible nod.

"Ralph," Grace began, "we have come across some information that may affect the viability of the development. Before we discuss this with you, we need some assurances, particularly regarding Hannah and her property."

He looked confused now. There was real uncertainty on his face. "What does Hannah have to do with the Woodmancote site? It's nowhere near her place."

"I have been impressed by your social values in the past, and that is why we have come to discuss this with you first." Grace let the sentence hang slightly. Ralph couldn't avoid letting his eyes wander towards Saric, who often looked menacing, even when he didn't mean to. "As a result of this information, Hannah has received threats regarding her home. We would like some assurances from you that whatever we discuss today will not affect her right to stay there."

In all the scenarios that Grace and Saric had planned for the previous evening, they had not once considered what came next. With a slightly quizzical tone in his voice that betrayed his continuing confusion, Lord Chandlerton asked, "Are we talking about Hannah's dodgy lease?"

Grace looked stunned. "What do you mean 'dodgy lease'?"

"Well, I'm aware that it's not in her name, if that's what we're talking about? It never has been. But this seems like a lot of fuss for that."

"Why have you let her stay, then?" This was no longer part of the strategy; Grace was genuinely interested.

"Because I like her. She pays her bills every month and provides a service to the community. That place is more than just a bookshop, it's a hub for the town. She runs outreach programs for young people and the elderly to read and write and discuss literature, and she donates excess stock to the school. She even lets amateur authors host their book launches there. I let her stay because she makes this town a better place. Or did you think all my talk about social conscience was just for show?"

Saric wondered how often anyone ever managed to render Grace speechless.

Then, to continue the unusual turn of events, she responded, "I think I did, and I apologise for that. Hannah's lease is important to the situation, but it's not the main problem. I will take your word that you will not do anything to her detriment as a result of what we are about to tell you."

"Of course not, I'd be happy to amend the lease if that would set your mind at rest, but please, let's get to the point here."

"Ralph, we have reason to believe that the planning permission on the site was obtained fraudulently, and that any development is likely to be extremely dangerous to its occupants. We have some evidence to support this, which we would be happy to share with you."

CHAPTER 22

Shortly after Helen and Ollie disappeared, Rob made a playlist of songs that reminded him of the times they had spent together. He listened to it over and over again, until the sense of closeness to them that it stirred clashed so hard with his growing sense of hopelessness that he had to avoid it completely. His finger had hovered over the delete button many times, but he had never been quite ready for that. On the way to the planning department, he put the playlist on and turned the car speakers up.

He drove too fast for the winding road that took him into town. Two cyclists in full Lycra were working hard up a hill. In their ridiculous costumes, Rob couldn't tell whether they were male or female. He pulled out to overtake, accelerated far more than was necessary, pulled in too close to them, slowed down briefly and raced off.

Stupid bloody cyclists, he thought.

Katy Perry was singing about fireworks now, and he could see Helen dancing. She had flicked off her shoes and was swaying barefoot on the grass. The final rays of the long summer evening had turned the world golden. She looked at him with such joy. He picked her up in his arms and twirled her around as she laughed. She let herself be held with total faith that he could never drop her. Ever.

Rob parked in a staff bay of the council building. He did not plan to be long. He was directed along a sparse corridor to an office. Room 27 was written on the front. He did not knock.

As he entered the room, he was surprised to find it was a shared office space. There were four desks, with jumbled papers all around. His planning official was, however, alone. He had presumably made sure of that.

"Mr Barrow?"

"Yes, that's me. You must be Inspector Fielding? Do take a seat. Before we start, can I see some identification please?"

"No, you can't. Sit down." Rob pointed at Mr Barrow's chair. The planning official was an unexceptional looking man. Early forties, a touch of grey coming through on the temples. He was heavily overweight, and his faced looked red.

"I can't talk to you if you don't show me your identification."

Rob ignored the comment. He wasn't naturally an intimidating man. He had a kind face and was the sort of person strangers came to for help.

But his face had contorted from the years of anguish, and the sparkle in his eyes was now only there when he needed it to be. He had seen Saric 'extract data' from helpless, average people many times, and he was confident he knew the process. He felt the muscles across his back tighten.

"You recently passed a planning request for the Woodmancote development. Tell me about it."

Rob knew he could only go so far with the information they had. No mention of the Neolithic mines. No mention of Hannah. His brief was to find out if the planning team were involved in a deception or whether they had been deceived themselves. That was all.

"Look, I don't know who you are, but you are clearly nothing to do with the police, so I must ask you to leave." Mr Barrow puffed the words out, and the colour in his face deepened.

"You are right, Mr Barrow, I am nothing to do with the police. I am a private investigator. My client has an interest in the Woodmancote site. We know that you passed the planning permission, and we need to know if you had a personal interest in that."

Mr Barrow breathed hard. He looked around the room, as if the answer to what to do next might be out there somewhere.

"My colleagues will be back any second." That was enough of an answer for Rob to know he had something to hide.

"I'm happy to have this discussion in public if that makes it easier for you. Tell me what you know."

"I don't have anything to tell. And even if I did, I wouldn't open up to you. Who the hell do you think you are? I don't have to answer to you."

Rob stood up. "I haven't got time for all this," he said, forcing himself not to shout. He lurched forward and grabbed the hair on the top of the podgy man's head. He forced his neck back awkwardly and look down at him. "Tell me if you took some sort of cut on this deal."

"I have . . . protection," Mr Barrow managed. He had tears in the corner of his eyes. "You can't do this to me. Let me go!"

Rob knew this should have been enough. He had somehow got the pitch wrong. Saric would have had this man's life story by now; he would never actually have to hurt this sort of person.

Rob thought how he could smash this man's face into the desk. He had seen that on films. It would hurt. Maybe he would talk then. He felt his own anger; it was carrying him off. This whole stupid project. This man was keeping him away from Helen and Ollie.

151

"I don't want to make a mess of your face." It wasn't a lie. "But I will."

Rob's muscles flexed and he wondered what it would feel like to hurt a man who could not fight back. What the crunch of bone would feel like.

Mr Barrow squirmed but put up no real resistance. Rob saw his eyes flash to a photo on his desk. It was a staged, professional shot featuring the planning official with a woman, presumably his wife, and a small boy in a wheelchair. The boy had plastic tubes running into his nose. Whatever the tubes were attached to had been strategically hidden from the shot.

Rob let go and picked up the photo. He stared at it for a long time. Mr Barrow let out a whining noise but did not move. "It's expensive," he said.

Rob put the photo down and walked out, without looking back.

As he turned on the engine, music blared out of the stereo. Rob flicked it off before he could identify the song. He did not want to think about Helen right now. He wound the windows right down and drove back to Saric's house in silence, sticking to the speed limit.

CHAPTER 23

June 2019

Texas's owner was called Mick. He was a tall man, and strong. To Ollie, he looked like he had been cut straight out of the surrounding rocks. Despite this, he moved with a natural balance that showed how comfortable he was in this terrain. He did not look like he would be familiar with handling children, which was true. But Ollie felt at ease with him anyway.

"You kids probably shouldn't be messing around out here," he said, as Ollie trailed behind him.

They were taking a different route back to the border. Ollie was fascinated by Texas, his saviour. The Community didn't keep dogs. Mick had encouraged Ollie to stroke Texas's back to say thank you. The dog seemed to accept the attention as a fair exchange. As they walked, Texas followed behind Ollie, occasionally sloping off for a few moments to sniff and poke around. Ollie wondered what drew her attention to those places and not others.

"Yes, I know," he said. "I'm sorry. I'm not supposed to leave the boundary. It isn't right."

"I don't care about that, boy," said Mick, with a warm smile. "I mean, it's dangerous for you to be out here without knowing how to take care of yourself. There's wildlife you need to keep away from, or know how to fend off, and holes to fall in and loose boulders to avoid, and all sorts of other things. You have to be taught how to get about in a place like this. You don't get taught that stuff in there, do you, boy?"

"No." Ollie felt ashamed that he hadn't been taught something that sounded so important. "Could you teach me?"

Mick stopped and turned to look at the child properly. "I could, but I don't think that's the life planned for you. I don't really know what you people do, but it doesn't seem to involve the need for you to come out here. And that suits me."

"Oh," said Ollie. He looked back hard at Mick.

"Come on," Mick said gently, "we had better get you back home."

As they approached the fence, Ollie saw something that scared him. There were people coming towards them. It was some of the Community's teenagers, and they were looking for something.

Mick saw them too. "I think that's a search party. Your friends must have raised the alarm."

Ollie stopped in his tracks. He wasn't sure why, but he was scared. He had broken a rule, and the Elders did not like it when people broke rules. They would punish him. When he got to spend time with his mum, she always emphasised the importance of doing what he was told and behaving himself.

Mick was looking at him strangely, as if he were confused about something. After a little while, he groaned a bit, like he was annoyed about having to do something. "Don't want them to see you, eh?" He didn't talk like the men in the Community; he kept missing out words. "Come on, then, this way."

He turned off the main path and towards the hill. As they walked, Ollie remembered something from when he was little. A warning not to go with strangers. Mick was a stranger, but that warning was from before. No one warned him about strangers anymore.

After a few minutes, they reached a high fence. Mick moved some overgrown branches from one side of it to reveal a gap. "Through there," he said.

Ollie followed the instruction and stepped into a large garden. It wasn't like a garden with flowers. It had lots of rows of different types of plants. There were old ladies kneeling along the rows and digging and cutting things. It reminded him of somewhere he knew, but he wasn't sure precisely where.

They didn't seem to notice him at first, but then he felt Mick's hand on his shoulder, and he was guided towards one of the ladies kneeling by the plants. She had a basket by her side that was full of the tomatoes she'd picked.

As Mick's shadow passed over her, she looked up and smiled. Then she saw Ollie standing in front of him and the smile disappeared. Texas bounded over to her, burying her nose into her side in the hope of some attention.

"Hi Julia," Mick said quietly. "I think we need some help."

Ollie wasn't sure how he felt as Julia took him in. He wasn't used to adults looking at him in this way, as if he might be interesting.

"So, who do we have here?" she said. She was still looking at Ollie, but the question seemed to be for Mick.

"Well, this is . . ." Mick realised he didn't know. "What's your name, boy?"

"It's Oliver."

"His name's Oliver," Mick explained.

"And where have you come from?" Julia asked, this time addressing Ollie directly.

Ollie looked confused. Where was he from?

Mick cut in. "I found him out in the wilderness. Or rather, Texas found him. He'd got himself in some trouble with the wildlife. His mates ran off. It looks like he'll take a beating if they find out, so maybe we should sneak him back in? Then he can call the whole thing a big misunderstanding."

"Hmmm," Julia said. "Well, we had better get out of here, then." She stood up with surprising grace. "Come along," she said to Ollie, taking hold of his hand. "This way."

The three of them marched through the garden, with Texas trotting along at Mick's heel. Ollie had never been inside The Lodge before. The building itself was unappealing. It had been part of the hotel once, but the Community had converted it as cheaply as possible. There were hard floors that were easy to clean and basic fittings throughout.

Ollie was led through one of the back entrances and into a sort of boot room. Julia did not stop there. "In twenty minutes, it will be time to prepare for lunch. All the ladies will go to their rooms to clean up. I can take you out through the front and point out the path to take back."

"OK," said Ollie. "Thank you."

"We can wait in my room until then," Julia added.

"Me as well?" asked Mick.

"Yes, I think so," Julia replied.

The three of them filed into a small room with Texas close behind. Ollie only had the faintest memory of an earlier life, which over recent years his mother had fought hard to keep alive. She talked of his room at home being full of toys, story books, colours and songs at bedtime. He thought he understood it, but no matter how hard he tried, he couldn't form a clear picture of it in his mind. The children's rooms in the Community contained age-appropriate things; some of them were for play, but nothing had been bought just for him. And there was little colour in any of the living quarters. The Chapel was the only room in the estate that was filled with rich, vibrant hues.

Even by Ollie's limited experience, the room he had found himself in now was sparsely decorated. The bed was a metal frame with a thin mattress and one pillow. The covers were white, except where they were stained. A metal-framed chair was neatly tucked under a battered, thin wooden desk.

Mick remained standing, while Julia sat at the desk and invited Ollie to sit on the edge of her bed. He could feel the springs and wondered what terrible thing she must have done to end up here. The grown-ups rarely spoke about this place, other than to tell them to keep away. For some children, the warnings were enough, but for others the natural instinct to explore was too much to ignore. The reports that came back from reconnaissance missions told of crazy women, flailing arms and people shouting at nothing. Ollie wasn't sure how much of it to believe. Why would the Community keep a load of crazy women? What was the point of them all?

Julia could see that he was looking at her with curiosity. "Do you know what this place is?" she asked.

"Yes," Ollie replied, before adding, "thank you."

"Can you tell me?" Her voice was soft. Ollie could tell she was used to talking to children, or at least had been once.

"It's a home for women that can no longer make a contribution to the Community." He spoke in a robotic voice, remembering the official line he had been taught.

"I see," said Julia.

"Oh," said Ollie. "I don't really understand. You seem normal. Why do you live here? I thought this place was for cr . . ." He caught himself before finishing the word. "Not normal women."

Julia smiled. "No one is normal, young man. Everyone is special in their own way."

"You mean in the eyes of the Great Lord?"

"No. I mean really."

Ollie looked puzzled, but he did not know how to come back on that.

"How old are you, Oliver."

"I'm nearly eight. And everyone calls me Ollie. If that's OK?"

"Have you always lived here at the Community?"

160

"Well, sort of." He looked at Julia, then at Mick. These people seemed different. Kind, perhaps. The way they held themselves, the way they spoke. It felt comfortable. It reminded him of his mum somehow. "I came here when I was not-much-more-than-a-baby." He said the phrase as if it were a single word, and the robotic tone came back to his voice.

"And do you know why you came here?"

"They came to collect me. Me and Mum. I think we were in a lot of trouble out there." He waved his arm to show Julia where 'out there' was. "I suppose I remember it a bit."

Julia sighed and looked out of the window for a long moment. Mick just stood there in silence.

"Well, that's the same as me, then, Ollie. I thought I was in trouble, too. So, I came here. But it turned out the trouble was not out there. It was right here—" she pointed to her chest, "—inside me all along. And when I found out the truth, I had to come and live here."

"But my mum knows the truth, and she doesn't live here," Ollie said. He immediately went red in the face. Under no circumstances was he supposed to tell anyone that. He didn't know why he had felt compelled to confide in this woman.

161

Julia leaned towards Ollie and gently picked up one of his hands, which she held in both of hers. Her skin was worn, but her hands were soft. She looked at him as if for the first time. Texas stood up. "And what truth is that, Ollie? Tell me."

Ollie felt a great weight pressing upon him. He wished he could wriggle out from under it. He wanted to share his secret. It would be an enormous relief. If his mum really was a crazy person, he wanted to know. And if she wasn't, he needed to know that, too. Tears formed in his eyes. He looked at Julia, then at Texas, and then up to Mick.

"Don't worry, boy, you can trust Julia," he said. It was enough.

"My mum says there's another truth. Something more important. And that we need to go home. My dad is waiting for us or might come soon. Either way, we are going to have to leave. And everything will go back to normal. And I'm not the person they tell me I am." He took a deep breath and let it out while the tears rolled down his cheeks. "Is Mummy crazy?" He was pleading for an answer now.

Julia pulled the lost little boy into her arms and let him cry into her shoulder. "No, Ollie, your mum is just fine," she said.

When Ollie's tears had subsided, Julia sat next to him on the bed. Mick took the seat and looked across the room at the two of them, giving nothing away.

"Ollie," Julia said, "would you like to hear a poem?"

"I don't really like poems," he replied, looking at the floor.

"I don't think you have heard these sorts of poems before."

"OK, then." He showed no real interest.

"Are you sure?" asked Mick.

"Now, then, Mick, poems are written to be heard. I can't keep it all to myself, can I? Not when its needed. Would you mind?"

Mick made no more comment. He got up and moved to the small wardrobe. He opened a drawer, reached into the back of it, twisted some sort of catch and pulled out a book. Julia was only allowed books that the Community deemed appropriate. These were on her desk. But there were some possessions from her life before The Lodge that she had managed to keep hold of. She had kept them hidden in various ways, until Mick had taken care of it.

*

Mick was an unexpected addition to Julia's life. The years after she had been placed in The Lodge were like a dream. She made no attempt to engage with anything, especially herself. She did what she was asked, and the routine of the days rolled into weeks, months and then years. In principle, The Lodge was engaged in doing what it could to support the Community. In reality, there was little output and most of the energy that was spent on the occupants was nothing more than containment. The women living there had a mixture of afflictions, ranging from total mental breakdown to early onset dementia. Julia was the only resident living there due to 'theological inconsistency'.

Mick had witnessed the Community arrive and evolve. He had little interest in it. He lived where he did so he didn't need to take an interest in things. But occasionally, he would find himself brushing up against his neighbours. He would see them scurrying around; there seemed little structure to what they did.

One day, as he and Texas were tracking a mule deer, the dog ran off and he followed her towards the edge of the Community. He came across three women standing next to a fallen section of chain-link fencing. Out of instinct, he offered his assistance. After a little discussion, the women agreed that this would be helpful, as it would mean there would be no need to bother the Elders over such a trivial task. In exchange for his effort, they gave Mick a bunch of herbs from their garden. A satisfactory relationship between them had begun.

It was through doing these odd jobs that Mick came to meet Julia. She was in the garden, and she looked different from the other women. She was clearly sad. The women in charge seemed certain of their purpose, while the others, whom Mick had tried to ignore, were troubled. Julia wasn't sick, but she was downhearted. When Mick first saw her, she was moving seedlings into individual pots.

"You'd do better if you soaked that soil first," he suggested.

"You'd do better if you minded your own business," Julia replied.

"Well, now, flowerpot lady, that's not very nice."

Julia stood up. "No, I suppose not. I guess I'm not used to being nice to people."

"Well, flowerpot lady, how about if I'm nice to you and you're nice to me. That's how it normally goes, I think."

Julia smiled. Her first one in years. Maybe it was wrong, but she liked it.

"OK. Let's try that, then."

And it was from there that they had got to know each other. Mick had come to understand a little of who Julia was. Maybe even a little of why she was that way. They took the moments they could. They talked. They wondered how life might have been if things were different.

After some years, Julia reached a decision and Mick wanted to help. So, when he had convinced The Lodge women that he needed to fix some plumbing, he gained access to Julia's room and built a false bottom in one of the drawers in her wardrobe. The hidden storage contained paper, pens, a copy of the *Adventures of Huckleberry Finn*, some jewellery, and a seemingly ancient book of nonsense poetry.

*

Mick passed the book of poetry to Julia. As she sat with it on her lap, Ollie was transfixed by the front cover. He felt something. A fear of the unknown wrapped in a sense of total comfort. He pulled himself into Julia, and there was something familiar in facing the sadness of this picture – and what this book might contain – under the protection of a loving arm around him.

She skipped to the back. Ollie had glimpses of pictures that he wanted to see more of . . . or else never see again.

She read him the poem.

He wanted to cry. Or fight. He wanted to make it end. There was too much sadness in the world. Why did it need to be captured here, in this poem, forever? The sadness will never end. The hope will never be fulfilled. He felt overwhelmed and stared at the floor.

"I think I have heard this before," he said.

"Well, maybe you have, young man. It's a famous poem."

For a few minutes, everyone sat in silence until Mick realised the time. "Better go, boy," he said, ending the moment. He took the book back from Julia and returned it to its secret place.

Whilst the rest of The Lodge busied themselves, Mick and Julia walked out of the front door.

"Take this path to the lake," Julia instructed. "Squeeze through the gap to the side of the gate and follow it round to the left. You'll know where you are from there. And tell the Elders the other children made everything up to get you in trouble. It will be your word against theirs. And never back down. They couldn't see the truth if it jumped up and smacked them in the face. Goodbye, Ollie." She bent down and kissed him on the forehead. He ran off.

As they watched him run down the path, Julia found Mick's big, rough hand and held it tight.

"What are they doing to those kids, flowerpot?" Mick asked.

"They're killing them."

Mick let her hand sink into his.

CHAPTER 24

June 2020

Over the next few months, Helen visited the town on three further shopping trips. She followed her plan closely and soon managed to convince the other members of her party that she was trustworthy. It wasn't difficult; it was in their nature to want to trust her. This was, Helen thought, probably how they had ended up wasting their lives in the Community.

By the fourth trip, she was allowed to fulfil small tasks with just her shopping partner and no further supervision. She helped to collect fabric from the haberdashery and candles from the general store. Luckily, the others overestimated how long these tasks took; they walked slowly and hesitantly, and Helen was able to carve out a few precious minutes to notice the pay phone in the sweet shop, or glance at a map on the wall by the town hall. The information was important.

Slowly, she built up a picture. She knew generally where she was because after escaping as a teenager, she had researched the Community online. She knew about its history and that it was in Nebraska, but what she needed now was local knowledge, such as transport links and communication options.

Helen's trips had furthered her distrust of the local police; she assumed from the Elder's meetings with the town leaders that the Community had influence over them. She sometimes wondered whether she was being paranoid; did people really pay off officials or was that just in films? Whatever the truth, she could not risk being found out now. She would not go to them.

In the best-case scenario, one phone call might be enough. She could make the call, go back to the Community as normal and wait for someone to come and get her and Ollie. But The Emergence ceremony was only weeks away and after that she would be forced to marry Daniel. The thought was unbearable. So, if she could not get help, she would have to carry out the more challenging plan. She would leverage all the work she had done with Daniel to get him to believe they needed to get away and build a new church in their own name. Between them, they could get hold of the keys to one of the vans, make some sort of distraction and just drive out of there. But they would need to know where to go. Somewhere they could drive to where she and Ollie could hide away for long enough to arrange a route that would take them far away and, ultimately, out of this country and to home. The first few hours would be key; she would need to know exactly where she was going.

It wasn't easy to gather this information. The people who served her in the shops seemed reluctant to speak to her. They were polite, almost deferential, in fact, but while they would happily chat with the other customers as they served them, about their children or the local gossip, they spoke about nothing with Helen except what she wanted to buy. How she longed for one of the salespeople to ask her about her own child, how he was doing and what trouble he had been in this week. She wasn't sure if this reluctance to speak to her was due to nervousness because she was strange and different, or whether there was something more sinister going on. Was someone in the town making sure shop staff didn't speak to the Community? The more Helen thought about it, the more that idea made sense. The Elders were taking a risk by letting the Community experience the outside world. The people in the shopping teams were terrified of outsiders, and they were kept in line by stories of the sin and terror that pervaded every aspect of their lives. But how long would that last if they started to speak to them? What if the team came to understand that the world was not only sinful but joyful and loving and full of wonder? Yes, it made sense that the Elders would want to prevent that.

Slowly, Helen managed to piece together some of the information she needed. She couldn't ask anything directly, of course, but there were other ways to gather intel. The lady who ran the shop where the

Community purchased its sewing supplies was incredibly apologetic that the linen they'd ordered had not yet arrived from her supplier.

"That's not a problem, I'm sure we can wait until next time," Helen had said sweetly. "Where do you order it from? Does it have to come far?"

"From Lincoln, but there was a crash on Route 80 earlier in the week, so the truck couldn't get through."

"That must be frustrating for you. Isn't there another way around?"

The older lady looked at her slightly strangely. Helen wondered if she had pushed her curiosity too far.

"You're not from around here, are you? Not unless you want to go all the way up to Sioux Falls and spend an extra three hours on the road."

"Oh," Helen said, trying to look uninterested. "When do you think it will be available?"

Through a series of conversations like this, Helen was able to piece together an idea of routes in and out of the town. There was only a single road running through it, and this went from east to west and connected the two interstate routes that ran from north to south across Nebraska. The nearest town that anyone outside the area would have heard of was

Denver, over the border into Colorado, but that was more than 275 miles away. The town had no train station, and a bus route ran through only on Tuesdays and Saturdays. The only real way in or out was by car.

Sitting in her room, Helen thought about who she would call when she got the chance. If she couldn't trust the local force, perhaps she could call the police in the UK, or maybe the British Embassy. The problem was that this would take up precious time. Public employees meant bureaucracy; she would be kept on hold and batted around between different departments. Besides, would they even believe her? Even in her own mind, as she prepared that conversation, it sounded like a hoax.

The obvious answer was also the most difficult. She should call Rob. His was the only number she knew by heart. And really there was no one else. As she thought of Rob, it was like a wall built up in her mind, preventing her from thinking out loud the thoughts she had been hiding from for the last five years. Would he answer? And if he did, would he even want to help her?

She had lied to him. From the day they met, everything she had told him had been a falsehood. Her family, her past, even the name he called her wasn't really hers.

173

And he had not come for her. Which meant either he had found out the truth and hated her for it, or he had forgotten all about her. By now, he had probably met someone else. After all, it had been five years. She pictured him with a new wife. She would be beautiful and kind and make him laugh. Most of all, she would be honest with him. Maybe they even had a child together.

She knew that she should be happy for him – he deserved that life – and she could even make herself think that thought, but deep down, she knew she didn't mean it. The pain of missing him burned just as hard as it had the day she was taken.

Because even though she had lied to him about a thousand things, she had told him the only truth that mattered; he was her soul mate and she loved him in a way that was deeper and more honest than anything else she had ever said to him.

And that is why she hesitated. Even though being apart from him hurt, at least while there was half a continent and a huge ocean between them, she could believe he was missing her, too. If the truth was that he hated her for the lies she had told, she wasn't ready to hear it.

Daniel burst into her room, interrupting her chain of thought. He looked around, as if someone might be hiding in a corner. He looked excited, like a child on Christmas morning.

"Martha, come with me, I have something to show you."

Helen was suspicious; Daniel had been overly keen to share all sorts of idiotic things with her in the past, but this was exciting him in a way she did not recognise.

"Where?" she asked.

"You'll see! Come on, we need to go now whilst the Elders are meeting."

Helen fixed a smile on her face. "Where are we going where you wouldn't want the Elders to see us?"

"You'll see!" He grabbed her hand and pulled her to her feet. Helen wanted to grab the cup off her desk and smash it into his face; how dare he pull her around like this? But she maintained her smile.

"Fine, OK, show me this secret, then." She made it sound like she was happy to play along. She was so close to executing her escape plans that she couldn't afford to break character now. And there was Ollie. She would do anything for him. The word 'anything' bounced around her mind as she let Daniel hurry her along a corridor.

Helen knew the set-up of the Community. The bedrooms were split into four areas. Unmarried men, unmarried women, children and

175

married couples. They were heading for the married section. Daniel strode out at a pace that left her uncomfortably half running, half walking. She felt like a child being pulled along by her dad for an appointment they were late for. They were right in the middle of the married couples' bedroom area when Daniel suddenly stopped. "Here we are," he said. He put his arms round her shoulder. He was hot with anticipation. Helen understood what was about to happen.

Daniel reached out, turned the door handle and pushed the door open. "Go ahead," he said.

Helen looked up at him and contemplated her options. She could scream and someone might hear and put a stop to things. But how far back would that put her? Daniel hadn't done anything wrong yet. Certainly nothing that the Elders would be unhappy about. She had to go in.

The double bed against the wall looked brand new and neither of them could stop looking at it. Made with crisp white sheets, it didn't appear that Daniel had slept in it yet. It was all in anticipation. There was a desk, some books and, opposite the bed, a large picture of Mary – a bigger version of the one that was in Helen's room. It would be looking down on the occupants of this bed. Watching everything.

"Look at this," Daniel said, directing her to the desk and pointing to a black frame. There were four sections to it, and it spelled out the word 'LOVE'. In the first quadrant was the same picture of Mary that hung on the wall. The second contained a photo of him and Martha. Her arms were by her side, and he had one arm clenched around her shoulder. The third was a picture of Ollie. He had a smile fixed on his face, which Helen recognised as his fake, 'this-is-the-face-you-want-to-see' grin. Daniel saw only what he wanted to see in it. The fourth section was blank.

"We will fill this section soon enough, my love," he said. He picked up the photo frame and gazed at it. "Our own child will be everything you could hope for."

Helen swallowed hard. *My son is already everything to me*, she thought. *And you will never take that from me. That space will remain blank forever, you absolute bastard.*

"Yes, my love, if it is the will of the Great Lord, our children will be everything to us," she said. She could not get the emotional intonation quite right, but Daniel was not really listening.

He put the frame down and sat on the bed. "I will make you happy here," he said, patting the sheets and summoning her to sit next to him.

This is going too far, she thought. She had not seen him like this before. She did not have his full attention. He was not even looking at her, at least not as another person. She knew exactly how he was looking at her. *With lust.*

"This is not the right way for us to be thinking. We must do things in the right way."

"So, soon, my love, this will be the right way." And then more to himself, "every night".

Helen grappled for a way to gain control. She had got used to pulling Daniel into the fantasy world she had created, where she could assume the role of the Great Mother. But she had to have his full attention. It was dangerous to the whole thing to try and slip into that world without him. The whole construct could be exposed. Another instinct was burning in him right now; something basic.

"Sit," he said. He was ordering her. She sat. He put his hand on her knee. He was not supposed to do this. He was breathing hard.

Helen felt sick. She was going to have to scream and fight and . . . and . . . and what? Lose all these years of work? She was so close. Could she really do *anything*? The word filled her mind. She put her hand on his and tried to gently lift it. His grip tightened.

"You're hurting me, Daniel. Daniel! You're hurting me!" Suddenly, she had his attention. He looked her straight in the eye. She had to strike now.

"You know who I am, Daniel. The great things that we shall achieve need us to *let go of everything* that we feel until *the right time;* now we should be at our most pure of heart. *It is time to go*."

The last suggestion was unsubtle, and more direct than she would usually opt for. She stood up as she said it and felt his hand slip away from her.

She walked straight out of the room before he could regain his composure. She felt him looking at her as she left. It hurt.

CHAPTER 25

Saric needed to do many things, and he was struggling to decide the right order to do them in. He needed to tell Hannah that she was safe, he needed to stop the development, he needed some time with Sense Check to put together a plan for visiting Julia Hawkins, and he needed to check in with Rob.

Grace seemed to read his mind. "I can deal with Gary Lambert if that helps."

"You shouldn't have to. The introduction to Lord Chandlerton was a favour; this is my project, not yours."

"I know, but I'm happy to do it. It's not a favour, there would be nothing owed, but you have more pressing things to deal with, and I'd like to help you, Saric. You have kept your word to Hannah already, and stopping the development is just the next step. And anyway, I'm pretty good at dealing with dodgy businessmen. Maybe even better than you."

As he concentrated on the road home from Franklin House, he could only see her out of the corner of his eye. He didn't want her to do anything for him out of some sense of obligation, but he figured she was being genuine. "Thank you, I'd appreciate it."

"I'll find a way for you to make it up to me one day," she said with a smile.

They drove in silence for a few minutes before Grace spoke again. "What are you going to do about Rob?"

"What do you mean?"

"Well, you know as well as I do that there is a good chance we are going to get back to your place and find him treating his wounds after picking a fight with that planning officer."

"I looked into the officer; he wouldn't have wounded Rob," Saric said seriously.

"That's not the point, Saric, he's not in control. You need to look after him."

"How do I do that? He needs to trust me, and I don't think he does."

"He does trust you. If he didn't, he would be storming that cult right now, but there are things that matter even more than trust, and a lost wife and child triggers a much more basic response than faith in a friend. You need to keep him with you, right where you can see him, and you need to get moving. He needs to see progress."

They spent the rest of the journey in silence. As they pulled up outside the house, a taxi was already waiting for Grace. Saric assumed she must have called it using an app on her phone. "I've got some things to deal with," she said. "I'll get one of my legal team to draft the new lease over the bookshop and I'll let Hannah know you need to speak to her later today. And don't worry about Gary Lambert, I'll deal with him. You go and do what you need to do with Sense Check. But remember what I said about Rob. You need to keep him with you, in more ways than one."

She leaned across the car and kissed him briefly on the cheek before exiting the vehicle. "I'll call you later to let you know how I get on."

Saric stayed in the car and Grace's taxi pulled away. He wondered if her goodbye had been a little colder than usual. Grace was right about Rob, he should have done a better job of taking care of him over the last few weeks, but he felt slightly unnerved that she had recognised that so easily.

It was usually easy to present the version of himself that he wanted people to see. In truth, most people didn't pay enough attention to see the other parts, but Grace seemed to see the whole of him. He liked that, but he also felt exposed; he hoped his weaknesses wouldn't scare her away. He didn't have time to worry about that now, though. Rob's car was in the drive, and he needed to see his friend.

Rob was sitting at his desk when Saric entered the office. His computer screen was on, but he didn't appear to be focusing on it. Instead, he was staring at the empty space on the wall ahead of him. Saric closed the door more heavily than usual, which seemed to bring his attention back from wherever it had been.

"How was the planning officer?" Saric asked as he settled himself behind his own desk.

"I messed it up. I went in too hard, and he saw straight through me. He threatened to call the police if I didn't leave. I'm sorry, mate."

"It's OK, we don't need him. Grace and I came to an arrangement with the lord." As he said it, Saric wished he hadn't. It sounded like he had replaced Rob with Grace, and that she had been a better partner.

If Rob noticed, or felt the slight, he didn't comment. Saric wondered if he was really paying attention or whether he even had the capacity to care about such things right now. He still felt bad about it.

"He's going to give Hannah a new lease for the shop and flat, which takes away Lambert's leverage," he continued. "Once he's done that, we can go to the authorities with what we know about the land and take him out."

Rob still didn't respond. Saric thought carefully; he didn't want it to sound like now he had sorted out Hannah they could move onto Helen, but he really did want to make some progress with Sense Check, and Grace's words of advice about taking Rob along with him were ringing in his ears.

"Sense Check has finished some of the analysis on the Nebraska site; if I look at the conclusions, can you start working on the logistics of getting us there?"

Rob looked at him, as if finally recognising he was in the room. "To Nebraska? When?"

"Just look at options for now, but I think in the next day or so. I have no idea if there are direct flights, so we will need to factor that in."

"What have you found?"

"Nothing yet. I need time to review the conclusions. As soon as I've done that, I will let you know. But I don't want the admin to hold us up when we get to that stage."

Saric turned his attention to his screen. After the breakthrough with the Nebraska location, he had requested a more detailed analysis of the area, and anything connected with Peace's Community there.

The primary sources remained the will of Helen's grandmother, Alice, along with the transcripts of the interviews with her lawyer and the priest. Sense Check would have cross-checked the information against anything in its databases, to either confirm or refute any facts or assertions within the inputs.

As a result of its work, Sense Check had developed a series of conclusions, which it provided along with details of how confident it was in their validity. It had also produced detailed analyses of each of the primary data sources, which were annotated with information on how they had been cross-checked and verified.

In an effort to speed up the process for Rob, Saric was tempted to skip straight to the conclusions, but it was important to follow the same strategy as they did with every other case, and that meant reviewing the primary data analysis first. As with most interview transcripts, Sense Check had highlighted much of the content as fundamentally irrelevant; the program didn't really understand small talk, although Saric had grown to realise that it was a necessary part of getting to the important statements. Both the lawyer and the priest were fundamentally honest men; Sense Check had not identified any outright lies or inaccuracies, although it had flagged several 'more data needed' inferences in the priest's commentary on religion.

What interested Saric now was the conclusions from the postcard. Grandcast River was a small town in Western Nebraska; it had a population of a few thousand and seemed to rely on agriculture as its primary economic activity. It was served by a single main road, which passed through the town from east to west, and it had no other significant transport hubs. Like many towns in that part of the US, Grandcast River was nowhere near anywhere, being isolated between the mountains and wilderness plains.

The town's website was of limited interest. It carried the usual content of out-of-date stories about market days and Thanksgiving events at the local high school. There was no reference to the Community, which was strange, as it was within the town's boundaries and its residents must have made up a significant portion of the population. There were, however, several strange references to "our generous benefactors" in stories about the regeneration of the high street, new equipment in the elementary school play area and a community centre next to the church.

"We're going to have to be careful," Saric said, mostly to himself.

186

Rob looked up at him. "Why's that?"

"This town's too well funded. There is nothing there generating any income beyond a few farms, but it's got a level of investment like something you'd expect in one of those new technology hubs. It's being run by someone, and I'd be willing to bet that's got something to do with the Community."

"Is that relevant? We're only going to speak to Julia; what does the town have to do with it?"

"I'm just gathering facts; I don't know when they will be useful, but I'd rather know what we might encounter so we can prepare for it."

Saric returned to Sense Check. At the turn of the twentieth century, the Lakeview Hotel had been a reasonably successful business, providing a stop-off for people travelling across the state to more interesting places. Later, as flights replaced road trips for long distance travel, it had repurposed itself as a hunting lodge. That had closed during the sixties and the hotel had lain empty for over a decade before Peace's Community had come in. On the town museum's website, Sense Check found old maps of the hotel. Apparently, it was of some architectural interest, which had merited preserving the documents. This was useful, because cross-referenced against the aerial photographs available on

Sense Check's mapping app, Saric was able to get a good idea of the terrain and access routes.

Finally, Saric turned to the Community itself. Sense Check routinely updated its checks for new information and had flagged some recent internet news stories, which revealed a possible recruitment drive. Several local papers across four different states had run stories about forthcoming visits by 'the Elders'. They were being led by a man calling himself Elder Gregory, who had the rather elaborate title of Global Head of Engagement and Enlightenment. The coverage across the various news sources appeared to be evenly split between outrage at dangerous forces coming to take away the town's young people and welcoming the 'true message' into the area. Saric wondered what might go on at these events. He had never been in any doubt about his own atheism but was interested in the faith of others, particularly when it involved people giving up their homes and families to dedicate their lives to it.

Elder Gregory must be an incredibly persuasive and charismatic man, Saric thought.

As his final cup of coffee ran out, Saric started the upload of the transcript of his interview with Lord Chandlerton. It was unlikely to be relevant to anything now, but it was data, and so it should be included.

He picked up his empty mug and wandered down to the kitchen, where he found Rob standing at the door and staring into the garden. It was early evening and still warm; in another world, this would be the perfect night for sitting outside, drinking crisp white wine and talking for hours. This wasn't that night.

Rob turned to look at him expectantly. Saric barely knew what to say, but nonetheless the words came out. "We are ready, it's time to go."

CHAPTER 26

August 2020

Life in the Community created many conflicts for Helen.

It was terrible being held against her will and seeing Ollie only under supervision, and with The Emergence ceremony and her subsequent marriage to Daniel growing closer, she felt a constant sense of unease. Most of all, she missed Rob. Even though she doubted every day that he would still want her, she knew that she had to find her way back to him. Every night when she looked up at the moon and the stars, she took comfort from the fact that Rob could see them, too. Even if this wasn't at the same time, they were there and they were constant.

On a practical level, her day-to-day situation wasn't too hard. She stayed in a comfortable room, had three meals a day prepared for her and was only expected to contribute to the simplest of tasks in return. She never had to worry about paying bills or whether she should try for the next promotion; she simply had to comply with instructions.

Community members rose at dawn and spent time in silent contemplation before breakfast. The morning was spent completing work assignments. Helen's usual tasks were sewing or prepping vegetables. After lunch, there were teachings and discussion groups for those who were not yet full members of the Community, and independent study time for the members and Elders. Evenings were spent in silent prayer.

It was boring, but it wasn't hard. Helen could see why it appealed to people. She hated that she had no autonomy and missed choosing what she would do each morning, even things as small as what she would eat or wear. But being told what to do was easy in its own way, as she had no responsibilities. Every decision was made by the Elders, who denied their own responsibility for the consequences by deeming them to be the will of the Great Lord. For those who knew nothing else, it was simple and straightforward.

Jessica was one of those people. She and Helen often spent their mornings together as part of their work duties. Over time, Helen had grown fond of her; she was kind and honest and although it did not appear so at times, she was also bright. What she lacked was curiosity. She had no interest in anything beyond that which she could see in front of her, or which was told to her by an Elder. Jessica was happy with that.

Helen had spent many hours contemplating whether it would be better to be like Jessica, being happy in the tiny, invented world in which she lived and never wondering if there was anything else.

There was a strong temptation to want this. For Jessica, the Community was the truth, and she was happy with that. She rarely felt emptiness or loss or pain of any kind. But even with that temptation, Helen knew that she would never want that life. She wanted to know the truth of the world, whatever that was, and even if it was more painful than the lie. In any case, to be capable of considering the question meant that Helen was aware of the alternative, and that took away the choice for her to decide to know anything less than she already did.

That morning, Helen and Jessica were sewing in a small group of young women. It was almost lunchtime and Helen was already thinking of whether she would be able to sneak a few minutes with Ollie that day. Lunchtime was often the best opportunity to see him, and she'd give him a few words of encouragement or just catch the smell of his hair.

In many ways, the conversation this morning was the same as would be taking place between groups of young women everywhere. Helen had talked about the same things hundreds of times with her own friends. She felt awful distinguishing between her real friends at home and the people in the Community, whom she pretended to be friends with to enact her plan and protect her son. The reality was more complicated; she loved these women like her friends at home, but she knew that one day she would leave them, perhaps hurting them in the process, and she had to be OK with that.

They had been teasing one of the younger, unmarried women because she had been seen speaking with one of the young men. Due to his unfortunately large nose, the group did not consider him to be a suitable match. Helen smiled slightly as the younger woman blushed. The conversation then moved on to whether one of the other women would have a boy or a girl when her baby arrived next month.

Helen had to remind herself of Martha's persona as the woman sitting across from her placed a gentle hand on her own stomach and told the group "I do hope it's a boy, my husband will be so proud if it is and I don't want to disappoint him."

The group assured her of the Great Lord's will, and she appeared reassured.

Charlotte, the woman who supervised their sewing group, was a kind lady and married to a well-regarded Elder. He wasn't one of the leaders and appeared to have no interest in being so, but he was respected by the leadership, who relied on his wisdom with the confidence that he was not trying to overthrow them. Unlike many of the supervisors, Charlotte allowed their conversation, but only if they were not too disruptive and completed their tasks. It was unusual for her to speak, however, so Helen was surprised when she interrupted.

"Don't look so sad, Martha, it will be your turn soon." It seemed that Helen had not hidden her disgust at the Community's sexism as well as she had hoped.

"What do you mean, Charlotte? I am not disappointed; I look forward to the baby arriving and pray that he is healthy."

"Of course you do, and soon it will be your turn. As you know, my husband Jacob leads The Emergence ceremonies, and he told me last night that your ceremony will go ahead at the next new moon. Once you have emerged you can take your place as a full member of the Community and fulfil your true purpose. You will be free to marry Daniel and give him sons of his own."

It was as if an invisible force had hit Helen in the centre of her chest. All the air disappeared from her lungs, as her brain seemed to forget how to instruct her body to breathe. She had run out of time. The new moon was only two weeks away. She could wait no longer, she had to bring the plan forward.

CHAPTER 27

From Saric's point of view, the choice to fly business class was simply a practical one. It was important to arrive well rested and he was unable to do this in the cramped seats of economy. As they stepped off the plane and into the dry Nebraska summer heat, he stretched to relieve the tension in his back but otherwise felt ready to face whatever lay ahead.

Rob had not been able to enjoy the relative comfort of their journey, as his mind ran through every possible iteration of what might happen over the next few days. He felt every minute of the six-hour time difference, which meant that he had not slept for more than twenty-four hours, even though the current time meant it was only just past midday.

On the plane, they had discussed the plan in hushed tones, trying to avoid the attention of the other passengers.

Both Rob and Saric had dipped in and out of Sense Check since their first attempts to find Julia Hawkins had led them to the Community in Nebraska. The headline details were straightforward to extract; plans of the Community's layout from its original construction were available from the town's museum, but they wanted more. This task was not well suited to Sense Check, though.

The Community took members in from all over the world, and into different locations. It wasn't easy to find any data of substance from which to build a base of knowledge. They could connect some individuals to the Community, but when they tried to follow the business interests of those people through public information, the trails were blocked by extravagant ownership structures – trusts, offshore holdings and partnerships. Sense Check wasn't really designed for the tasks. It had been set up and developed to follow more direct logical processes, testing assertions and filling out the background of particular individuals. Unpicking this organisation needed a much wider viewpoint. These people were careful about the trail they left, and they clearly did not conform to the contractual norms of business deals. When a formal agreement could be made based on a handshake, or more likely a solemn promise, it did not get recorded.

One thing that was certain was the presence of money. And lots of it. Saric wanted to know where it came from, and who it benefited. He got nowhere. Given the complexity of the arrangements in place to make it disappear, he assumed they must be generating cash from more than simply accepting the assets of new members. He found possible links to politicians, pharmaceutical companies, publishers, universities and other bodies of influence, but again, any hard connection was impossible to prove.

Whatever lay behind this whole thing, Rob and Saric agreed on the plane that they wouldn't approach the Community immediately but spend some time getting to know the area first.

While it was unlikely that an interview with Julia Hawkins would yield much new information, it was important to plan for other eventualities, and that meant understanding the surrounding geography and the politics of the local town. Rob had argued that they should simply knock on the door of the Community and ask to speak to Julia, but Saric refused to entertain the idea. Given that Sense Check was primarily designed for UK analysis, he felt exposed by the limits of what it could contribute to their background research, but he also felt that too many risks were inherent in this approach. In any case, they had been told that the Community members didn't speak to the outside world, and he doubted simply being there in person would make a difference.

"What if there's more to this than we think?" he had asked, as one of the cheery cabin crew offered them yet another drink. "We don't know enough about this place; we need to know what we are walking into."

197

Rob conceded that Saric had a point, although he acknowledged only to himself that this had more to do with an odd feeling in the centre of his stomach than any detailed strategic analysis.

One wall of the airport terminal was lined with desks for a variety of car rental companies. They chose one at random and hired a large but unremarkable grey SUV. It was the kind of car that a person might see a hundred times within just a few miles of driving, and that was exactly what they needed.

Grandcast River was a four-hour drive to the north of the airport. Back in the UK, this would be a relatively long drive, but considering the huge scale of the US, it was practically next door. It had been a long time since Rob had driven on the other side of the road, and it took him a few miles to get used to the unfamiliar controls and road signs. Once they were on the main road, however, he enabled the car's cruise control, and the miles flew past on the long, straight road that ran through the centre of the state.

They stopped at a motel around ten miles outside of town. The Community was a further twenty miles past that. They had decided on the plane that two men with foreign accents checking into the local hotel might make them stand out. After all, this was a small town, and not one that appeared to have a thriving tourist industry or a diverse population. While there was little risk associated with standing out, Saric still felt strongly that it was not worth taking it.

"Are you sure we're not overthinking this?" Rob asked him. "We only want to speak to someone; we're not planning to rob a bank. Why all the secrecy?"

"I don't know," Saric had replied. "But in my experience, it's better to plan for the worst. If it's not necessary then we haven't lost anything, but sometimes it is necessary. If we check into the hotel in town, people might ask questions. In a motel by the side of a main road between large cities, we're just another two businesspeople working away from home."

"You can be really paranoid sometimes, you know that."

"I do, but paranoia has kept me alive on more than one occasion, so we'll stay outside the town."

The motel was situated directly on the side of the main road, next to a small diner. Both were well maintained but looked like they had seen better days. Rob hadn't travelled around the US before, but he felt like he knew this place; it looked like all the motels he'd seen in films. There was a small office at the end nearest to the diner. To the right of that was a two-storey building with eight doors and eight windows on each floor. A metal staircase ran up the side of the building to enable the residents of the top floor to access their rooms. At the front were sixteen parking spaces, each numbered to correspond to the rooms. There were cars in three of them.

Rob waited in the SUV while Saric went into the office. Shortly afterwards, he returned with two keys. "Seven and eight," he said through the window. He walked along the row of doors, stopping at the two furthest ones on the ground floor.

Rob pulled the car into space number eight and stepped out into the mid-afternoon heat.

Saric tossed him a key attached to a large wooden keyring with a number seven burned into it. "Let's meet in there in an hour," he said, nodding towards the diner at the other end of the car park.

Rob's room looked exactly as he'd expected. Twin beds with tables, a desk with a coffee machine and mugs. At the back was a door to what Rob assumed was the bathroom. The only natural light came from the small window next to the door.

He threw his luggage onto one of the beds and kicked his shoes off as he sprawled across the other one. He had an hour to kill so decided he could afford to spend twenty minutes of that resting. Then he would take a shower and meet Saric.

•

Slowly, Rob became aware of a banging noise coming from somewhere around him. He reached out an arm to grab his phone, but there was nothing where the bedside table should have been. The knocking continued.

"Rob, can you hear me?" came a familiar voice.

Rob opened his eyes and took in the unfamiliar surroundings. The illuminated red numbers on the digital alarm clock at the side of him read 17.18. He had been asleep for more than an hour and was now late for meeting Saric.

"Yes, sorry, I'm fine. Can you give me twenty minutes?" he called through the door.

Exactly eighteen minutes later, Rob walked along the path towards the diner. He had showered and changed his clothes and was feeling a little more awake. The restaurant was brightly lit, with a counter that ran along the whole of the back wall. Behind it, Rob could see into the kitchen, where a large man dressed all in white was cooking. Built-in tables lined the other three walls. Most of them were empty. Saric was sitting in one to the right side of the door, looking out of the window at the main road.

Rob sat opposite him, and they were soon joined by a waitress, who poured coffee from a large glass pot into the empty mug in front of Saric. "What can I get you?" she asked with a bored smile.

"Coffee, please," said Rob, trying to buy himself a few seconds to take in the huge menu, which was printed on a laminated card in front of him. In the end there was just too much choice, so he followed Saric's lead and ordered a cheeseburger.

"Nice sleep?" Saric asked with a flicker of amusement.

"Sorry, mate, I don't know what happened. I only meant to close my eyes for a couple of minutes."

"It's fine, you needed the rest. I've scoped out the area."

"You've been out already?" Rob was annoyed that Saric had left the motel without him.

"Only briefly. I drove out to the town to see whether it would be of any use to us. I didn't even get out of the car. It's pretty small. There's really only a single street of shops; the usual things you would expect, I think, a supermarket, a post office and a town hall. Beyond that there are just residential properties laid out on a grid of roads. I learned nothing of interest."

Despite saying he had not learned anything, Saric spent the next few minutes talking Rob through the detail of what he had seen, using a map of the area that he had picked up at the motel's front desk. Saric's observational skills were incredible, and by the time their food arrived, Rob felt like he had been into town himself. While he wasn't sure what use this information would be, he was pleased to know it and wondered again what aspect of Saric's mysterious past would have led him to this degree of detailed recollection.

Rob generally tried to eat healthily at home. He worked too hard at his training to waste calories on junk that didn't help him meet his optimum protein intake, but he had to admit his cheeseburger and fries were excellent. As they ate, Saric outlined the plan. "Tomorrow, I'd like to visit the Community and see what we can find out about the place. If they are welcoming, then perhaps we can speak to Julia, and if not, well, we'll come up with another plan."

"I thought you didn't want us to draw attention to ourselves. Why wouldn't we just go ahead and make an appointment with them?"

"We just don't have enough data to know what kind of reception we'd get. I'd like to keep our options open for now."

The two men carried on their discussion for an hour or so, before Rob's fatigue started to show. They agreed to settle in their rooms and get some rest before starting again with fresh minds in the morning.

CHAPTER 28

August 2020

Daniel's enthusiasm for their marriage, and the rights it would bring him as a husband, was a new dynamic that Helen had not properly foreseen. As Martha, she had built a fantasy world within Daniel's mind, where she could embody the Great Mother and provide insight into the true church. This was a church that for now only they could truly understand, and when it was revealed to them it would become the basis for the whole Community. Helen had found many ways to use this influence over Daniel's faith to get what she needed from him, and to stay informed of the Elders' plans.

Throughout the time she had been back at the Community, the prospect of marriage had been an almost constant discussion between Daniel and Helen, and amongst the Elders. It was a difficult balance. The Elders knew that matrimony would settle her down and give a focus to her energy. But as a prospective Elder himself, Daniel should not be burdened with an unbeliever; that just wouldn't be right. And so, The Emergence had become critical. They couldn't wait any longer for Helen to go through it. She was starting to hold Daniel back from his rightful status.

Some Elders had suggested that Helen should be replaced with a more appropriate wife. Helen's father objected to this, on the grounds that it would be detrimental to Ollie's development in the faith. His mother had to be seen to have given herself to the Community. This may have been enough in itself, but when coupled with Daniel's unswerving commitment to Helen, or Martha as he knew her, there was enough to convince the Elders to go through with the plan.

Helen had seen enough of the Community as a child to get a sense of their view of marriage as being balanced between husband and wife. But this was a child's view. Her own marriage had been a true one of equals. She had never felt like Rob had wanted to possess her. She realised now that she had not given the idea of marriage, and what it would mean to Daniel, enough consideration. He had been taught that she would become his. This was upsetting the balance of power that Helen had crafted in his mind.

Worse than this, it was clear that she was confronting Daniel's most basic physical urges. She would be his, and he could, at last, take everything he wanted from her. For so many years, he had held all these feelings back. Temptations had been resisted and the surges of feelings he did not have the words for were coming back to his mind now. A huge weight that had been pressing against him for years was clearly starting to make cracks in his defences. She could see in the way he looked at her recently that he wanted so much to let those defences burst and have those feelings carry him away.

Helen knew that her control over Daniel's faith was not going to be enough to get him to carry out her plans. She was going to have to harness this new power inside him, too, and so she invited him to come to her room to join her in private prayer. It wasn't normally accepted for unmarried men and women to spend time alone together, but Daniel had been given special permission to come and go as he thought necessary, in order that he could aid her with her progression back to the true faith.

He was due in five minutes, and was never late, so Helen prepared the environment. She took out a bra from her wardrobe and positioned it at the end of the bed. Then she took a spare dress and laid it over the top of it. She arranged the clothing so that the bra sat under the dress in the right place, with the smallest bit of the strap poking out. Finally, imagining herself sat on the edge of her bed, she moved her desk seat to a position where her imaginary self would be perfectly placed between the clothing and the large picture of Mary, the Great Mother.

When Daniel arrived, she was on her spot on the bed. He came in without knocking and stood looking at her for a moment. He noticed the clothes on the bed, of course, and seemed a little taken aback.

"Sit there," she told him. And he sat.

He wriggled, seeming a little off balance. "You said you wanted to speak to me before class. Is there something you would like me to explain?" he asked.

Helen was concentrating hard but maintained a serene expression. She gently matched his breathing pattern and mirrored his sitting position. After years of manipulating Daniel's mind, she no longer needed to work hard to get into his head. But the well-worn groove they had established had become quite gentle. He had accepted his place in their plans to rebuild the Community in the true faith. He knew he would be the rock upon which that church would be built. Guided by his direct communion with the Great Mother, he would know what to do, and when the time was right.

But until now, Helen had not set that timeframe. Keeping Daniel in the holding pattern of 'soon' created much less risk of resistance. It had become easy. At least for Helen.

Now she had to make 'soon' into 'now'.

"Daniel, I think it's time we talked about something important." She saw his eyes dart towards the clothes and then back to her again. He must have realised she'd noticed, but his expression gave nothing away.

Their breathing had harmonised now, and she started to slow the pace. He followed.

First, she would link herself with the picture of the Great Mother in Daniel's mind. She continued. "I think we have both noticed what is behind me now." She flicked her eyes in the direction of the picture on the wall. Daniel felt the Great Mother looking at him. "The time of thinking has passed; I know you can feel that in you now. I can feel it, too. The Great Mother has spoken."

Her next step was to draw a connection between Daniel's profound sense of religious truth and his newfound, more basic urges.

"It would be right to wonder where you are feeling her voice. It might be in feelings that you have never felt before, the ones you are now experiencing." She knew he would search for any new feelings and, by accepting her suggestion, would frame those as part of his religious certainty and something within the control of the Great Mother. With the smallest movement of her body, she shifted the direction of his gaze to her left; the hint of bra strap coming out from under her dress seemed to be the only thing in the room. To bring him back to her, she moved her sitting position. He followed. Her feet were planted on the floor, and she looked him straight in the eye. "Wherever you experience those changes in the way you feel, whether that's in your heart, mind or body, it's the will of the Great Mother making herself known to you. The stronger those feelings become, the more we can know that the time is close."

Again, she targeted her suggestions to frame his physical urges as a sign of a more profound but non-specific truth. "Soon we will know the time is here. The Great Mother will make you feel it."

Daniel had slipped into a trance and was following her words without question.

Helen continued, subtly changing her tone to layer in suggestions. "You and I must pray to the Great Mother, *which is me*, and you, together. Knowing that has always made you strong. Stronger than all the others. The time has come for you, and *me, as the Great Mother* will reveal the truth. As you look at me now, you know you can *feel all those feelings inside you* that make you strong. As you look, *the Great Mother makes you feel those feelings* to give you that strength. And we can both wonder how you know that it is only through the Great Mother that you know those feelings can be fulfilled. Through the truth. And that truth must be revealed. And we shall burn away all the lies so that the truth can be felt by all."

Now she moved onto preparing him for leaving the Community. "When it is time, you will know. *We will leave* the lies and return the truth. *The Great Mother will take you far away* into the full truth. She will only return you when all is prepared. The Emergence will be nothing compared to the revelations that will follow for us. Everything that The Emergence could do for us will be done tenfold. *We shall go so far* from the lies. *So far*. They cannot follow where we will go, for they cannot know the truth until we return. And then they will know, for you will teach them."

As a final step, she wanted to unite Daniel's feelings of desire and his absolute devotion to the teachings of the Great Mother. She stood up, took a couple of steps to the picture of Mary and lifted it off the wall. As intended, Daniel's attention started to drift from her. She changed the timbre of her voice to nudge him back into the moment. Then she said, "I love the Great Mother. She shows me everything there is to know." She stepped back over to the bed. "*She truly is the truth behind everything.* Every thought and *every feeling*." With that, she placed the picture of Mary's face at the top of the dress lying on her bed. The bra strap was still visible. The image was grotesque.

"Shall we go?" she said. Helen was done. For now.

CHAPTER 29

The next morning, Rob and Saric met at the same table at the diner where they had eaten dinner the previous evening. The same tired-looking waitress had greeted them and taken their order, and the same chef was currently cooking eggs and hash browns for Rob and pancakes with bacon for Saric.

Rob had wanted to leave at first light and reach the Community as early as could be considered socially acceptable, but Saric insisted they eat first and aim to arrive at their destination by midmorning. As they sipped their coffee and waited for their food, Rob continued to challenge Saric on this point.

"We are arriving completely unannounced, and I think it's polite to let them start their day before we do that," Saric protested. His coffee was hot and strong, and it gave him a little more patience than usual to revisit the same argument they had run through twice the previous evening.

"I'm not sure I care if it's polite or not. I just want to know whether Julia is there and, if she is, what she can tell us. And anyway, since when have you worried about social niceties?"

212

"I worry about them if they make people more likely to help us. And besides, the food here is good; it might be a long time before we get an opportunity for lunch."

After they had filled up with carbs and caffeine, they began the drive to the Community. It wasn't far and the roads were clear, so they made good progress. Saric drove carefully, taking in the terrain and mapping it against the electronic and paper maps that he had previously studied. He wasn't sure why he did this – it was more instinct than a conscious process – but he found that it calmed his nerves and allowed him to focus.

They turned off the main road and onto a narrow track, which must once have been the driveway to the hotel. It was lined with trees, which had the appearance of needing much more water than the land around could provide. As the long track wound around the side of a large, rocky hill, they saw the main building ahead of them. It was much larger than it appeared in the photos and was spread over three floors and across three separate sections or wings. Around the main building were a series of smaller, single-storey lodges.

Three cars were already parked under a small, covered area to the right of the main entrance. Two older model trucks carrying the usual knocks and dents of vehicles maintained for utility, and a brand-new

Mercedes. Saric pulled up at the end of the row and shut off the engine. "Remember to let me lead this, like we agreed," he said.

Rob nodded his unhappy acceptance, thinking Saric didn't trust him to keep his nerve during the meeting. In reality, there was a more practical reason to stop Rob talking too much. There was a small but material chance that Julia Hawkins was sitting in the building in front of them. The evidence indicated that she was Helen's mother. If those two things were true, there was also a chance that Helen was within the Community's walls. The probability of that was smaller than the chance of Julia being there, but not zero. And if she were there, it was also possible that she didn't want to be found and that whoever answered the door would be briefed to be on the lookout for British men in their mid-thirties asking strange questions.

Saric couldn't stop Rob accompanying him to the door, but the less he spoke the better.

One half of the main building's heavy, wooden, double-width front door was open, so they walked straight into a large space that must have once been the hotel's reception area. It was furnished sparsely with furniture in the same wood as the door, old-fashioned paintings of country scenes and large posters of children and families with improbably wide smiles. Big and shiny, they looked out of place in the

214

room. To the left of the main door was a wide desk and behind that the entrance to a small office area. A man of late middle age stood up from behind his desk and walked out to the reception, smiling with almost as much enthusiasm as the children in the photos.

"Gentlemen," he exclaimed, with his arms wide, "welcome to our Community! I am Carl, and I am delighted to meet you. Please, come in and take a seat. Can I get you anything to drink?"

Carl motioned them into a seating area to the other side of the reception. It was more modern than the room they had just left, with luxurious furnishings. Biblical images replaced the country scenes on the walls and glossy brochures were spread out on the circular coffee table, around which six armchairs were arranged.

Rob glanced at Saric who nodded back. This was not the welcome they had been expecting, and Carl seemed receptive to conversation. They took seats next to each other and he came and sat with them. He appeared happy to see the two strangers who had just arrived unannounced at his front door. "You must have seen our promotions?" he said. "It's not often we get walk-ins these days, I must say. Most people make their first contact online, but it's lovely to meet you anyway."

Slowly, Rob understood. Carl was a recruiter.

215

"As I said, my name's Carl and I have lived here in the Community with my wife for more than thirty years now. We have brought up two successful sons and one beautiful daughter, who all still live here. They have families of their own now, and my sons have promising futures ahead of them in our leadership team."

"It's lovely to meet you, Carl," said Saric, his accent stronger than usual, "we have heard lots about this place, and we wanted to experience it for ourselves."

"Well, it's lovely to have you here. I'd love to give you a tour and tell you all about our principles and lives, but first, I'd like to hear more about you. Tell me what brought you here."

Saric thought quickly; honesty was not yet the right approach, at least not completely. There was an opportunity to gather more information, but they needed to keep Carl onside. Saric was unsure of what he would be expecting to hear. He thought back to the conversation with Father Rupert; these places played on the needs of the lost and lonely.

"My friend and I met two years ago at a church support group. We'd both recently lost our wives and were grieving. We became friends and have since come to realise that our lives have lost the meaning they once had. I have had a very successful career in business, but this means little without someone to share it with. The world today, being full of sinners, is no place to find that meaning. My friend, whose faith, I must confess, predates my own, heard about this place many years ago from his father, who had a friend who moved here. He mentioned it to me recently, and we knew we must visit to find out more. I do hope we have not inconvenienced you by arriving unannounced, but we have travelled a long way."

As Carl looked at him, Saric wondered if he had overplayed the story. Was it all too convenient? But Carl's smile didn't waver.

"Not at all, the Great Lord encourages us to extend our hospitality to visitors, and this is what we shall do. But tell me—" he was looking at Rob now, "—what is the name of the friend of your father? Perhaps he still lives here."

Rob looked again at Saric for reassurance and received another nod.

"I believe her name was Julia, Julia Hawkins."

Rob tried to sound casual as he said it. This was meant to be a half-remembered name of someone he had never met but that had featured in a story told by his father. For the briefest moment, Carl's smile faltered. The look of shock was gone almost before it appeared, but Rob had seen it, and so had Saric.

"Yes, I remember the name—" Carl had regained his composure, but there was a marked change in his tone, "—she no longer lives here, I'm afraid. I believe she moved on to another calling."

"Oh, that's interesting. I don't believe my father heard from her after she came here, so I didn't know that. Do you know where she went? I'm sure he would like to get back in touch with her."

"I don't. She made her own choice and left us. We did not follow her after she chose that life."

Rob's heart sank. He had felt so close to something, like it was within his reach, and now it had gone again.

Carl stood up. "Excuse me, gentlemen, I have something to attend to."

He left the room, leaving Saric and Rob sitting in silence. They exchanged a glance but said nothing. A couple of minutes later, Carl re-entered. "Gentlemen, I am very sorry, but an urgent matter has arisen. I will not be able to show you our community today. It has been lovely to meet you." He stood by the door expectantly, urging them to leave.

Saric reviewed his options. There was something here he did not like, but he wasn't sure what that was. Julia's name had triggered this

218

response, but why? They could refuse to leave, of course, but it was clear they were not going to get any more answers. They needed to find another way.

Saric rose slowly and walked out of the room. Rob followed. "Thank you for your hospitality, Carl. I hope we meet again."

There was no smile in return.

As they walked across reception, they spotted three men standing in front of the desk. They said nothing, but their gaze did not leave Rob and Saric until they had got into the car, started the engine and begun the return journey along the long drive.

CHAPTER 30

Saric took them straight back to the motel. As they drove, they didn't talk about the exchange that had just taken place. Both men wanted to take a moment to process their thoughts.

The man they'd just met was polished, but he had an edge that Rob hadn't liked. It felt as if he had wanted something from them. Looking back, Rob felt a blast of anger. He should have seen through this charlatan immediately.

So, if he was going to discard what he had been told, what should he believe? Was Julia Hawkins here or not? If she was, Carl didn't want Rob and Saric to know. Rob couldn't draw a conclusion, but he had no intention of leaving it there.

Back at the motel, Rob and Saric sat in the restaurant and drank coffee. Saric had anticipated Nebraska would present him only great mugs of diluted instant coffee, and he had been happily surprised to find the long drip brew rich and bittersweet. "I'll run that discussion through Sense Check," he said eventually, "but I don't think we'll find anything extra in it."

"Agreed," said Rob, and then he explained how he had hoped for more.

Saric listened closely to his friend. "The exchange was unsatisfactory, but we do have some new facts to work with," he said.

Rob raised an eyebrow.

Saric continued. "We can now conclude that this group would like to welcome new joiners. We presented ourselves as possible entrants. They wanted us. Then they did not. Either Julia Hawkins is here, or she is not. If she isn't, and Carl's story is true, then she was here and has moved on, and there is no reason for them not to accept us into their group. Or, she was never here, in which case lying that she was is completely ludicrous. Or she is here, and they don't want us to know."

"Yes, I see what you mean."

Saric had rationalised the feeling Rob had recognised from the moment they reached the Community.

"So, she is there, then?" Rob asked, half to himself.

"I think we need to work with that assumption, yes," said Saric.

"OK, what next?"

During the silence of the car journey, Saric had already mentally compiled their list of options.

The easiest approach was to simply walk in and demand answers, using whatever means were necessary. In Saric's assessment, there were three significant downsides to this plan.

The first was simply one of numbers. There were perhaps eighty residents in the Community. Allowing for those unlikely to get involved in a fight, such as children and the elderly, that left, perhaps, forty people. After some consideration, Saric also eliminated women from his risk assessment. He had learned over the years, sometimes to his benefit and sometimes to his cost, not to underestimate women, but the Community appeared to have a very traditional view of their role, which Saric doubted involved much investment in developing their combat skills.

That left, perhaps, twenty men in the Community who might try to stop their entry. Twenty against two. Saric had fought against less balanced numbers and won – his training counted for a lot in these situations – and Rob was developing nicely, too.

Yes, if it were just about numbers, he would still like this option.

222

Which brought him to downside number two. This was rural America. It was reasonable to assume that the residents of the Community were in favour of exercising their rights under the Second Amendment. He should assume they would be armed.

Again, this wasn't necessarily a problem. Weapons could be obtained, although without his contacts it might take longer to do so here, and it risked escalation, which brought him to problem three.

In the UK, he had been useful to the police on more than one occasion. Many more than one, in fact. This meant that they had a certain amount of tolerance if he sometimes stepped outside the strict application of the law to get results, particularly if those results also helped to get them the answers they wanted. In America, he had no such contacts; if they were caught breaking the law they were on their own, and if Sense Check's analysis regarding the influence of the Community on local town officials was correct, it was unlikely that the police force would even be impartial.

For now, despite the other options being more longwinded, he had to rule out a direct approach. They had the photo of Julia from 1987, and some sense of what she might look like now, but Saric wasn't sure he would recognise her even if he saw her.

For a moment, he allowed himself to consider whether Sense Check would benefit from some kind of facial recognition functionality, to link the images in its database to real time inputs. It would be easy enough to program, but that was for another time.

They needed more information. And it was information about a fundamentally secretive group. The public facing recruitment strategy, the website and the press releases were one thing, but these were just what they wanted people to see. He and Rob needed to know about other things. Who was there, what did they do and, ideally, how were they funded and controlled? Sense Check was working on this, but the organisation hid its tracks well. Nothing was held in the cloud and the funding was routed through a complex structure of overseas trusts that was proving difficult to unlock.

This had led Saric to the option he now suggested to Rob. "If we can't gather the information we need digitally, we will have to use a more traditional approach," he said. "What we need is someone willing to talk to us, and we know now that we aren't going to find that in the recruitment office. In my experience, people don't talk when they are part of a group, especially one with rules telling them not to. They talk when they are alone; either because they want to impress someone or because they want to share what they know with a person they trust. They might see that it is in their interests to do so."

Saric paused and Rob nodded, not wishing to consider what he meant by the latter part of Saric's reasoning.

"We need the chance to speak to one of them alone. Someone senior enough to know what is going on but not so senior to be part of the leadership. Maybe someone a little disaffected. I think our next step is to find that person and try to convince them to help us. We've already concluded that there isn't enough data available to us yet to enable Sense Check to draw meaningful conclusions, so we need to watch them, understand their routines and structures, and, if we can, identify a chance to speak to someone who can tell us where Julia is and, most importantly, what happened to make Carl so scared of her."

Saric spent the rest of the evening in his room, running various iterations of the same searches through Sense Check. Many things about the Community didn't make sense, but a general feeling of something not quite right wasn't the basis for an enquiry. Instead, he tried to itemise the matters that concerned him and focus on these in order.

First and foremost, there was the Community's organisational structure and financing. It made little sense that it was able to sustain itself, and its influence on the town of Grandcast River went beyond that. It should be possible to piece this together; companies had to file documents with the authorities, and, if you had the right contacts, even the finances of individuals could be tracked. The problem was that the Community was sophisticated. There were trusts and shell companies in exotic locations. Did that really make sense for an organisation that was all about religious contemplation and stepping away from the evils of modern life? Saric wasn't convinced.

Secondly, there were the movements of Julia Hawkins. What had happened to her to make her take Helen and leave everything she knew to move halfway across the world and live with strangers? And how had Helen ended up back living with her grandmother some five years later? Saric wasn't sure this was important, but he thought that understanding Julia's choices would be critical to discovering what she had done later.

Finally, there were logistical matters. He wanted to find out about the patterns of the Community that might reveal answers to the other questions.

As Sense Check met another dead end, Saric's phone rang. He picked it up and pressed the accept button without checking the caller ID. "Yes?"

"Hi, Saric, how are you?" The voice at the other end of the line soothed away much of the frustration he had been feeling.

226

"Grace, hi. How are you?" He said it too quickly, the words running together.

"I'm good, thanks. I thought you might like an update on the Gary Lambert situation. But first, tell me, how are things there?"

"Frustrating," Saric said honestly. "There's something going on here, but I can't put it together correctly."

Over the next ten minutes, Saric talked Grace through his appraisal of the location and their trip to the Community. He spoke methodically, not missing out details to keep Grace's interest or exaggerating to overstate his conclusions. Grace listened intently but silently, not interrupting with questions or opinions. Saric then outlined his plan for the next day. Only when he had finished speaking did she respond.

"I can see why you are frustrated. I thought this was just a trip to interview a woman about a will, and now you are dealing with all of this. But Saric, are you missing something here?"

"What do you mean?" He tried not to sound defensive at this suggestion.

"Well, you are worrying about ownership structures and complex financial arrangements. That's all very interesting, but is it relevant?"

227

Grace was one of the few people Saric knew who could comment that funding structures sounded interesting without a hint of sarcasm, but the point resonated.

"You think it's unrelated?" he challenged.

"I don't know. Perhaps it is and perhaps it isn't. But it's not what you are looking for. In the end, what you need is Julia. Are you sure there isn't a simpler way to get to her than through the numbers?"

Saric was quiet for a long time.

"Anyway," Grace moved on, "do you want to know about Gary Lambert?"

"Of course. Is Hannah OK?"

"She's fine, Saric, I saw her yesterday. She insisted on taking me for dinner to thank me for helping to sort things out for her, although I think that was just a cover story to spend an evening questioning me about you. Honestly, if she ever decided to stop selling books, that woman would make an excellent interrogator. No one is safe when she wants information!"

Saric could hear the warmth in Grace's voice and enjoyed the thought of the two women chatting together.

"What I wanted to tell you is that I looked a bit further into Gary Lambert's business dealings, and it seems that this isn't the first time he's picked up land very cheaply and then made a fortune by getting planning permission on sites that no one else thought could be built on. Returns on land vary enormously, of course, but for land with development potential the price can usually be compared to similar sites in the area.

"It seems like his land is always cheaper to buy and then always makes a lot more profit than those other sites. It doesn't make sense. I have met the guy and he's not that good.

"I hope you don't mind, but I called your mate Inspector Stephens and suggested that he might like to have a look at what's going on. I've sent him enough details on the sites and the numbers that even he should be able to piece it all together."

Saric felt that Grace was being a little unfair on Inspector Stephens, who was a solid policeman who had proved helpful over the years.

"Thank you, Grace," he said sincerely, "but please be careful. Lambert won't like this if it puts his money at risk."

Grace laughed. "Don't worry, Saric. I've dealt with worse people than Gary Lambert before. You don't have to protect me, you know."

"But I didn't ask you to get involved with those people. If anything happened to you because of you working this case . . ." he trailed off, unsure of how to finish the sentence. "And maybe I want to protect you, even though I know you don't need me to."

"Take care of yourself, Saric." And with that she dialled off and Saric returned to his computer.

CHAPTER 31

September 2020

Tomorrow was shopping day, which meant that the group heading out were brought together to discuss and allocate the forthcoming jobs.

To be sure of getting a chance to break out and make a phone call, Helen had to be paired with Jessica. She was highly trusted, and it had not taken Helen long to recognise that she had been given the job of getting close to her. She knew the Elders hoped Jessica's clarity of faith and her certainty of how to live a correct life would be a positive influence. In fact, her role as a spy had operated in reverse. Helen told Jessica what she wanted the Elders to hear, which had accelerated her ability to gain the freedoms she needed to build an escape plan.

But she could not completely deny that she enjoyed Jessica's company. In a way, her simpler view of the world was relaxing. There was nothing to be confused about. She wondered if she would miss her when she left.

The shopping group had two new additions, a brother and sister from Chicago, who had completed The Emergence ceremony the previous year. Helen didn't know much about them and would rather they were elsewhere. When they weren't allocated the same tasks, their shoulders dropped, and they looked at the floor as if they might cry.

For pity's sake, thought Helen.

The brother looked up briefly, then back at the floor. He took a deep breath before speaking. "I was just wondering if, perhaps, for our first trip, just for the first one, of course, we could go in the same team, well, because, you know . . . I just thought . . ." He took a sideways look at his sister, who did not make eye contact. "Sorry," he said.

The Elder looked at him as if he had been speaking Russian, and then carried on. "Helen and Jessica, you will be doing the pharmaceutical trip, as usual. They have been sent the list."

Good, thought Helen. The pharmacy was towards the end of the main shopping area and a good place to break away. The pharmacist, Mr Tibbs, was a tall, bald man in his late thirties. He had a kindly face, and he seemed to enjoy Jessica's company. His gentle manner meant he was the only man in the town that she did not shy away from. Helen had spent the last few trips helping to build this relationship. She could be confident that Mr Tibbs would be looking forward to their visit tomorrow, and that he would, as usual, make them a coffee whilst they waited for him to package up their order.

232

As the Elder droned on about some pointless change to the way they were to record stock going forward, Helen leaned over to Jessica, put her hand on hers, and whispered in her ear. "Do you remember the birds in the park we saw last time?"

"Oh, yes," said Jessica. "They were so pretty."

The 'park' was a rough grassy area behind the row of shops but it contained a small pond and was a refuge for the town's wildlife. The children played there, their little voices singing out with delight as they ran around for no reason other than they could. A space on one edge of the pond had been designed to attract birds, which the locals would feed with seeds and scraps of bread. Before she had been joined by Helen, Jessica had never had the confidence to walk through the park. Now, though, she could hold tight to her arm and follow along as Helen strolled them both along, as if it were the most natural thing in the world. Just in case they were told not to do it again, Jessica had never reported their park visits.

"I have kept some bread," Helen whispered, "for the birds."

"Oh."

Helen could see the conflict on Jessica's face. "It's OK, sweetness, we won't stay long. But wouldn't it be lovely to see them sing for us, just for a few minutes?"

Jessica conceded that it would indeed be lovely. "But will we have time?" she asked. They were not supposed to dawdle, and an inexplicable gap of time would be shameful.

"We will find a way to grab a few minutes," Helen reassured her, looking her straight in the eye and reaching for every bit of trust she could extract from her friend.

"OK, I'm sure you're right," Jessica said.

That's the right answer, my little spy, thought Helen.

CHAPTER 32

Saric seemed to have drawn a conclusion. "We have light until about eight thirty, I suggest we take a look at this place. I want to know if we can isolate someone while they are outside the compound and easy enough to get hold of. We need to ask a few questions. Maybe you can do it your way. If not, we might need to resort to some more basic techniques. Regardless, we need to determine who is inside this place."

"Yes, OK, let's go and take a look," Rob agreed. He was frustrated. He didn't know what Julia Hawkins looked like. He wanted to get into this place and shout her name over and over. He had not anticipated a situation where people would want to keep him away from her. He felt lost. He knew he was struggling so he agreed with Saric. He had to trust his friend now.

Saric had packed carefully. He had as much surveillance kit as he could explain away as for use while wildlife watching. He didn't have any weapons, although if it came to it he had established how to access guns on the street. When he did that preparatory work, it occurred to him that he might be verging on paranoid, but as he started playing out the options to progress the situation, he was reassured by the knowledge.

For tonight, though, all he needed was his binoculars or, to be more accurate, his father's binoculars, as he always thought of them.

They drove off, again in silence.

The terrain made Rob feel uneasy. Alien. *Where the hell am I?* he thought. There was green around them, but not British green. It had a different quality to it. It was as if it had grown out of rock, not earth. It felt inhospitable, as if even the land itself did not want them there.

Saric interrupted his thoughts. "We need to aim for the high ground to the west of the property. There's a track that leads part of the way, but we'll need to walk the rest."

"That's fine," said Rob, who felt that some physical activity might help to release some of the frustration he felt about the lack of action. "But why aren't we just parking up at the end of the drive? Wouldn't that give us a better sense of who is coming and going?"

"I doubt we'd see much. It's not like they are commuting in and out every day. And there is nowhere to the south where we can observe them without being seen."

"Who do you think is watching?" Rob almost laughed at Saric, until he saw the expression on his face.

"These people worry me, Rob. Something here doesn't make sense, and until I understand what that is, I'd rather not take any chances. We'll watch from the ridge to the west so that we can observe the interactions. We'll see anyone coming and going from there anyway."

They parked the hire car at the edge of the road and Saric took two bags from the back seat. He handed one to Rob, as he threw the other one over his right shoulder. Then, without consulting a map, he stepped off the road and onto a trail leading into the woods. The path was wide at first and marked with wooden way markers. After a few minutes, the main trail veered to the left and Saric turned right. Rob followed. Still with no map, Saric guided them to a winding path leading up a steep hill. The trees were tall but thin and their branches did not begin until several metres above Rob's head, so the path remained fairly open. As they walked, the hill got steeper and rockier, and the trees became sparser. At the tree line, Saric turned sharply, and they followed a ridge further to the east.

They had been walking for perhaps an hour when Saric paused and looked down the hill.

"There." He indicated the valley below, where Rob saw the Community property.

237

They were to the northwest and, therefore, viewing the property from the other direction to that which they had seen earlier in the day. The main property was in front of them, but they were now viewing it from the side. To the right they could see the driveway, which now led away from the front door. Interspersed around the grounds were the single-storey lodges and closer to them still was a large lake and a larger, barn-like building. It was fenced in, and the gardens were being used for vegetables.

Rob thought it strange that there were fences around the rest of the property. It looked like the hill line, lake and woods formed natural boundaries, and in any case, they were a long way from anywhere.

Saric unpacked the binoculars and a blanket and found a space from which to observe. He had arranged for the waitress at the diner to provide them with coffee in the thermos that he had bought at a service station on the way from the airport. He brought that out, too. If anyone happened to come across them out here, they would look like birdwatchers. It was unlikely that anyone from the Community would even look in their direction, but he ensured they were adequately hidden anyway.

It was late afternoon, and there was a lot going on below them. People were moving between the different lodges in pairs and small groups. There appeared to be very little chatter and most people seemed deep in thought.

Many of them walked with purpose and, despite the beautiful evening, few stopped to take in their surroundings. Saric was reminded of his time on military bases, where each person had a role. There was a routine here and anything unusual would stand out. That might be helpful, or it might be a problem.

After half an hour, a group of children emerged from one of the lodges. There was, perhaps, twelve of them, and they ranged in age from around four to early teens. The children were more animated than the adults, but a strict-looking woman was marshalling them hurriedly into the main building.

After that, the adults emerged from the lodges and walked towards the main building. There was a collective sense of purpose.

Dinnertime, perhaps, or time for worship, Saric thought. Either way, it appeared that the whole Community was gathered in the main building.

A short while later, two women appeared from the main building. They were in their mid to late forties. Behind them, two younger men were carrying two large steel trays, the kind that Saric had seen when large groups of people were being catered for. The men followed the women to the fenced-off building below them. One of them removed a key from her pocket and unlocked and opened a gate, before taking one of the trays. The second woman took the other tray, and they carried them to the front door of the barn. Meanwhile, the men waited outside, slouching against the fence.

A short time later, the women emerged. The trays were gone but they now carried two large wooden boxes full of muddy vegetables. They passed these to the men, locked the gate and returned to the main building. No words were exchanged.

"I'd like to know what's going on in there," Saric whispered to Rob, nodding at the barn.

"And I would like to know what you are doing here," said a voice behind them.

Startled, Rob jumped to his feet. Saric raised an eyebrow and stood up more slowly. He took a good look at the stranger, as if making some sort of calculation. The stranger seemed to do the same. A dog joined them and stood by the man's feet. It showed no aggression towards either Rob or Saric.

240

"You move very quietly," said Saric. Rob absorbed the calm in his voice and relaxed. "My name is Saric, and this is Rob. We are taking a look at the Community down there. We have an interest in it."

"Well, well. This I have not seen before. My name is Mick. I live here, not there—" he pointed at the Community, "—my place is round to the west. What on earth are you two doing watching that lot from up here?"

"It's rather a long story, I'm afraid," said Saric. "Do you know them well?"

"I know bits. Why don't you just go and see them?"

"We tried that. It didn't work out," said Saric.

Now Mick looked intrigued. "Really? Troublemakers, are you?"

"We're just looking for someone," said Rob, speaking for the first time.

"British, eh?" Mick said. "And you? I can't place you."

"I dare say not," said Saric. "We would be very grateful to hear what you know about this place. The person we are trying to find might be in trouble."

"They're all in trouble down there, I'd say."

241

"What do you mean?" Rob cut in.

"They don't seem right to me," said Mick. "The way they carry on."

"Will you help us know a bit more about them?" Rob asked. "We mean them no harm. We just really need to find the person we're looking for."

"OK. Let's go back to my place and get coffee. You can tell me what this is all about and, if I believe you, maybe I will help."

Mick's home was a small cabin located deeper in the woods than Saric and Rob had walked through to reach their lookout spot. It was made from wood so weathered that it looked to be part of the landscape itself. Smoke rose from a small metal chimney at one end.

The door opened into the main living area, which included a small kitchen and dining table, as well as two armchairs set around a woodburning stove. At the other end of the room, two doors led into what Saric thought must be the bedroom and bathroom. It was clean and tidy but old and worn. Everything in the room had a function but for two photos sitting on a small shelf by the fire. One was black and white and showed a young couple. The age of the photo suggested they were Mick's parents. The man was in his late twenties. He proudly donned his uniform, his large hand resting on the shoulder of the small woman. She was younger than him by maybe ten years. She was smiling but her eyes looked sad.

The other photo was of a much younger Mick. He was standing proudly in a uniform like his father's.

Mick filled a large, cast-iron kettle with water and placed it on top of the wood burner. He sat in one of the armchairs and then, realising there were two men in front of him and only one chair, nodded towards the dining table. Rob took one of the chairs and pulled it up between the armchairs where Mick and Saric now sat.

"Do you live here alone?" Rob asked, politely.

Mick laughed. "Look around you, see any woman's touch here? No, it's just me and Texas," he said, patting the scruffy grey dog, which had settled itself on the footstool in front of Mick's legs, "we do well enough on our own."

"Have you lived here long?" Rob persisted, partially out of politeness and partly because he wanted Mick to like him, although he wasn't yet sure why.

"Thirty years, ever since I left the army. It was my parents' cabin before that. I moved here while I got back on my feet and never left. A quiet life suits us both." He petted the dog's head again. "But we are not here to gossip, tell me what you were doing out there on my hill."

While Mick brewed coffee, Rob told him.

"Helen and I met when we were at university. People talk about love at first sight, and maybe that happens for some, but this wasn't that. At the start, we were friends first and foremost. We were both away from home for the first time, and a little lost in a world full of people who seemed to know exactly what they were doing. Helen's parents died when she was very young, and she was brought up by her grandmother. I think she had a very sheltered life before university.

"She was studying psychology and I history, so we didn't have lectures together, but we had lots of time off between classes. We would study with each other during the day and spend our evenings in the pub discussing what we had learned and the questions it had raised, wondering why no one else seemed interested in anything bigger than what they were going to wear on Wednesday night or whether their most recent one-night stand would call them again.

"She became my best friend, the one person in the whole world whom I could tell anything without worrying about how they would react. I was honest with her about things I couldn't tell anyone else.

"As time passed, we spent more and more time together, until one day, early in our second year and while sitting in the student bar, I looked at her and realised I was in love. And it was like I had always been in love with her but hadn't known it until that moment. I knew I wanted her to be by my side every single day and for the rest of my life.

"When we graduated, we bought a little cottage together. We couldn't afford it really and it needed so much work, but we both wanted something that was ours forever.

"She got a job as a psychological therapist in a hospital but continued to study, as she wanted to extend her understanding of neurology. I became a teacher. We were happy together. Her job was important to her; it was a vocation, really. She wanted to help people to understand their own minds. There were many times over the years when she could have taken more highly paid positions with better opportunities to progress her career, but she would always turn them down, saying they wouldn't further her ambition.

"Four years after we graduated, Helen became pregnant with our son, Ollie. She had always been certain that she didn't want children, and I had accepted this decision as a part of being with her. It was a surprise, but from the moment we found out she was expecting, neither of us could imagine any other future but the three of us together.

"It was important to Helen that Ollie was cared for by his family in those early years, so we both agreed to work part-time. Back then, it was unusual for a father to do this; my school even made a big fuss about it in the local press. I guess it was good PR to demonstrate its commitment to supporting flexible working. But it meant that I got to spend a day a week at home with my son, and it allowed Helen to continue building her career, so I didn't care what people thought.

"We did all the things that young families do; we visited the park and ate ice cream on the beach, and we were just so happy. Helen's grandmother had passed away by this point and she had no other family, but we were enough for each other, and my dad was always on hand if we needed him.

"And then, one day, when Ollie was three years old, Helen took him to the park. She often took him on a Saturday morning, while I caught up on marking. He used to love to climb the trees and look for dinosaurs. They were supposed to be home in time for lunch, but they never showed up. That was five years ago."

Mick sat completely still as Rob's story poured out of him. "And you think they came here?"

"Not quite," said Saric, picking up the story. "We have found a link between this Community and a woman that may have been Helen's mother." Saric couldn't help himself from including the caveat to his statement, given the warning Sense Check had provided about there being no direct necessary link between the facts and that conclusion.

"And it's her you're looking for?" asked Mick.

"Yes, it's her," said Saric. Silence filled the room for a moment whilst Mick sat in thought.

"What can you tell us about this group?" said Saric eventually.

"Not much, really, they have been here for almost as long as I have. They bought out the old hotel and have been fiddling around with it ever since. There was about thirty of them at the start, I suppose, and then they recruited a few more over the years, to what you see now. They mostly live in the main building, apart from the poor dears they stick out in that old barn you could see from the ridge. They call it the Lodge. I sometimes do a bit of work for the old girls, fix stuff up for them, but I've never been past the Lodge. It's not a happy place. I've only bumped into those from the main house a handful of times. I guess they think I'm a bit of a nut stuck out here on my own. But they've never bothered me."

"Do they leave the Community for anything?" asked Saric.

"The only time I see people come and go on a regular basis is when they go into town for supplies. They do this on the last Thursday of every month. But they don't talk to anyone; they're not exactly a sociable bunch."

Tomorrow, thought Rob.

"Anyway, I thought you said they aren't going to talk to you. I can't really see how you are going to find out the names of the people in there. Do you know what the woman you're looking for looks like? How old do you reckon she is?"

"She would be around sixty-five. We have an old photo from when she was younger, and a mock-up of what she might look like now." Rob reached into his pocket, pulled out his phone and brought up the original picture of Julia Hawkins as a young woman. Mick took the phone from Rob and looked hard at it.

"Hmmm," he said. "What's her name?"

"Julia Hawkins," said Rob.

"Hmmm," Mick said again.

Texas stood up and walked to Mick's side, looking carefully at Rob.

"Not seen her."

"Do you want to see the older version? It's supposed to be pretty accurate." Rob took the phone back, changed the photo and handed it over.

Mick took a quick look. "No, sorry, guys, I don't recognise her."

Rob felt uneasy. There was a conflict here. Until this exchange, he had found Mick to be very open. His body language was confident, but Rob did not feel like there was anything being masked. Now there was a clear edge in him.

Saric noticed Rob's unease and decided to change the subject. "Why do some of the group live in a separate gated area?"

"That's where they keep the old and infirm. But only women. It's sort of like an asylum, I suppose."

"How odd," said Saric.

Mick had nothing to say to that. Instead, he stood up and announced they would have to wrap it up there. "I'll show you back to where I found you," he added. He wasn't offering, just stating a fact.

"That won't be necessary," said Saric, "but thanks."

"You shouldn't trust those gadgets of yours to get about up here," he said. As the comment hung in the air, Saric exchanged a look with Mick by way of an answer.

"Thank you, Mick," said Rob. "We appreciate your help."

CHAPTER 33

"What did you make of that?" Rob asked Saric once they had reached a safe distance from Mick's cabin and were certain he could not hear them.

"Very interesting," Saric said thoughtfully. "He is lying, of course. I am certain he knows her."

"Yes, but why?"

"I am less sure of that. People lie to protect themselves or someone that is important to them. I can hypothesise about what Carl and his colleagues might gain from keeping Julia away from us – perhaps she is of some value to them or poses a threat – but Mick is different. What does he gain by lying to us?"

"I don't know, he seems like a loner to me. If he has tried so hard to keep to himself for all these years, how does he know anything about her at all? And if he does, what is stopping him from telling us?"

"We'll work it out," Saric said, hoping that he sounded reassuring.

"So, shall we return to the observation point?"

"No, we're losing the light and I don't think we will learn anything more today. Let's head back to the motel and plan for tomorrow."

•

The next morning, Saric found Rob waiting at their usual table in the diner. The waitress was refilling his coffee cup and Rob's dishevelled appearance gave Saric the impression that it was caffeine and not sleep that was fuelling him.

The waitress saw Saric enter and placed a new cup of coffee on the table. She gave him a flash of a smile and then busied herself wiping down the already clean tables around them. Saric liked the waitress, she was competent and polite without being unnecessarily friendly, and he approved of her industrious attitude to work.

Saric thought about Grace and the advice she had given him when he last saw her. Rob needed a friend to be there for him while his hopes of this being the lead that found Helen were torn away. He wished he could be that friend, but he did not know how.

If their roles were reversed, Rob would know. He would have the right words. So would Hannah, or Grace. But not Saric. The words would come out wrong; they would be muddled and confusing and he would make the situation worse. Instead, he would do what he could and follow the facts. "I have a new plan," he said. It sounded harsher than he had meant it to, but he needed to keep Rob focused. It wasn't time to worry yet.

"What's that?" Rob barely looked up from his coffee, which he was stirring slowly, while gazing at the liquid spiralling around the edge of the mug.

"Mick told us one important thing yesterday. We missed it in all the confusion. Today is the day when they buy their supplies. That means a number of them will be in the town. If there are eighty people there, that must require a shopping party of at least six, maybe ten. All we need is one of them."

"But yesterday you were adamant that we had to gather more information before approaching anyone."

"Agreed, but that was yesterday. Plans have to change in response to new information, and our information tells us this is the best opportunity to find out what is going on in there. I need you to finish that coffee and get in the car. I want to get there before they do."

Rob and Saric knew that once they got to the Community they might have to think on their feet. It seemed perfectly possible that even if she was there, Julia Hawkins might not want to see them. Community life

253

was hard to research, and it certainly wasn't open. They had imagined different scenarios of how they might gain access. Rob was frustrated to have been shown the door just at the mention of Julia Hawkins' name.

Prior to meeting Mick, as they had sat looking down at the Community, they had contemplated what they might do to extract the information they wanted, should they get a one-on-one with a member of the group. They had allowed the lazy assumption that everyone would know each other. Now that Mick had explained there was a separate area for elderly residents, they were less confident of that. Overnight, Saric had plugged the fresh data into Sense Check and played with some scenarios. It seemed clear that it would be better to target an older member of the Community. Sense Check had drawn the conclusion from publicised information that recruitment drives targeted young adults. Older members were likely to have been in the Community for a long time. If Ms Hawkins had moved on years ago, they may remember her. On the other hand, if she was isolated in the way Mick described some of the residents being, they may have been around long enough to know her from earlier days.

The more challenging question was how to extract the data. Saric pointed out that there could be many perfectly legitimate reasons for why the person they spoke to simply wouldn't have the knowledge they wanted. This slanted the approach away from the more brutal options.

254

They might have to go through several targets before getting to someone with the information they needed, and a missing Community member would be an immediate cause for alarm. It would take too long, be too messy and put everyone on alert. Out of habit, Rob mentioned there was also a human cost, which Saric acknowledged could also be viewed as a factor.

Saric looked at Rob for an answer.

"OK. What have we got that they might want?" Rob thought out loud.

"I think that depends on what you mean by 'they'," said Saric. "They, the people of the Community, seem mostly fairly ordinary. I guess they just want normal-people stuff. The Community as an organisation seems to want money, power and influence."

"I'm not sure they do want 'normal-people stuff'," said Rob, "but I get the point. It seems to me that the one thing we have that they would want is our souls. Before we mentioned Julia Hawkins, Carl seemed very enthusiastic."

"They can have mine," offered Saric, "if they can find it."

255

"I don't think we have time for them to go looking for that," smiled Rob.

Saric was pleased to see the smile back on his face, even if just for a moment.

"No, this time, I think you're going to have to trust me to go and sell my soul to one of these morons," said Rob. "The double act is too hard to explain."

"OK," said Saric. "We isolate the one we want, and you offer them your soul. Then what?"

"Then they tell me if they know a Julia Hawkins."

"I think you might need to refine that bit."

"It will come to me," said Rob. "It would be better if we could find a woman."

"Why?"

"Middle-aged women love me."

"Fine. We'll find you an old woman to manipulate."

Rob couldn't quite tell if Saric was making a joke or not.

CHAPTER 34

The town was smaller than Rob had expected. As the car travelled from the diner towards their destination, the area only slowly grew more populated. Houses around here were large and spaced out, often with miles between them.

As they approached the outskirts of the town, the houses grew a little closer together, forming streets with neatly fenced gardens until rural farmland turned into the suburbs. It took little more than a minute for Saric to drive from the outskirts to the centre of the town.

He parked at the side of a wide road and turned off the engine.

"Where do we start?" Rob asked.

"It's only just past nine, and we have no idea when the targets will arrive. Our objectives for now are to gather information and to find a place to wait and watch."

"And where were you planning on gathering that information?"

Saric looked along the street. When he had driven through the town on the night of their arrival, he had noticed the types of businesses here.

257

The high street was dominated by a large supermarket, but there were smaller premises either side of it, including a post office, a hair salon and a hardware store. They needed somewhere where they could start a conversation with someone who knew the town well enough to understand its relationship with the Community.

The supermarket was large enough that there would be lots of employees who might be willing to talk, but the nature of somewhere that big meant it was unlikely they spent much time chatting with customers. If they were lucky, they might find someone local to the town who knew about the Community that way, but it seemed just as likely that an employee chosen at random would be new to the area and, therefore, clueless.

The other shops were more likely to be the sorts of places where staff would know their customers. They were smaller, so conversations would take place as transactions were processed. Gossip and scandal would be shared out with the change.

The staff at the pharmacy and post office would probably have a good knowledge of their customers, but they would no doubt be keener on confidentiality.

Saric thought briefly about trying the hairdressers. The people there would be sure to know what was happening in the area, but one look at the place told him it was not the sort of place where he or Rob might drop in to get a trim. They would stand out immediately, although it would give them a chance to test Rob's theory that he could charm any middle-aged woman presented to him.

The hardware shop seemed the best choice. It was small enough that it would have only one or two employees. Maybe even the owner worked there, and perhaps they had lived in the area for a long time. And Saric could discuss tools much more confidently than he could hair products.

"Let's try over there," he said, nodding towards the shop's dusty windows.

As he stepped out of the car, Rob felt like he was also stepping back in time. There was something old fashioned about the shops that lined the high street. Other than the supermarket, there were no big-name stores, just a series of what seemed to be small, independent businesses. There weren't even any coffee chains, just a café on the corner across the road from the town hall. The people were different, too, slower somehow. It was like no one was in a hurry to get anywhere, which was perhaps because there was nowhere to go.

They crossed the road and entered the shop; a bell rang as Saric pushed the door open. There was no one at the counter to the left of

259

the door, so they spent a few minutes browsing the cramped but orderly aisles. It was the wonderful sort of shop that seemed to stock every item a person might need around the house or garden. Saric picked up a few items as they moved around, and by the time they reached the counter again, a young man was standing behind it.

"Can I help you, sir?" he said politely.

"I'd like these, please," Saric said, his accent opaquer than ever, "and do you stock binoculars?"

"We do, sir, let me show you."

The young man looked tiny as he walked next to Saric. He was unusually thin and his blue polo shirt, which carried the logo for the shop, seemed far too big for him. Rob followed them towards the back, where the outdoor pursuits items were stocked. Rob felt a strange sense of discomfort as they walked past cases stacked with guns and ammunition.

"We have quite a range. Are you looking for anything in particular?"

"We are here to watch the wildlife. I understand that you have wildcats here and we are hoping to see some. And the birds, of course, so something suitable for that would be best."

The assistant started talking Saric through the various options and Saric gave every appearance of being interested in what he had to say.

"Do you know the area well?" Saric asked, "only we went up to the top of the hill line by the mountain trail yesterday and we didn't see much. Would there be somewhere better to observe the wildlife?"

"Oh, I wouldn't go there, sir, that's a strange place. And it's where the crazies from the Peace group live. There'd be too much noise to see proper wildlife there. You'd be better off heading further west, out towards the start of the Rockies. It's a bit more of a drive but the wildlife there is great. There's good hunting, too."

"What's the Peace group?" Saric asked, while examining the binoculars the assistant had just passed to him.

"You haven't heard of them?" There was a look of genuine astonishment on the boy's face. "I thought everyone knew about the Community."

"I'm not from around here," Saric said, although the assistant didn't react as if that explained it. Rob wondered if he had ever left Nevada, or Grandcast River for that matter.

"Ever since I can remember, we were told to stay away from them. They come and recruit you and then make you give up your money and your family, and you are never allowed to leave again. And if you try to leave, they lock you up so you can't get away.

"My dad always told me to stay away from them. He said be polite and don't make them angry but stay away. They come to the town sometimes to do their shopping. My friend Billy's sister joined a few years ago and he hasn't seen her since, but she came into the shop to pick up their order one time, and it was like she didn't know who I was."

Just then, a presence appeared behind Rob.

"What are you doing, Marcus?"

It was an older man. He was wearing the same polo shirt as the assistant, which was tight on him to the same extent that Marcus' was loose.

"I was just showing this gentleman our binoculars, Mr Shaw, he's interested in bird watching."

"Well show him, then, you don't need to be talking about anything else."

"Sorry, Mr Shaw." Marcus looked embarrassed.

"I'd like to buy these ones," said Saric, holding out the pair in his hand, "and the other items, please."

"I'll take it from here, Marcus," said the older man. "Please go and clean the storeroom."

As he rang the items through the till, Mr Shaw apologised for his employee. "This is a good area, you know, and despite what you might have heard, our neighbours are excellent people who do nothing but good for the town."

"I had heard nothing different," said Saric quietly. "Thank you for your help today."

The bell chimed again as they left the shop and made their way to the café on the corner to wait for their targets.

At 11 am, two identical vans drove down the high street.

"Take a look at that," said Saric.

Rob nodded, and they both watched as the vans moved through the high street before turning into a long drive that Saric knew would take them to the back of the supermarket.

"Looks like our guests have arrived."

Rob nodded again. "Let's go and get some groceries, then."

The two men got up. Saric paid the bill, and they left the café. Rob suddenly felt conspicuous. When Saric was in this mood, Rob thought he seemed a couple of feet taller than usual. Rob felt his own demeanour change, too.

I just want to find the woman that might know where my wife and son are, he thought. *Why won't these bastards just help me?*

He reminded himself to stay focused.

Back on the street, the foreign air hit his throat. He felt out of place. Overwhelmed, perhaps.

What the hell is going on? he thought.

The last five years of his search for Helen and Ollie seemed to cram into his mind all at once.

This might be the last lead we ever get, he thought. *What if I mess up? What am I even going to do or say?*

Saric stopped walking and looked at his friend. He put a big hand on Rob's shoulder. "Don't worry. When the right time comes, we'll know what to do."

Saric spoke the words with such certainty that Rob had no choice but to accept them. Rob looked at the floor, took a deep breath and then lifted his head with a broad and welcoming smile on his face. It looked only a little deranged. Saric figured that it would have to be good enough, and in any case, it was better than any smile he could manufacture for such an occasion.

"Remember, first off we find the right target. Then we find the right opportunity. We'll separate here but remember to do nothing inside the store except look. Got it?"

Rob said he understood. Saric went in first, and Rob saw him pick up a basket and wander off into the shop.

Rob waited a minute and followed Saric in. Inside the supermarket, the air conditioning made him feel a little off balance. *Hot-cold-hot-cold,* he thought. *Stupid bloody part of the world*.

He picked up a basket and focused on looking like a friendly but unremarkable shopper.

Both men had agreed it seemed unlikely the Community would be shopping for eighty or so people by picking groceries off the shelf, so Saric had undertaken to go straight to the back of the store and poke around for activity. Rob was to stay in the main shopping area.

Rob wandered around, accumulating the most unlikely basket of shopping, as he picked things off the shelves without the slightest interest in what they were. He looked up and down the aisles and saw no one out of the ordinary. He hoped Saric was being more successful. Just as he processed the thought, his partner came round the corner of the aisle and paced over to him.

"We have a target. Buy what you've got and meet me outside. They are on the move."

He glanced at the shopping in Rob's basket. "Maybe put the baby food back first," he added, "we look weird enough out here already."

And he was off.

Rob did as instructed, and then he found Saric back on the street. He was looking intently for something and was clearly processing his thoughts.

"There are six members here. All in male-female couples. Four of them are at the back of the store ticking off their order and loading it into the vans. They are uninteresting. An older couple has left them to go down the high street. If I heard them right, it's something to do with their post. They are in the building down there with the red frontage. They aren't hard to spot."

"You want to follow them in there?"

"No. I want to isolate the woman. For you. I have a plan. I shall make a distraction, then it's over to you."

"What distraction?"

"You see those men working on that scaffolding?"

"Yes."

"They are lazy. They have only single-bolted those connector joins, and they have missed one out altogether. One nudge and the whole thing could come apart."

"I see," said Rob. "We can't just stand here waiting."

"Maybe we should go back to the café," suggested Saric, but before they could discuss things further, the target couple reappeared on the street.

"Right, let's do it," said Saric. He strode off at such a speed that Rob almost had to break into a jog to keep pace.

Halfway between them and their target was the shop with the two-story scaffolding up against its front. The two men were at the top of it working on the surrounds of the windows. When they were ten meters away, Saric said to Rob, "Isolate the woman", and then he burst into a full sprint.

"Look out!" he roared as he ran. Reaching the scaffolding, he ripped one of the poles out of place. The whole structure swayed. The workmen howled and grasped for something to grab hold of.

"Your upright was just about to go!" Saric shouted up to them. He wrestled with the pole, taking the weight of the higher platform and throwing the workmen around.

"Oh goodness," screamed the woman from the Community. Her companion looked terrified.

"Help me," Saric said to the man.

"What do I do?" he replied, stumbling forwards.

Saric proceeded to control events. The old man was instructed to put his weight onto the now loose upright, whilst Saric barked his orders, creating such a sense of tension that everyone in the vicinity, including the men themselves, were genuinely concerned that the workmen's lives were hanging in the balance.

The old lady was rooted to the spot and clearly terrified.

"Please, come with me. You shouldn't be here if something terrible happens. Let me settle you with a hot drink while it gets sorted out."

She let herself be guided across the street and into the café. The man who had served them earlier was now involved in the rescue attempt, but Rob placed his order with a young woman who was possibly the owner's daughter.

"Here, have some camomile tea," he said to the old lady in his most soothing voice. "That was quite scary. Did you see what happened?"

"No, I was just walking along the street towards the Post Office with my husband when that man shouted, and we saw the scaffolding fall. I hope no one has been hurt." Her voice was honest and open; Rob liked her.

"I'm sorry, I haven't introduced myself properly. I'm Rob." He offered her a hand and a charming smile; he was being every inch the handsome English gentleman that romantic comedies had led Americans to expect.

"I'm Delia, and my husband is Don." She shook his hand politely, although there was an awkwardness to the interaction.

Embarrassment, Rob thought.

269

Delia sipped her tea. "Thank you for your kindness, I was quite scared."

"That's not a problem at all, I'm glad to help."

"Where are you from?" she enquired. "Your accent is not from around here, is it?"

"No, I'm only visiting. I'm from England. Do you live in the town?"

"Oh, I love England! We visited once, years ago. We went to Tewkesbury; do you know it? It was lovely, so much history."

Rob nodded vaguely but no contribution was needed, as Delia continued. He noticed that her bright tone had dimmed slightly, as if she had checked herself. "We live close by but not in the town itself. We are part of a religious community, devoting our lives to the service of the Great Lord."

Rob's heart raced. This was his opportunity, and he had to get it right. He had thought at length about how he might find out where Julia Hawkins was, especially as the direct approach had failed with Carl. He needed something more subtle, but he didn't have much time.

As he'd lain in bed staring at the ceiling of his hotel room in the dark, he had thought about what Helen would do in this situation. She was an expert at understanding people's minds and how they worked. Meanwhile, Rob's own ability to read people was more instinctive than scientific, relying on gut feeling rather than anything tangible. Helen practised analytical techniques to decipher meaning where others saw only confusion. She had often talked to Rob about what she was reading. While much of it was beyond his understanding, every now and then something would stick.

As he sat in front of Delia, the way forward became clear to him. He was no longer in a coffee shop in Nebraska, but in his armchair in the cottage.

*

"You should be careful, you know, Rob," she had said with a smile.

"Why is that?" He looked up from the book he was reading. Helen was sitting at the dining table, her books laid out in front of her. She had been reading and taking notes. Rob remembered the way she pulled her hair back from her face while concentrating, and how she chewed her pen when she was thinking about how to say something. He could smell the coffee in her mug and the daffodils that she had picked from the garden and arranged in a vase on the table.

"I'm reading about how to tell when someone is lying to you. If you think they are, there are ways to doublecheck."

"Oh, yeah?"

"Yes. Imagine you've told me on the phone that you are at the pub with your brother, but I think you are out with another woman. Well, instead of asking you where you are, I could instead say something like, 'Did you get stuck in the traffic caused by the accident on the high street?' If you are at the pub, you would know that there was no accident and tell me I must be mistaken, but if you aren't, you'd be stuck. You would have no way of knowing there hadn't been an accident, so you would probably agree with me, which would prove to me that you are lying. Even if you didn't say yes, you would have to hesitate while you processed how you should answer, and then I would know for sure anyway."

"Interesting theory. Doesn't sound very scientific, though; not your usual kind of thing."

"No, it isn't. In reality, it wouldn't prove anything; everyone would react differently in that kind of situation, so you can't draw any conclusions from it. But it's interesting anyway, and I like to ensure you know just how much power I have."

She had smiled then, and Rob had got up and walked across the room to stand behind her chair. He'd put his arms around her and kissed the top of her head, knowing that was one test she would never have to apply to him.

*

Back in the coffee shop, Rob looked at Delia. "You don't mean the Peace Community?"

"Yes, have you heard of it?" Delia looked surprised.

"It's such a coincidence that we should meet like this. I have travelled here to visit the Community. I believe that it is my true path to devote my life to the service of the Great Lord, and that the Community is the greatest servant of the truth." He paused for effect. "I have read a great deal about the life that members lead, and I intend to join, if I can. In the UK, I have followed a routine of quiet reflection for many years, but I have been told that the Community will help me to fulfil my purpose."

Delia's eyes lit up. They had been right; the acquisition of souls was important to the Community. Whether for good reasons or bad, Delia wanted to recruit him. She would want to help him now.

"I have been in correspondence with my aunt; she is a member of the Community, and she has told me that she will introduce me to the Elders and support me to become a member. I arrived here today and intend to spend the night in town before meeting her tomorrow afternoon."

"This is excellent news; it must be a sign of the Great Lord's will that we should meet here today. Tell me, who is your aunt?"

"Her name is Julia, Julia Hawkins."

Delia's reaction was not what Rob had expected. She did not deny that she knew Julia or tell him that she had passed away or left the Community. That was good news. Julia was there, Rob was sure of it.

But there was something strange in Delia's response. A hesitation, as if the idea of Julia writing was possible but did not quite make sense to her. Rob did not know what to make of it.

"That's lovely, I'm sure she will be delighted to see you after all this time. And I am sure you will make an excellent addition to our community. Tell me, do you have any questions about our life that I can help you with?"

Rob struggled to think of something to ask. What would someone worry about when they were considering giving up every aspect of their way of life for the service of some greater purpose? The concept was alien to him.

At that moment, Don walked through the door and straight towards Delia. "We have completed the task," he said to her softly, "I think we should go and finish our errands now."

Delia stood up and smiled at Rob, who politely rose from his seat to say goodbye. Don reached out a hand and shook Rob's. "Thank you for looking after my wife," he said, before leading her back out onto the street.

CHAPTER 35

In the past, Helen and Jessica had travelled into town with Don and Delia, a kindly older couple who had lived in the Community for longer than anyone could remember. Today, though, when they arrived at the departure point at the front of the main building, they were greeted by one of the Community's Elders.

"Good morning, girls," Elder Jacob said with a smile that hinted at something Helen could not quite place.

"Good morning, Elder Jacob," Helen and Jessica replied in unison.

A wave of fear passed through Helen. She had a plan for today, which was threatened by unexpected changes to the itinerary. Why would they change the assignments when they had been so carefully planned the night before? This hadn't happened before. Could it be that they knew what she was planning? Was that why they had assigned Elder Jacob to supervise? He was a leader and would be empowered to watch her every move. With him there, she wouldn't be able to get away for long enough to enact the plan. There wasn't another trip before The Emergence ceremony, so if she couldn't complete the plan today there wouldn't be another opportunity before her marriage to Daniel.

Before she allowed panic to set in, Helen caught herself. She had to work out what was going on, control what she could and amend the plan if needed. There wasn't much time, but she had the car journey ahead of her; perhaps she could amend her ideas.

"Elder Jacob, I wasn't aware that we were accompanying you today. Has there been a change of plan?"

Elder Jacob sighed. "We have decided that the new members of our party require further support with the trip and have paired them with Don and Delia for today," he said, referring to the siblings from Chicago who had been in the meeting yesterday. "You and Jessica will travel with me and can carry out your tasks while I conduct an important meeting with the mayor."

Helen's heart leapt; all was not lost.

"And you will be pleased to know that Daniel will also be joining us," Elder Jacob added, just as Martha's husband-to-be walked around the corner.

Helen's eyes opened wide, but she concentrated on maintaining her self-control.

"Hello, Daniel," Jessica said with a beaming smile. "How fun to have you with us today, too."

Elder Jacob raised an eyebrow. "We do not make these trips for fun, Jessica."

Jessica shrank in on herself and mumbled something that was half an apology and half an explanation. Helen resisted her desire to tell Elder Jacob to grow up. "What are you doing here today, Daniel?" she asked.

"While you do your chores, Elder Jacob and I will be dealing with important Community business."

OK, I can probably cope with that, thought Helen.

"But I will find you when I am done, and make sure that none of those outside influences have troubled you. You are, after all, my betrothed. You know I have never thought it right for you to be out there."

"How long do you think you will be?" Helen tried to ask the question as if it were quite incidental.

"Not long, I'm just here for the introductions this time."

"Oh." This was not how Helen had wanted this day to go at all.

The old van, which Helen and Jessica were sat in the back of, seemed to travel more slowly than usual. Helen's mind raced as she mentally rehearsed the steps she would take to secure those few precious moments that would allow her to get to a phone.

Helen had come up with her plan over many months. In fact, it had started years ago. There were two parts to it. The first was simple, at least in theory. She would find a phone and call Rob. It sounded simple, but the reality was more complicated. She had eventually earned the trust the shopping party, scoped out the area to find a public phone and engineered Jessica's behaviour so that she might buy herself a few minutes to get to it and make the call. Rob would need to move quickly. She would have preferred for him to have more time to get help to her, but she could not control the timings of the shopping trips. If the call went as she hoped, and she knew he was coming, she would have the couple of days before The Emergence and the three days before the ceremony itself to play with. But what if he didn't answer? Or couldn't help? Or wouldn't?

Then she would have to resort to the alternative plan. She didn't want to do that, as it would destroy too many lives, but if no one was coming to help she would have to act before The Emergence. Remaining in the Community after that wasn't an option.

As they arrived at their destination, Elder Jacob pulled the car into a space behind the town hall. It was at the other end of the town from the supermarket, where they usually parked, but conveniently located for the pharmacy and the park. Helen was pleased; Jessica looked nervous.

"It's OK, lovely," Helen said quietly, placing a reassuring hand on Jessica's. "I know the arrangements have changed but look at the sky and at how beautiful it is. We should share the joy of our surroundings."

Elder Jacob turned in his seat to look at them. "You have your assignments, is everything clear?"

Helen nodded. In the wide backseat of the van, Jessica appeared to be trying to disappear completely.

"Daniel and I have an important meeting with the town governors, which starts shortly. It will last no more than two hours, so it's important you are back at the vehicle by then. I don't have time to wait for you. Is that clear?"

Helen nodded again. "Thank you, Elder Jacob. I hope your meeting goes well."

Elder Jacob said nothing but stepped out of the car.

Daniel took hold of Helen's arm and pulled her close to him. "I will come and find you when I get out."

There was no time to convince him otherwise, as he turned and bounded off after Elder Jacob.

The pharmacy trip was the most important part of their duties and would take up most of their time, but also on their list was the sweetshop for the children and the haberdashery. Helen's plan required them to do the pharmacy first. She wasn't sure how long she had before Daniel reappeared, and it was important that she made the call before he re-joined her. There was no chance then of him letting her out of his sight.

"Come on, Jessica, let's go and collect the medicines. I'm looking forward to seeing Mr Tibbs again, he might even have those biscuits you like."

They walked side by side towards the illuminated green sign of the pharmacy.

Like all the other shops on that side of the street, the pharmacy was a single-storey building. Inside there were three aisles stocked with the usual items. These led to a counter, which stretched across the whole width of the back wall.

To avoid the need for Jessica and Helen to deal with money or lists, the order was called ahead by the Community's nurse. While no one had ever explained the process to her, Helen had never been asked to pay for the items here, so she assumed that was also settled on the call.

As far as Helen was aware, the Community nurse had no formal medical qualifications, and her solution for most ailments tended to be rest and prayer, with added painkillers if the patient was particularly lucky. Nevertheless, there were always two or three large paper bags to be collected from the shop.

Mr Tibbs saw the two women as he bid goodbye to an ancient-looking man at the till. As the man slowly turned on two canes and made his way towards the door, the pharmacist greeted them warmly. Helen had liked him from the first time they met; he was a genuine sort and seemed to have a real affection for Jessica.

"Ladies, it's great to see you. I hoped it would be you collecting today. I'm so sorry, but I haven't quite finished packing your items. Do you want to come and wait in the back?"

Helen enjoyed this ritual, knowing that Mr Tibbs had no intention of packing anything before they arrived, just so that he could make them coffee, offer them biscuits and spend a bit of time in Jessica's company. He worked in the pharmacy alone and, as far as Helen could see, most of his customers were in their seventies and eighties. He enjoyed the company of two women around his own age, and he was also harmless and made Jessica smile.

Jessica accepted the invitation eagerly, but Helen pulled her aside. "Why don't you wait with Mr Tibbs, and I will run over the road and pick up the sweets," she said quietly. "This way, we will have a little spare time to visit the park before meeting Daniel."

Jessica frowned deeply. She looked up to Helen and it was unlike her to contradict anything she suggested. "I'm not sure, you know we are not supposed to leave each other. What if something happens to you?"

"I'll only be at the other side of the road; you can see the door to the shop from here." Helen nodded at the large window, which ran the entire width of the front of the shop. It wasn't quite true; the sweetshop was just out of sight, but Helen said it confidently and thought it unlikely that Jessica would contradict her. "I would worry about you, but I know Mr Tibbs is a good man and a good friend to us, so he will keep you safe." She paused, allowing time for Jessica to consider the options, and then, just for good measure, added, "With sunny weather like this, I am sure the birds will be singing extra sweetly today."

"OK . . . yes, you are right . . . but do be quick, Helen."

"Of course, the list is short today; I will be back before you have finished your coffee. I'll just need the money first."

Unlike the list for the pharmacy, the one for the sweetshop was short and inexpensive. Even after all this time, the Elders didn't trust Helen to look after the money, and so this was Jessica's job. Helen thought it strange that a religious organisation priding itself on living modestly and without luxury went out of its way to buy sweets, but she had learned early on that what the Community said and what it did were two different things. The promise of sweets as a reward for compliance was a tactic they shared with parents all over the world. Little treats kept the Community children happy and stopped them asking awkward questions.

Hesitantly, Jessica took a small envelope from the pocket of her dress and passed it to Helen. The Community members never opened the envelopes, they just handed them over, and nor did the assistants take the money out until they had left the shop. Helen thought it was odd, but if there was cash inside that was enough for her.

"It's all in there," said Jessica.

"Thank you," Helen replied. Then, without knowing why, she reached out and hugged her. If things went well today, she would be gone soon, and she had come to think of the younger woman as a friend.

Pressing the envelope into her pocket, Helen stepped out into the street. There was some commotion by the building site at the other end of the road, but she didn't have time to worry about that now. As quickly as she could without drawing attention to herself, she hurried across the road and to the sweetshop, which, despite its title, contained a strange amalgamation of different products.

The front was stocked with the type of items tourists might like to buy; as well as sweets, there were ornaments, guidebooks and other products that might commemorate a holiday to Grandcast River. Most of the items looked like they had been on the shelves for years, which made sense to Helen, as she had never met anyone in the town who wasn't a local and couldn't imagine who would want to holiday in a tired town in the middle of nowhere with no attractions. It was a different story at the back of the shop, where fishing and hunting supplies were on display. Rural pursuits were a way of life in this town. The shop was run by a husband-and-wife team, and while the wife was usually sitting at the counter knitting, the husband would be busy chatting to customers about recent sightings of whatever animal they were trying to shoot that season.

None of this was important to Helen right now. The most important thing in the whole world was on the wall by the maps and guidebooks – a pay phone.

Pulling her eyes away from the phone, she walked up to the counter and greeted the wife warmly.

"You on your own today? Where's your friend?"

"There was a long list to collect from the pharmacy, so she is doing that while I'm here."

"Oh. Well, how can I help you today?"

Helen handed over the list and the woman read it slowly. "That's no problem, I'll just put it together for you. I'll only be a few minutes."

As the woman placed her knitting under the counter and stood up, Helen seized the moment. She opened the envelope with the cash in it. It was way more than they could possibly be spending on sweets, hundreds of dollars more. She had no time to consider what that meant and pulled out a ten-dollar bill. "Would you mind changing this note for me? I've been asked to make a call to a potential new member."

The woman looked at her strangely but took the cash, opened the till, and handed her a number of coins. These felt strange in Helen's hand; not only were they American and unfamiliar, but it had been five years since she had handled any money.

When she was sure that the owner was occupied picking the items for the order, Helen hurried towards the payphone and shoved some coins in at random. She had rehearsed dialling the number in her mind a hundred times, making sure she remembered the country code. It was 11 am in Nebraska, which she was pretty sure meant it was 5 pm in the UK. School would have finished but Rob would probably be running some after school club or marking or preparing a lesson. There was no point in dialling the landline, he might not even live in their house anymore, so she called his mobile.

Her hand shook and she felt clumsy, terrified that she would misdial; there was no time to waste. She finished dialling and there was silence.

Please connect, she thought.

After what felt like minutes rather than seconds, a strange ringing started. This was to be expected, as she was dialling from overseas. She waited, barely able to contain her frustration. After a couple of rings, it stopped. She heard a familiar voice.

"Hi, this is Rob, leave a message."

Emotion welled up inside her. He was alive! Despite her disappointment, she had planned for this eventuality.

"Rob, it's me, Helen. Ollie and I are fine, but we need your help. We were taken from the park and are being kept in a religious community just outside of Grandcast River, Nebraska. You'll find the location online. There's a lot I need to tell you, that I should have told you already, but please, for now, I need your help. Please can you alert whatever authorities you think can assist; I'm going to try and escape if I can, but I need to protect Ollie, too. Please, Rob, I'm so sorry. I love you."

Her hand shook as she hung up the receiver. She took a moment to blink the tears out of her eyes and turned to see the man and wife staring at her. Back at the till, she handed over the open envelope containing the rest of the money for the sweets. The message gave her hope but it wasn't enough; she didn't know if Rob would pick it up in time and even if he did, would he help? She would have to move onto option two.

Helen stepped out of the door and bumped straight into Daniel.

"Found you!" he declared. "I'm all done with my meeting." He didn't wait for a response and went on, leaning in and talking in a loud whisper.

"The residents of this town make such little sense. They go about this place as if it has meaning, but they see nothing of the truth. I'm not sure I'll have the patience Elder Jacob has with them. It's tedious. *They* are tedious. And anyway, I have other things on my mind right now."

He looked at her in the way a child would look at a long-sought-after toy, having finally saved enough pocket money to own it. Then he noticed something. "Are you alone?" he asked.

"Not really," said Helen. "Jessica is just over the road dealing with the pharmacy order."

"But you're not supposed to be away from one another, are you?" Daniel looked more confused than angry.

Helen took his hand and squeezed it. Then she leaned into him. Looking him straight in the eye, she said, "The time is so close. Closer than we thought. I feel so close to you, Daniel. The Great Mother has shown me the way. The path. It has all opened up. I needed to come here alone for some personal provisions. For us. Don't you see?"

"I'm sorry; what do you mean?"

"I no longer need The Emergence, Daniel, the Great Mother has let me know. It is time for us to become one and rebuild the Community with the truth."

Daniel's eyes were wide. He had known this was coming for so long, but now it had finally arrived. His moment. Their moment. Together. Fully together. He opened his mouth but couldn't form any words.

"Come and see me after dinner and I will talk you through what we have been commanded."

"Yes," said Daniel, and Helen let go of his hand.

"Now we must collect Jessica."

As they walked back to the pharmacy, Helen wondered if she could still give Jessica her trip to the park. It seemed unlikely with Daniel here. It was a shame to let her down, but it couldn't be helped.

The fuss at the end of the street seemed to have died down.

CHAPTER 36

As he climbed into the car, Rob's phone rang again. It was a number he didn't recognise.

"Hello," he said curtly, keen to get back to the motel and a large bottle of cheap whisky.

"Rob, hi, it's Mick."

Rob fought the urge to hang up. His encounter with Delia had left him confused and frustrated. "How can I help you?" he said eventually.

"It's probably better that you come here. There's something I need to tell you."

"Mick, I'm tired, can't you tell me what it is?" Rob looked over at Saric, who was starting the ignition, and shrugged.

"No, Rob, it's better that you come here. There are some things you need to understand."

Rob sighed. "OK, we'll be over in around an hour." It would take them that long to get back to the Community and hike up to Mick's cabin.

"No. I need you to get here at 6 pm. That's the only time that will work."

Rob dropped his phone from his ear to check the time, the screen showed it was just past midday.

"Alright, we'll be there. See you then."

•

Later that afternoon, Rob followed Saric back towards Mick's cabin in the woods. Now they knew where they were going it was quicker, but Rob felt a huge sense of disappointment about their day. He had thought his encounter with Delia would give him certainty about what had happened to Julia, but all he had was more questions. And he felt no closer to answering either them or the ones he had started with.

Saric, on the other hand, was feeling more optimistic. They had gathered more information from Delia and her husband, Don, who had helped him on the building site, than they could have hoped of getting. Sense Check would find something. The fact that the answers made little sense gave Saric confidence rather than cause for concern; the more unusual the set of circumstances the more likely it would yield a unique conclusion. And they really needed a conclusion.

Saric was wary of Mick. He had formed a positive view of the man due to his composure, accuracy and evident skills in the mountainous terrain. However, none of that made him any more comfortable about being summoned to an isolated location to meet with him for an unknown reason. His training had taught him to plan for all potential scenarios, even those that seemed unlikely. Mick had seemed friendly enough, but there was an edge to him that Saric couldn't read. Rob's instincts could not be trusted right now, and this meant Saric had to plan for the possibility the encounter might be hostile. Mick was involved with the Community somehow, and everything that Saric had learned told him that its members were willing to use any means available to secure their success.

As they rounded the final ridge, they could see Mick's cabin sitting peacefully in the clearing, smoke still rising in gentle tendrils from the chimney. Saric took a moment to assess the scene. Everything was quiet. The sensible option was to walk away. He didn't trust Mick, and while they would easily overcome the older man hand to hand, he was the only one who would be armed.

But the time when sensible was an option had passed. This was damage limitation now, and Rob wouldn't walk away. Cautiously but confidently, Saric stepped onto the porch, where a rocking chair was positioned next to an old dog bed. He made his way to the door and knocked.

"Come in," came Mick's voice from the other side, "it's open."

As he pushed the door, Saric saw Mick standing in front of him. He was aware but unthreatening. He also wasn't alone. In the armchair by the wood burner was a woman in her late sixties. She was wearing a long linen dress and an expression that Saric could not read. Some strange mix of fear and expectation, he decided.

Rob's voice was quiet beside him; he sounded somehow far away. "Julia?" he said hesitantly.

It was Mick that responded. "Come in, gentlemen. We have a lot to discuss and not much time."

The woman stood up. "Yes, young man, my name is Julia. Julia Hawkins. Please sit." She directed them to the dining chairs that had been positioned to allow them to face each other. Mick moved to Julia's side.

Rob and Saric sat down as directed, as did Julia. Mick stood next to her. An alert Texas sat at Mick's feet, unsure how to read the mood of the room.

"Mick tells me you two gentlemen have been looking for me?"

"Yes, we certainly have," replied Rob.

"And you hope I can help you find your wife and son?"

"Yes."

"Tell me what you told Mick. I want to hear it from you."

Rob looked at Saric, who nodded. Rob explained how his wife and son had disappeared. And how they had spent five years looking for her. And how the will of Helen's grandmother had given them Julia's name. And how an old postcard had brought them here.

Julia listened to the whole story without interruption, her face twisting with emotion as Rob spoke. At the end of the narrative, Rob paused, before asking, "Julia, are you Helen's mother? Do you know where she might be?"

"You poor child. I'm so sorry for the pain you have suffered. I'd always hoped she would get freedom forever."

"Helen, you mean?"

"No. Not Helen. Not my sweet Helen. Helen was freed from this world many years ago. But your Helen; that's another story."

295

"I'm sorry, I don't understand." Rob was impatient for more but held himself back from trying to rush the woman. She was in pain; they could all see it.

Mick put his hand on Julia's shoulder and Texas stood up. "You don't owe these two anything, Flowerpot," Mick said. "Are you sure you want to go on?"

Rob twitched, as if he might stand up. Now it was Saric's turn to put his hand on Rob's shoulder.

Two steps and Mick is no longer part of this discussion, he thought. *Even if he was in the marines some decades ago.*

But it was an instinctive thought that needed to be balanced against the other options.

Before Saric could draw a conclusion, Julia reached up to find Mick's hand, gripped it tightly and spoke again. "I'm afraid I do owe this young man, Mick. If it were not for me, he wouldn't have been in this position."

Texas sat back down.

"Helen, I mean your Helen, has a story, too. Her real name is Martha. She was born in the Community in 1985, around the same time as my Helen. She was only a little girl when I arrived here. You are right that

296

Alice Johnson is my mother. I know it would have broken her heart when I left her." She paused for a moment before continuing. "I'm sorry, it's all a little jumbled up in my mind. To tell you about your wife, I must first tell you about my daughter.

"Helen and I moved here when she was twelve. I was running away from a lot of things; I know that now. At the time, I thought we were moving towards the truth.

"My marriage to Helen's father had broken down a couple of years previously and things were . . . difficult between us. Helen and I ended up living back with my mother, Alice.

"Just when I thought I was going to spend the rest of my life at home, I met a man, Thomas, who offered us a different future. To try and support us, I was working a couple of evenings a week in a bar, although in reality, my mother was paying for almost everything. One evening, Thomas came in for a drink and we hit it off. He was American and in the UK on business. He told me he was divorced, too, and he seemed to understand something of the pain I was in. His business involved the church, and he took me along to some of their services. They were like nothing I had seen before.

"My mother attended church every Sunday, I think that's what people of her generation did, but I had stopped going with her as soon

297

as I was old enough to make my own decisions. This church was different. There were no hymns or sermons, but instead the speakers talked of real-life problems and how these happened because people failed to understand the truth. They offered solutions and could make things better.

"I fell in love. With Thomas but also with the Great Lord. I figured they could offer me the life I had always wanted. When Thomas asked me to move to America with him and join him in his community, I knew it was the right thing to do.

"My mother wasn't happy about any of this, of course. I was moving halfway across the world with a man I had known for a matter of weeks. She had never been further than a day trip to France. But I knew it was the right thing for Helen and me, so, eight weeks after our first meeting, we got on a flight and moved to the Community here."

Julia paused; it was clear that telling this story was painful. They gave her time.

"I don't know how much you know about the Community, but I will assume that if you have managed to find us from a town name on a postcard, you have done your research."

Saric nodded.

"What you won't know from the advertising and recruitment strategy is what it's really like here. As a new arrival, you spend three weeks in a separate location, learning the ways of the Community. The idea is that it gives potential new entrants time to assess whether the Community is the right place for them. People leave through choice and people are asked to leave. The process is said to be one that tests faith, but really what it tests is compliance. Will the entrants cause trouble or ask awkward questions? That's the real test.

"During those three weeks, I didn't see Thomas once. He had gone straight to the Community. I worked hard and did as I was asked, and I was eventually permitted to enter The Emergence. You have heard of The Emergence, of course?"

Saric nodded again. Rob could not move.

"Three days in the wilderness. Three days and three nights. It's mostly staged, of course. It's not in their interest to let you starve or freeze to death. But it's terrifying. I genuinely thought I might die. It breaks you down to a point that I didn't even know was possible. And then eventually you are admitted to the Community and the relief is immense. Unbelievable. And because you are so happy to be there, you don't ask any questions.

"At least Helen was spared that. Children don't go through The Emergence until they are around thirteen. It's unusual for single women to be in the Community with a child, but after The Emergence, they found us a double room in the women's wing. I thought that Thomas and I would be together again, but he had left to go on another recruitment trip, and it soon became clear that he wouldn't be returning for more than a few days at a time.

"I was happy enough, though. Day-to-day life was quite easy really, and we were far away from our problems in the UK. As long as you stuck to the rules you could get by quite nicely. And Helen seemed happy; she made friends with the other girls here and I knew she was safe, away from the influences that might have led her astray back at home."

Julia's mind seemed to wander slightly, and she stared out of the window for a long time. Texas rested her head against her knee.

Carrying on as if she had not paused, Julia continued. "One of Helen's friends was a girl called Martha. I believe she is the person you know of as Helen. Martha's father is one of the senior Elders of this community. He is a man of great faith and little kindness. Martha was the same age as Helen, and they became extremely close. Despite her father's position, Martha was kind to Helen and wasn't worried by the fact she was of little standing in the Community.

300

"There is a hierarchy here, you see. Many relationships are formed to manage power dynamics, and to progress one's own position within this hierarchy. Martha was just a child, of course, but she had not fallen into that trap. I liked her a lot. She was bright, too. More inquisitive than most of the children here, who rarely seem to understand that there is a world beyond the confines of the Community. Martha was interested in life outside. Helen told her stories, of course, but she would ask me, too. She was amazed when I told her that women attended university and had careers as doctors and architects and engineers. Life isn't like that here, you see. There's men's work and there's women's work, and the two do not mix.

"Life in the Community was not what I had expected, but we were reasonably content. I missed my mother and often thought of returning to her, but we hadn't parted on good terms. Besides, I was too proud to admit she was right, and that Thomas had not been who I thought he was. Even if I had wanted to leave, I had no means to do so. As you know, we are a long way from anywhere here and I had no easy access to money, no means of transport and, at that time, no means to communicate with the outside world.

"Then, three years after we arrived, Helen became ill. It started with a cold but quickly progressed to something more serious. Medical care here is provided by the matron and closely controlled by the Elders.

301

"I called the matron, of course, and she gave Helen some treatment, but after a couple of days her fever got worse and her breathing more difficult. I asked them to call a doctor, as she needed to be in hospital, but they refused. They told me this was a test of Helen's faith, and that the Community would pray for her. I begged them to call a doctor and later an ambulance, but they insisted the Great Lord would look after her.

"The next day, as I sat beside her bed, my darling Helen passed away. They told me her faith had not been strong enough."

The room fell silent. Rob felt exhausted. The questions swirled around in his mind. He looked at Saric, and Saric knew it was his turn to take up the discussion.

"That is a very sad story. I'm very sorry for you. I can only imagine how it feels to lose a child." Saric paused. "You said that Rob's wife's name is Martha. Why do you say that?"

"Martha was Helen's closest friend. She took her death hard. Her parents simply could not understand. For them, Helen's path had been chosen by the Great Lord. I truly believe they think she was lucky to have made her way to 'everlasting glory' in such a short time. Martha couldn't see it. She came to me to share her pain. We cried together and talked together, and I think, in the end, we both came to a realisation. We saw

302

what they were doing. It was all lies, just stupid, pitiful, comfortable lies."

She let out a long sigh. "I couldn't stop the whole thing, it was too big. What could I have done on my own? They are believers." The way she said it, the word sounded dark and malign. "But I decided I could save Martha. We agreed it together. I set up the whole thing with her. I still had a place in the Community then, so I stole some money and we got her out. It wasn't easy, but I managed to get in touch with an old friend. I made her believe she was coming for me. Martha and I got out through the fence, and I gave her Helen's passport, some money and an address. I made my friend take her and I stayed behind to see what I could do to buy her some time; maybe throw them off a bit. Martha didn't want to leave me behind, but I promised her I'd be fine and would get word to her to let her know. That must be the postcard you saw."

"And you sent her to your mother?" Saric said.

"Yes. Where else? I told Martha to never contact me, and to never speak of this place to anyone." She looked at Rob. "Not even the ones she loved."

"Martha," Rob whispered, trying the name. He didn't like it.

Mick stiffened. A tear trickled down Julia's face.

303

Saric leaned forward in his chair. "Is she here, Julia. In the Community now?"

"I don't know. I don't leave the Lodge. But Mick and I met a boy called Ollie. He was about the age of the son you described. Do you have a picture?"

Without speaking, Rob took his phone from his pocket. He didn't need to find a picture. Helen – could he still call her that? – and a three-year-old Ollie filled the screen as soon as it came on. Julia took the phone from him.

"Poor boy," she said. "Yes, I think he's here. Grown, of course, but yes, that's him. He spoke of his mum." She looked at Mick, who nodded in solemn agreement. "It looks like you have found your wife and son, young man."

Rob sat back in his chair. The words seemed to bounce around inside him. He felt his heart racing, adrenaline erupting throughout his body. He tried to breathe deeply to get some control, but it was no use. He stood up and tried to find something to focus his gaze on, but everything looked and smelled strange – he couldn't grasp onto anything. The confusion overwhelmed him. He lurched to the front door, stumbled onto the porch and threw up. It seemed to bring some relief, and, as he pulled in some breaths, he became aware of his big friend's arm wrapped around him.

Texas ran around in circles. Mick was kneeling on one knee talking in a low voice to Julia. As Saric brought Rob back into the cabin, she placed a hand on the rough skin of Mick's cheek. Rob and Saric caught the end of their discussion. "My sweet little Flowerpot, of course I will. I know I don't say it, but—" he became aware that he was being listened to, "— just because you don't say something, doesn't mean it isn't true."

"I know," said Julia, and she kissed him lightly on the cheek she wasn't holding.

"Now, we need to figure out how to get you to your wife and son."

The sudden change to the practical altered the mood in the room. Everyone shifted their body position. Texas stood alert, ready to go.

Mick looked at his watch. "We need to get you back," he said.

"OK. Yes, you're right." She turned back to Rob and Saric. "You're not going to be able to get in there. Not without an army. And even then . . . no, we need to get them out. I will go to them."

Mick raised an eyebrow. "You can do that?" he said. He didn't sound convinced. She assured him she would find a way with such confidence that it seemed immediately settled.

"Fine. Get my phone to her," said Saric. He took it from his pocket, changed the settings and gave it to her. "There's no code to open it now," he explained. Julia looked unsure. "Don't worry about it, Helen will know. Tell her to phone Rob as soon as she can."

Saric looked at the remaining charge on his phone's battery. "I'm afraid you will need to get this to her soon, or the battery will go dead. Tomorrow, ideally. Definitely not later than the day after."

"I will try and get it to her tomorrow, then. Morning probably. I can't risk them finding your phone before we get to use it. Will it ring if someone calls you? I can't have that."

Saric explained the phone would make no noise or light up in any way until Helen used it. Then he turned to Mick. "If she can get to the Lodge, we can get them out through the fence, right? Then back up here through the woods and out of here?"

"Yep," Mick confirmed. "My guess is it won't take them long to start looking, though. If they've gone all the way to England to bring them here, I reckon they want them in the Community pretty bad."

Saric stood up. "Once they are outside of that fence, they will never be going back."

Mick nodded.

Unless they want to, thought Saric.

It was a dark thought, and one he had promised Grace he would never share with Rob.

"Good luck, Julia," said Saric, "and thank you."

Rob took Julia's hand and held it for a long moment, but he couldn't form any words. Julia understood.

Saric guided them back to the road in silence.

"You drive," Saric said when they got to the car. He opened the boot and pulled his laptop out of a bag. "I need to take control of my phone."

Rob drove them back towards the motel with his mind swimming with thoughts.

"He can't look that different," he said at last. "If Julia can recognise him from my old photo, I guess I will, too. Dad always said I'd recognise him however old he got."

Saric had no idea what the answer to that was, but it didn't seem that Rob really needed a response. "Let's fill up the car on the way back," he said. "We might need a full tank."

CHAPTER 37

Leaving Rob a voicemail had left Helen with a dilemma. If she'd spoken to him, she would have known whether he was coming and could wait if he was. But a voicemail wasn't enough. He might not pick it up and, even if he did, he might choose not to get involved. As she couldn't rely on the message, she had to move onto the backup plan.

Her quietness at dinner as she contemplated her next move didn't go unnoticed.

"What's wrong, Martha? Did you find today tiring?" Jessica asked her.

"Yes, I suppose I did; there was a lot to buy, wasn't there," Helen said thoughtfully, "but tell me, how was your coffee with Mr Tibbs? What did you talk about?"

"He is such an interesting man. He told me all about how his mother is getting on since her retirement. And he has just got a new cat. He said his old cat isn't too happy about it. I think I would like to have a cat one day."

"Jessica, do you ever wonder what your life would be like away from the Community?"

"What do you mean?" said Jessica, as if Helen were asking if she had ever considered relocating to the Moon.

"Do you ever imagine a different life? One where you would live away from here? You could get a job and buy things you like. Perhaps you could get a cat, or maybe you could even fall in love with someone like Mr Tibbs."

Jessica looked shocked now. "Martha! That could never happen." Helen could see that she had also embarrassed her. "Why would you even dream of something like that? Life away from the Community is sinful; we see that every time we visit the town."

"Do we, Jessica? Tell me, what sin did you witness today? I'm not sure. I think there is goodness out there, and maybe even happiness. What if I said I could take you away, to somewhere where you could decide your own future?"

"No, Martha, the Good Lord has shown us the way. Our lives are here, that is His intention for us. And soon you will marry Daniel and your life will be complete. Perhaps the Great Lord will even bless you with a child."

Helen wanted to remind Jessica that she already had a child, but she knew the younger woman meant no harm by what she said. She also knew that she wouldn't be able to save her.

After dinner, while silent prayers were taking place, Daniel found Helen walking in the grounds by the lake. While most people chose to pray in the chapel, silent meditation in the grounds was also permitted, allowing them to steal a few words in private.

While asking after her, Daniel stood much closer than she would have liked. She explained that the Great Mother had visited to tell her the time had come to test the true faith.

"What did it feel like?"

Helen was slightly taken aback by the question, which was more inquisitive than Daniel could usually manage.

"What do you mean?"

"When she came to you, what did that feel like?"

Helen looked at the man standing opposite her. It was a long time since she had really done that. He was younger than the image she kept in her mind, and more innocent. Despite all the cruel things he had done to her, and intended to do in the future, there was a kindness there. He really cared about her soul, and he wanted to save her.

Helen tried to summon up a description of what it might have felt like, but the explanation felt weak. "I felt complete and certain, as if the path that has always been there for me was suddenly clear. Until that moment, I didn't know it even existed, but as soon as she visited me, it was as if I had always known. I hope one day that your faith will become strong enough for you to feel that, too."

Daniel bowed his head.

"But now the Great Mother has a task for us. She has given me clear instructions, and you must follow me, Daniel."

"Tell me, Martha, what must I do?"

Helen explained the plan. It was simple enough, but Daniel still looked confused.

"Why, Martha?"

"It is a test, to see who has the faith to follow the true path. There must be a test so that we can prove we are worthy. It's the right thing to do."

Helen held Daniel's gaze, keeping his attention for as long as possible while he processed the information.

"I understand."

"We must start the plan tomorrow. Meet me after morning prayers outside the chapel. We will pray together for the Great Mother's guidance and then we will follow her path."

CHAPTER 38

As Julia left Mick's cabin, the phone felt heavy in her pocket. This was despite it being tiny compared to the devices she remembered from her life in the outside world. When she had moved to the Community, phones had been large with tiny black and white screens. The gadget that Saric had just given her was something else entirely; it was thin and almost all screen. There weren't even any buttons; she would have no idea how to operate it if called to do so.

When Mick had come to her in the garden that afternoon, there had been something different about him. He'd looked heavier somehow. She had immediately known something was wrong.

When he told her about the men he had just met and the story they had relayed, she understood why. Losing her daughter while knowing it was her fault had left her deeply hurt. Over time, she had confided in Mick over that pain. He was convinced that the Community Elders were to blame and tried hard to convince her that she was not at fault. Julia struggled to believe him, but she welcomed the sentiment and was helped by the fact that someone else clearly cared about her feelings.

By bringing the news of Rob and Saric to her, Mick would have known he'd be opening up wounds that were only just starting to heal.

Julia had spent many hours wondering what had happened to Martha – calling her Helen did not feel right even in her own thoughts – and had imagined many futures for her. Ultimately, she had resigned herself to the fact that she would never know her fate.

Finding out that Martha had found happiness with Rob had been good news, but she was distressed when Mick told her that Martha might be back in the Community against her will.

A lifetime of experience had taught her to be sceptical of other people's motives, and even before Mick told her his belief that she should meet the men, Julia had resolved to do so. She needed to look Rob in the eye and understand his intentions. Martha would never have returned to the Community voluntarily, but she might have left Rob for good reason. Men were not always kind, and Martha might not want to be found.

Leaving the Lodge to get to the meeting with Rob and Saric wasn't difficult. While they weren't exactly prisoners, they were overseen by one of the residents, a woman of Julia's own age called Nora. Nora's husband had been a senior elder, but when he died of a heart attack she had been asked to move to the Lodge.

315

Instead of seeing this as a rejection, Nora had taken it as an opportunity to grasp some standing in the leadership by overseeing the members. In practical terms, this meant she acted as a liaison between the main Community and the Lodge, organising deliveries and reporting back to the leadership on any issues with the women. Julia also knew that part of Nora's role was to keep an eye on her.

When Julia helped Martha to escape, she became a danger to the Community. They could not let her leave because of the risk she would tell the outside world what happened there, but equally, she could not be allowed to live among the main population, where she might continue to be a disruptive influence. Life in the Lodge was a convenient way to keep her under control. Even then, the Elders saw her as a risk; she had embarrassed them, and they did not like it. Nora, therefore, took it upon herself to spy on Julia. When the opportunity arose, she read her letters and listened in to her conversations.

The only opportunity Julia had to get to the cabin was in the early evening just before dinner, when the Lodge's residents were permitted to visit the chapel to pray. She slipped away easily enough, out through the same gap in the fence that Mick often used to visit her.

After meeting Rob, any concern she held over his intentions disappeared. His pain was raw and real; she understood it and wished

316

that she could ease it. When he had shown her the picture of Martha and Ollie looking happy and healthy, she knew that she had to do whatever she could to help.

Julia had liked Ollie immediately, and she understood now why she had felt compelled to share Helen's favourite childhood poem with him. It was hugely personal to her, but reading it to the boy had brought her joy rather than pain. He was Martha's son. Now she knew this, she could see it in his face. He had her smile. Perhaps on some level, she had recognised that when they met.

As she reached the boundary to the Lodge, she squeezed through the gap in the fence before pulling the branches across to cover it as best she could. Mick had asked her more than once to leave through that gap and not return. It would be easy enough and, despite the Elders' misgivings, she was quite sure they wouldn't pursue her.

She would be happy with Mick in the cabin. They hadn't spent much time together, but she felt closer to him than she had felt to any man in the past. They understood each other in a way that Julia could neither understand nor explain.

But Julia could not leave Helen. After her death, the Community had laid her to rest in the burial plot at the foot of the hills. Julia was permitted to visit her grave sometimes, and no promise of happiness

317

with Mick could tempt her to give up those visits and the opportunity to spend time with her only daughter.

She entered the Lodge as the other women were returning from evening prayers and walked into the dining room. Julia didn't want to be near them tonight, so she went straight to her room to rest and wait for what was coming tomorrow.

CHAPTER 39

Rob was completely drained as he and Saric sat down to eat in the motel diner. They spoke briefly about what would happen if Helen called and the exact instructions to give. Saric linked Rob's phone to his laptop so Sense Check would record everything. There was not much to plan for. They just needed to agree when she could get to the Lodge fence with Ollie. If there was a problem with that plan, Rob would have to improvise.

"Don't start talking about anything else," Saric warned Rob. "You'll use the battery, and we might need the phone." Then he added, "You can talk to her for the rest of your life," and immediately wished he hadn't; it sounded so melodramatic. Rob smiled at him and said he understood.

Back in his room, Rob sat on his bed. He knew there was no chance of anything approaching proper sleep, which frustrated him because he wanted to be fresh for whatever the following day had in store. He took his phone from his pocket, plugged it into its charger and stared at it, imagining Helen's voice coming out.

Looking at his phone, he became conscious of a stack of unread messages, unopened emails and missed call alerts.

All stupid junk, he thought to himself.

He decided to have a clear out; if by some accident he didn't pick up Helen's call he wanted it to be obvious. As he got into his missed calls, he saw an American phone number with a voicemail attached. He put the phone on speaker and played it.

Helen's voice hit him so hard that he almost didn't hear the first few words. He *had* missed her call. The message was only a few seconds long and he replayed it the instant it ended.

For five years, he hadn't known whether she had left him or been taken from him. Now he knew.

I am coming for you, my sweet darling, he thought. *I am coming.*

Five years of uncertainty was washed out of him in an instant. She wanted him to come to her. At the same time, five years of hatred and anger for those stolen years without his wife and son were able to take their full shape. He stood up and started pacing the room, his body shaking with rage, as he thought, *I am going to destroy them all. Every one of these bastards. I'll tear them all apart.*

He played the voicemail again to hear her voice one more time. It soothed him. As long as he could hear her voice, the rage could wait. He could feel the little chubby arms of his beautiful son wrapped around him. He could feel Helen's warm body snuggled into his on the sofa. *They'd taken it all away from him.*

But now he knew that they hadn't just taken that from him, they had taken it from all three of them. He realised the voicemail opened up yet more questions, but he knew one thing for certain.

I'm coming.

CHAPTER 40

The small desk in the motel room hadn't been big enough for Sense Check and all the reference materials that Saric wanted to work with, so he had settled on the spare bed, his back propped up with pillows and the laptop across his thighs.

They had gathered a lot of data today and he needed to process it before the morning. He had uploaded Julia's story and Sense Check had cross-referenced it against the data they had already gathered. It matched. He was satisfied that the woman they had met today was Alice Johnson's daughter and the mother of Helen Johnson.

He was also satisfied that the Helen they were looking for was not Julia's daughter.

The rest was conjecture. Nothing in Sense Check could prove the rest of Julia's testimony — that their Helen was born in, and had escaped from, the Community. They held no official records of births, marriages or deaths and, if these events were recorded anywhere, it was not connected to the Nebraska address. Saric thought it likely that the Community believed the source of authority for such matters did not reside with the State Registrar.

Even if he could find evidence that Martha existed, he couldn't prove that Martha and their Helen were the same person. And even if he could, what would it matter?

He put Sense Check on the bed and turned to the maps. Rob's instinct was to storm in all guns blazing, either figuratively or literally, and carry Helen and Ollie out in whatever way necessary. Saric knew they needed more than this. They needed a plan.

Using the information they had gathered from the observation point, the daily schedules available from the Community's website, data about power usage and local transport reports, Sense Check had identified the weak points in the Community's defences. The whole Community ate and prayed together, which meant that there was an hour each evening when they were all in one place. There were periods of movement just before and after these times, and movement meant confusion; moments when discrete intruders might not be noticed, and absences not missed.

There was an opportunity there.

They knew that the Community boundary was fenced, but that wouldn't be hard to get through. Access would be easy but slow. Apart from the main driveway, which would be observed, they would have to enter from either the mountains or the woods. Saric wondered whether

323

an eight-year-old boy would be able to walk in the mountains for the three-mile hike to where they would leave the car. He knew very little about children.

Rob would know, but Saric knew that he could not ask him.

He no longer had his phone, so he used his headset to dial Grace's number from his laptop. The line rang for longer than usual and Grace sounded a little odd. "Saric? Is everything OK? How is Rob?"

He didn't like the urgency in her voice. "Yes, fine thank you. Are you OK?"

"It's just before 4 am here. I was worried something had happened."

As she said it, he realised his mistake. "Grace, I'm so sorry, I completely forgot."

"It's fine." Her voice was lighter now; she turned her camera on as she flicked on a light and he was pleased to see her face, despite her bleary eyes. "My alarm will be going off soon anyway. What do you need?"

He contemplated his answer to that question for a moment. "Just someone to pull apart the plan, I suppose. This needs to go right, and I

324

need someone to make sure I'm not missing anything. There are things that you and Rob understand that I don't always see. We found Julia."

Saric relayed to Grace about meeting Mick and Julia, and about what they had learned in the town. He explained the Community in detail and conveyed his plan to rescue Helen and Ollie. "What am I missing?" he then asked.

"It's a good plan. Very comprehensive. I agree that it would be better to get them out without being noticed if you can, but you need to plan for the alternative. I'm sure you know that."

He nodded. The back-up plan had been ready since day one. Grab and go. Whatever means necessary.

"But Saric," she continued, "you need to plan this on the basis that you won't have Rob with you."

"There's no way he'll stay here, if that's what you mean?"

"No, not that, I know he'll be there. But he won't be of any use to you. We know what is at stake for him. You need to manage him as much as any other unknown factor in this situation."

She paused while Saric reflected on this. She was right, of course.

"You say this Mick has a military background. Would he be useful to you if you needed some support?"

Saric was silent.

"You have to trust someone, you know."

Saric wondered whether he trusted Mick. He had no reason not to, but he had known him for barely more than twenty-four hours.

"You're right, thank you."

"Saric. Be careful. I know what this means but don't let the emotion take over."

"I won't, Grace, thank you."

"Call me when it's over."

"I will. Goodnight, Grace."

"Good morning, Saric," she said with a smile, as she rang off.

Unlike Rob, Saric would sleep well that night; rest was necessary to prepare for the day ahead of him. As he switched off the lamp, he made a promise.

I'm coming.

CHAPTER 41

September 2020

Back in her room, Helen sat on her bed. Her mind was firing in lots of directions at once. The idea for tomorrow was simple enough. A distraction at the right time and off they would go. She no longer really doubted that Daniel would do what she needed of him. If anything, over the years she had done a better job with him than she could possibly have hoped. His recent enthusiasm for their union had the potential to cause trouble, but even that she had managed to repackage in a way that gave her control. She wondered what it would feel like to dump him on the side of the road somewhere and drive off.

Helen had spent time recently working on her own mind, too. The Martha the Community wanted was a mask she had to wear, but it was not her. Whilst she had become practised at it, to the extent that it no longer required constant attention to achieve, it was still a burden to carry the alter ego around in her mind. And on top of that, she had to be able to drop into yet another character of the Great Mother. She was unsure which was more difficult or more tiring. She wanted rid of them both. Now, as she considered it, if tomorrow didn't work out, she wasn't sure she would be strong enough to keep up the whole façade any longer. Even for Ollie.

To try and find some peace, she eased her mind into other areas of thought, but it was no use. The places in her mind that could bring her relief were so wrapped up in the world before this nightmare that they took her straight back to the importance of tomorrow. Oddly random thoughts came and went. Things she missed and wanted back. Other than hymns and classical religious pieces, she had been starved of music for so long that she wondered how it would feel to turn the radio up and dance.

What will Ollie make of proper music? she thought.

She suddenly felt scared. *Can I still dance? Will music still make me feel the same way?*

She lay back in her bed, with little hope of any quality sleep. She felt cold, overwhelmed perhaps.

Please let me get back to my husband, she silently pleaded. *Please let my son feel the warm arms of his father around him and hear him say it will all be OK. If I am paying the price for something I've done, surely that debt is settled.*

"Please, please, please," she heard herself say out loud.

Was that Martha's voice or mine? she wondered. *I am so lost.*

She opened her eyes and found herself looking up at the picture of Mary that the Community had recast as the Great Mother.

She sat up and shook her head, as if literally trying to throw the thoughts from her mind.

No! You don't get to do that, Helen. You know who you are.

A surge of adrenaline flowed through her.

Those bastards don't get to beat you. Tomorrow you start the journey home.

CHAPTER 42

At 6 am, Rob decided it was OK to get out of bed. He had drifted in and out of something approaching a light sleep for some hours and was relieved that he could finally consider the day to have begun.

He stood in the bathroom in his underwear and looked at himself in the mirror.

I had better shave, he thought. *I want to look my best to see Helen today.*

Since hearing her voice on his phone, the idea of seeing her and Ollie had not left his mind for a moment.

I wonder if she will mind that I have got so big? he thought. She always liked him the way he was before, and now he looked different.

I can go back to how I was, can't I?

Rob got dressed quickly and went to Saric's room.

Saric was waiting for him. "Sit down, Rob. Let's go through a couple of things."

Rob sat next to Saric at the little dressing table in the room, and both turned their attention to Saric's laptop. Saric showed Rob the location of his phone; it was in the Lodge as planned. He demonstrated how he could track the phone and explained how he could see a mirror of its use. If someone made a call they would know, and be able to listen in.

Having reassured Rob that this element of the plan was in place, and they were ready to react, he wanted to talk to him about the other elements of the work he'd done the night before with Sense Check.

"There are some aspects of this I don't like," Saric said.

"Go on."

"Julia's story is consistent, but we are reliant on both her not having lied about her intentions and her ability to execute her part of the proceedings." Reading back the transcript of the discussion in the cabin, with all the emotion removed, had considerably lessened Saric's enthusiasm for the plan.

"She'll do it," said Rob. "You saw her."

Saric made no comment on this statement and returned to the practical aspects of the plan.

"If we get away with drawing them to the Lodge, and out of the compound, I'm quite happy with the plan." Saric looked at Rob and concluded he didn't have his full attention. "Our back-up plan needs to have some parameters."

Saric flicked around the screen and brought up Sense Check's transcript. "See here," he said, pointing to a section of Julia's speech, where she said, "You're not going to be able to get in there. Not without an army. And even then . . ."

Sense Check had flagged the statement as unlikely to be true, given the US army consists of around 1.4 million people and there was an estimated eighty people in the Community. Whilst just another example of how Sense Check's literal system didn't cope well with metaphor, it had made Saric reflect on what they might find inside the Community compound. According to the program, based on a cross-reference with other US closed communal groups, there was a ninety-five per cent likelihood of the Community possessing weapons. Julia's turn of phrase insinuated they may be heavily armed. And worse, that they would feel entirely comfortable firing on anyone who tried to break in.

Rob couldn't ignore it. He was enraged and wanted a reckoning, but he was still able to recognise the risk.

"We can't pull back from this now, Rob," Saric said. "And if something goes wrong, it could expose Helen. I think we need to move today, come what may." Saric's face looked tight. Rob caught the look in his eye, and it made him shudder. "If it comes to it, Rob, I'm going in. I'll be quick, but it won't be clean."

Rob wanted to complain that he should go in with Saric if it came to that, but at that moment, he felt the enormous gulf between them. Rob knew he would be in the way. Saric sensed the tension. "I'll need you on the perimeter to create a distraction," he said.

"Whatever it takes," Rob replied. "If it does come to it, you'll need to go in armed. How are we going to organise that?"

"Mick will oblige."

"Are you sure?"

"I won't be asking."

•

They had agreed the previous evening that they would wait at Mick's cabin until they received Helen's call. Julia had said how she hoped to be able to get the phone to her during the morning, but she had been unable to be any more specific. Waiting at Mick's gave them proximity

333

to the Community, while, Saric hoped, being far enough away to be able to keep Rob calm until they heard from her.

They parked in the usual spot and made their way to the cabin. Saric had his tablet now, tracking his phone. He checked it regularly as they walked. He knew he would hear it if Rob's phone rang, but he wanted to make sure the signal was maintained throughout the journey. He kept an eye on the tracker. His phone was still in the Lodge, which meant Julia had not yet moved towards the main house; they had time.

Mick was waiting at the door when they arrived. He was staring across the woods in the direction of the Community, apparently oblivious to their approach. There was an expression of great concern on his face. At that moment, Saric recognised just how much Mick must care for Julia, and what not knowing if she was safe must be costing him. Like Saric, Mick was a man of action; it would be hard for him not to race after Julia and attempt to rescue her from the danger that she was undoubtedly putting herself in.

Mick nodded at them and walked indoors. Texas waited on the first step for them and nuzzled at Rob's hand before turning to follow her master inside.

"Any word?" Mick asked, knowing there wouldn't be and not really expecting a response. He nodded towards a cabinet in the kitchen. "You might want to have a look through there, Saric. Might be of use to you. I assume you haven't brought your own."

Saric opened the door and found a small selection of weapons. Hunting items mostly, including a decades old but perfectly maintained Marlin 336 rifle. It would not be Saric's weapon of choice, but under the circumstances, he thought it would be sufficient, and he was glad Mick had made the offer. It made other things easier.

"Thanks, mind if I take this one?" Saric said, examining the rifle. It was old but well maintained.

"No problem, just leave me the M14."

Mick held Saric's gaze, as if challenging him to say that he was going alone. Saric remembered his conversation with Grace. Mick could be useful to him.

He nodded. Both men considered the matter closed.

CHAPTER 43

Helen worked hard to look as normal as possible during her morning routine, despite knowing what the day would bring. She finished morning prayers in the chapel and, as she walked out of the large ornate doors, it hit her that this was it. Today she was going to take Ollie and, with Daniel, get out.

As instructed the night before, Daniel came over to meet her. As he broke away from the group of men he was talking to, he had that familiar broad smile across his face, as if he had just won first prize in some competition. But as he approached, his mood seemed to shift.

"I have been praying, Daniel. There is something you must know. But not here."

"Let's walk, then," he suggested.

Helen wanted the more intense atmosphere of her room. "No, we must be private. My room," she said, and walked away. Daniel paced after her. Even this close to The Emergence and their subsequent wedding, they should not have been going to her room alone in the middle of the day. Helen wanted Daniel to be in the mood to break rules.

As soon as they got to her room, she told him to sit, pointing at her bed. Another broken taboo.

She pulled the desk chair around and sat right in front of him. She looked both urgent and completely serene. Daniel knew he was going to hear something important.

"The Great Mother is with me. It is divine. I have received total clarity. Oh, the joy, Daniel. Such joy in my heart to share what I now know. I have known that you must be with me, Daniel. We all know how clear that truth is. But my darling, it is so much more."

Daniel was fixed on Helen. He wanted to know it all.

"You are the one! You have been chosen. The Great Lord himself is coming to you tonight. You know it is true. You have seen the signs. Daniel, why do you think I was brought back here? Why were the Elders guided to join you to me? Why have we been made to wait all these years for our truths to emerge? We will become one, Daniel, but not just as husband and wife. We are here to bring the truth. The full truth that is being revealed at last. Everything is part of that plan. Yes, you can see it now. Feel it. It is so obvious."

She paused. Daniel absorbed the truth that he was the chosen one for the Great Lord's work. It was obvious.

"But, oh, Daniel, tonight, when the Great Lord comes to you, you will be blessed with absolute grace. You will shine. All truth will be clear to you, through you, in you. We will rebuild the Community in the certainty of that truth. You will bring this Community to its proper place."

"I . . .I . . . I . . . er . . ." Daniel could not bring a full sentence together. Helen looked at him as he realised he was the full truth. The Great Lord had selected him.

That's right, soak it all up, you arrogant little bastard, she thought.

Suddenly, Helen leaned forward and took both of Daniel's hands in hers. "It can't be here. We can't be here. The Great Lord is very clear. We must leave this place as a new family, into the wilderness of the outside world. Only then, from the outside, can the Great Lord come to you."

"Why?" Daniel managed in a high-pitched voice. He sounded like a little boy.

"We must be in the wilderness of the outside world. The Great Lord must prepare you for a triumphant return. Whilst we are away, he has work to do here. They will be prepared for your arrival and will know they have been saved when you come back."

"I see," said Daniel.

"We have to go, as soon as possible."

"I see. How?"

"You must take the first steps of your new leadership, Daniel. This is your Community now. You must do whatever is needed to do the Great Lord's will. If we do not follow His instructions, they will try and stop us. They won't let us leave together. We must take steps. After lunch, go to the office and take the keys to one of the cars, or the vans; it doesn't matter. Once you have the keys, we must distract everyone, so they don't see us leave."

"What do you mean?"

"Don't worry, my darling. The Great Mother has made it very clear what must be done. You must cleanse the Community of its false ways. From the ashes of their ignorance, you can rebuild their faith. We cannot leave this place with its old ways undisturbed. We must burn away the old ways for the new shoots of truth to start growing whilst we are away."

Daniel looked confused.

"The chapel, my darling. It must burn. You must take it to ashes, and when you return, you will arise from the flames! The new church will be built in you! You must give them the gift of flames. The Great Lord demands it!"

"Yes. Yes. Of course. The chapel will burn. And I will rebuild it. Yes." He took a deep breath and looked deep into Helen's eyes. "I am ready to receive the Great Lord."

Helen was now confident that she had Daniel primed for action. The look in his eyes told her that he would do anything to fulfil his destiny. "Go now," she said, "I will signal to you when the time is right. Then you must take the keys and join me. Do not let them see you. If they do, you must make an excuse."

He stood up and she followed him. They were face to face now. She reached out and gently touched his arm. "If the Great Lord's will is done, we will be together this evening."

Daniel left the room full of purpose and bravado. Helen sat for a moment. The timing for the next part of the plan was both critical and fragile.

*

Helen would often steal a few moments with Ollie at the end of lunch, before he returned to lessons and she to her work.

That would be their chance. There would be the usual busy time while dishes were cleared and washed, and the dining room was tidied where their absence might not be missed for a few minutes. But it would only be a few minutes, so they needed to use them well.

Until then, there was very little to do but try and appear calm.

Helen had thought for a long time about whether she could arrange to take some items with her. Some clothes perhaps, or provisions from the kitchen. There were practical considerations, of course, but most of all she hated the idea of ripping Ollie from everything he had known for the last five years with no warning and nothing that was familiar to him.

She felt pain across her chest as she remembered Squashy Dog, the toy that the then three-year-old Ollie had cried for to comfort him when they had been taken. She'd had no words to explain to him that the toy was still on his pillow, where it had been left that morning when they headed out to the park. She wondered if it was still there.

How would her child ever trust her again when she was about to put him through the same experience for the second time in his eight short years?

For one reckless moment, she wondered whether it was possible to obtain some money from the envelopes of cash that were passed around on shopping trips, but that sort of thing would be noticed. Instead, they would leave with nothing and trust that they would be able to get far enough away from the Community to find help before they ran out of fuel.

Helen made her way to her morning chores. She was assigned to the kitchens today and spent the next couple of hours chopping onions for the evening meal. They made her eyes weep, but for once she was glad of this, as it hid the emotions she was struggling to contain. From the kitchen, she made her way directly to the dining hall. Jessica was already seated, and Helen made herself busy until the chair next to her was taken. She knew Jessica would have been trying to save the space for her, but she couldn't bring herself to lie to her only friend in this place. They would not say goodbye.

The meal passed slowly, and Helen felt as if she were a piece in a giant game of chess. The Elders and the other senior members were one set of pieces, and she, Daniel and Ollie were the other. She had to keep a careful eye on proceedings to plan a route and put her pieces together in the right place, while ensuring their opponents were focused elsewhere.

Helen became aware of a conversation going on around her, but she could not hear the words. It was as if she were underwater and listening to the chatter going on at the surface.

"Martha, dear? You look to be a hundred miles away? Are you feeling unwell?" one of the women asked her.

Helen stared at her, knowing she should respond but failing to find any acceptable form of words. Thankfully, the Elder leading her table answered for her. The men here could always be relied upon to do that if a woman was asked a question that appeared in any way taxing, and the Elders were the best at it of all.

"Of course she's alright, she's just excited for her Emergence on Thursday, and after that she will experience the day she has been waiting for her whole life, when she becomes a wife and – soon, I hope – a mother. What has she got to be down about, it's every girl's dream? That's right, isn't it, Martha?"

Become a wife? Helen thought. *You think my dream is to become a wife? And to a man like Daniel? He has done nothing to deserve my love. He is nothing to me. And I am already a mother.*

She wanted to scream, but instead she smiled and muttered something about feeling overwhelmed. Most of all, she made sure she kept track of all the pieces.

At some silent instruction from the head table, the leaders signalled that the dishes should be cleared, and the human cogs of the great machine that was the Community started to turn. Everyone had a job to do, and they completed them with a solemnity that seemed unnecessary.

Helen took her share of the plates towards the drop off point by the kitchen, ensuring she timed her arrival so that she passed Daniel, who was marshalling the rearrangement of the chairs.

"The time has come. The Great Mother would have you fulfil your promise," she whispered. Daniel nodded conspiratorially, like a poor actor in a second-rate spy thriller, and slipped off towards the offices.

Next, Helen moved towards Ollie, who was waiting in a corner with the rest of the boys. They were trying to look like they were helping, but really, they were doing little other than trying to avoid being told off. Ollie's eyes lit up when he saw her and then dimmed slightly. He was eight now, and too old to look pleased to see his mother in front of his friends.

She motioned for him to follow her. Ollie glanced around his friends and then complied.

"Mum, we learned about the animals this morning. The ones that live in the woods, and I knew which one was a wildcat, and Elder Nathan was very pleased with me." The words tumbled out and Helen felt another pang of guilt at taking him from what was probably the only home he remembered. But the pieces had moved too far now. There was no going back.

"That's brilliant, Ollie, I am so proud of you. Now, tell me, would you like to go on an adventure?"

CHAPTER 44

Saric, Rob and Mick sat in silence for a long time. Texas, who was used to being outside and on the move, was restless for a while but had eventually given up and was lying in the corner with one eye half open, just in case. Eventually, the silence was broken.

"She's on the move," Saric declared.

They all shifted position and then fell silent again. Whatever Julia had needed to do or say to leave the Lodge and head towards the main Community building had been done. They could see she was walking along the path. She paused for a few moments and then carried on.

It wasn't a long walk from the Lodge to the Community – five minutes according to Sense Check – but it seemed to last forever. In the cabin, no one spoke or moved.

Eventually, Julia made it to the main entrance to the Community.

"Turn it on," Rob said.

"Turn what on?" asked Mick.

"My phone has a microphone in it," Saric explained. "I can access it from here." Mick looked unsure. Saric added, "We can't overuse it, it will drain the battery."

"We can hear her?" said Mick.

"Yes, we can."

"Oh, right."

"If she stops moving, she's probably interacting with one of them. Then we'll listen. Just in case."

Rob looked at Mick. "She'll be fine. Don't worry."

Mick stood up. Texas rushed to his heel. "She better be alright. I told her I would look after her. I intend to keep that promise." Then, to no one in particular, he added, "she hasn't got anyone else."

"She's inside the building," Saric said. "Let's listen in."

He flicked on the phone's microphone, and they heard Julia's voice.

". . . understand you were not expecting me, but nevertheless, I must see Elder Nathan immediately. You know we do not bother you for nothing. But there are some things that Elder Nathan must know. Or

347

would you like me to take you into my confidence, too? Would you like to be responsible for dealing with our womanly requirements?"

Another voice mumbled just out of the microphone's range.

"My dear boy. Do you think I would be here demanding to see Elder Nathan if Nora could have dealt with it for me?"

Saric flicked the microphone off again. Both Rob and Mick looked at him with impatient confusion.

"We can't run down the battery, whatever she is doing is going to take a while. But I do think we need to get a bit closer."

Saric had already packed the items from Mick's store into the bags he had brought with him. He threw one across his shoulder while passing the other one to Mick, who did the same. A silent understanding passed between the two men; one born of a shared understanding of what it means to enter a battlefield. They each loved people who might get hurt in this, and they owed it to each other to protect them. Whatever that required.

As they navigated the steep path through the woods towards the boundary line, Rob wanted to run. In what direction, he wasn't sure. Part of him wanted to race as fast as he could right into the middle of the property, find Helen and Ollie wherever they were, and take them both using whatever force was necessary to overcome the bastards who had stolen them from him. But even as he made his way down the slope, the other half of him recognised that he needed to stick to the plan and accept help.

Saric's thoughts took him towards more practical matters. He kept one eye on the dot on the screen that was Julia. She was in the building now, moving between rooms.

She won't have long before someone stops her, he thought. They needed some luck now. They needed Helen to be in one of the first places Julia looked.

It was the middle of the day and Julia was in the dining room. That made sense, of course. Dining was a communal activity for the residents of the main building, which was good. It meant there was a high chance Helen would be there. It also meant there would be a lot of eyes on her, and on Julia when she arrived.

Suddenly, the dot started moving away from the dining room and back out towards the bedrooms. It was moving more purposefully now, no longer stopping to look in doorways, and with an obvious destination in mind.

Saric called to Rob and turned up the speaker so they could listen to any exchange that might take place.

He could hear that Julia was moving quickly; her footsteps were heavy and close together and the muffled quality of the sound told him that the phone was still in her pocket. There was a man's voice. She was talking to someone.

Then suddenly, "Martha". Her voice was urgent but quiet. She was trying to avoid attracting the attention of anyone but the intended audience. "Martha, wait."

Saric adjusted the settings on the microphone, improving the sound quality as far as he could. It would burn the battery faster, but this was important now.

The other voice said something about rooms. It was a voice that Saric had not heard before, but which he immediately recognised as a threat.

"Martha, please, wait. It's me, Julia."

The footsteps stopped. There was a pause, long enough for a person to stop, turn around and take in a familiar face that hadn't been seen for a long time.

CHAPTER 45

Daniel marched straight into the office and stood in front of the clerk on duty. "I need the keys to one of the vans."

"Sorry, what? I wasn't expecting anyone to be going out today. It's not on the schedule."

"You do not need to concern yourself with that," Daniel said with a smile. "I have told you I need a van, right now, and that is all you need to know."

"But it's not on the schedule," the clerk protested, confused.

Daniel leaned over the clerk, his big frame dominating the smaller man. "I am the schedule!" he said, his broad smile not breaking for a moment.

The office clerk was convinced. Daniel had a point. In his entire life, he had always done the right thing. He was the spirit of the Community. Everyone knew it. If Daniel could not be trusted, who could?

The clerk handed the keys over and told Daniel the licence plate so he could pick it out.

"Thank you," Daniel said. "I will remember this. You are a good man."

"Er, OK. Thanks."

Keys in hand, Daniel headed off to the parking area. He did not need to get to the car yet. He needed fuel.

The scale of the task had sat in his mind since the Great Mother had spoken to him. He was ready to rise and fulfil the truth that would be revealed to him from the ashes he would leave behind.

His future wife had given him the Great Mother's instructions, but Daniel knew the voice of truth was diluted by Martha's sweet, innocent nature. The Great Mother spoke of ashes, and poor Martha spoke only of creating a distraction, as if the point was getting out. Quite wrong. The point was coming back!

He entered the code to access the parking area. He was pretty sure he knew the code for every area in the Community, although obviously not for the safe. He walked to the garage and let himself in. Shelves and cupboards lined the room, with a range of basic car essentials neatly arranged. Screen wash, oil, filters, and so on. And, most importantly for Daniel, fuel. Lots of it. If the Great Lord ordered the Community to move on, they would not be reliant on the local town to fulfil that command.

Daniel picked up the nearest two petrol cans, shook them to check they were full and marched off back the way he had come.

The route back to the chapel from the garage took him up past the dining hall, through the old reception area, past the children's rooms and on towards the men's area. Architecturally, the chapel was a mirror of the dining room. When it was a hotel, it had been the ballroom. Now it was the centre of the Community, literally as well as spiritually.

Daniel should have looked odd as he strolled through the Community corridors carrying two full cans of petrol, but no one looked twice. He was so comfortable with what he was doing that his face and body language betrayed nothing of his intentions.

As he walked past the reception, he saw his old friend behind the desk looking puzzled. "What's up with you?" he asked.

"Oh, hello, Daniel. No, nothing really. Do you remember mad old Julia, the crazy witch woman?"

"Yes, of course. I haven't seen her for years. I sort of thought that she was maybe dead."

"Well, she just turned up. Demanding to see Elder Nathan. She looks old."

353

"Ha! Well, she is old, I suppose." And then to himself, "I will correct her soon enough."

"What?"

Daniel looked at him with some sympathy for his ignorance.

"Well," the receptionist continued, "she shot off the wrong way anyway."

"Which way?" Daniel asked, not really interested in the answer.

"Off towards the children's rooms. I think she got confused because Martha just headed off that way with Ollie."

"Oh," said Daniel, as he strolled off. "If I see her, I'll tell her."

As he turned the corner into the corridor of the children's rooms, he saw an old woman listening at one of the doors.

Could that really be Julia? he thought. She looked so old. He knew the stories about her, of course, but had only a few memories of seeing her when he was a child. When it all happened, he had thought it odd that she had betrayed the Great Lord; she had been so kind before that, and funny. But as he got older, he had learned the full truth. She was, quite simply, mad.

"What are you doing?" he asked as he strolled towards her.

She clearly did not recognise him. "Young man—" she looked him up and down, noticed he was carrying two fuel cannisters, made some sort of mental calculation and carried on, "—I'm looking for Martha and Ollie. I've forgotten which room they are in. Do you know?"

"Yes, of course I know," he replied. "This is my community. I know everything."

"Oh," Julia replied, a little taken aback by the odd answer. "Please can you tell me which one is their room?"

"*They* do not have a room, mad woman. She has a room, and he has a room. You should remember that."

Julia knew better than to rise to such an obvious opening into conflict. "Please can you help me?" she asked.

Before Daniel could respond, Ollie and Martha appeared at the far end of the corridor. They did not look up and hurried off in the opposite direction.

With surprising agility, Julia sprang off after them.

Daniel watched as she ran after his future wife and son.

As Julia got closer, she called after them. "Martha. Martha, wait. Martha, please, wait. It's me, Julia."

CHAPTER 46

Helen span round when she heard her name. At the other end of the corridor were two figures.

The first was familiar to her. Daniel was holding two large cans of petrol. She hoped he had the keys but was pleased in a small way that he had also thought about fuel.

It took a moment for her to place the second person. She hesitated, not quite believing her eyes. Was the woman at the other end of the corridor really Julia?

It was as if she had just run straight into a wall. When Helen had been brought back to the Community, her father had told her that Julia had died shortly after helping her to leave. He said it was from the grief over losing her daughter.

But the woman in front of her was definitely Julia. She looked older, and she had aged more than the twenty years between their last meeting, but now, in this corridor, it was as if no time had passed at all.

"Julia!" Helen's voice did not sound like her own, and for the briefest moment, she felt like a fifteen-year-old girl again, about to leave home for the first time to travel halfway across the world to live with a woman she had never met. But she also knew there was danger here. Daniel would have been warned about her; she wondered if he knew who she was.

"Ollie, can you go and wait in your room for a few minutes, please?"

Her son sighed but did as he was told.

"My darling, Martha!" Julia covered the length of the corridor in just a few steps and embraced Helen, holding her so close that Helen could feel her heart beating. There were tears in her eyes, of happiness to see Julia again and of sadness and pain for all the years they had spent apart. The hug seemed to go on forever, and for a long time, neither woman said a word.

"What are you doing, old lady?" Helen had forgotten that Daniel was there, still clutching those ridiculous fuel cans. "You are not allowed to be here. Please leave."

Julia smiled at Daniel; one arm still wrapped around Helen. "Now, young man, what kind of way is that to speak to your elders? I have matters to discuss with Martha, and I would value some privacy. Please leave us alone."

Daniel seemed unsure over how to deal with such a direct response. Julia merely stared at him. Neither of them moved.

Eventually, Daniel found the words. "Whatever you have to discuss with my future wife you can say in front of me. We have no secrets."

Julia's eyes did not flicker.

It's as if she knows, Helen thought.

"Yes, dear, that's lovely. Martha and I are old friends and I just wanted to share some words of wisdom with her before the wedding. To make sure everything is a success."

Daniel just stared.

"Now, my dear, do you really want to hear the details of what we women discuss before a wedding?"

He was uncomfortable now.

Helen smiled sweetly, making sure her eyes fully met Daniel's. "Please, my love, give us a few moments, I am sure that it will be worth it."

"OK, but no more. You have interrupted our preparations." Daniel retreated a few steps but stayed within listening distance. Helen wondered what it was that he expected to overhear.

"Now, let me look at you." Julia took hold of Helen's upper arms and turned her so that she was facing her directly. In doing so, she moved ever so slightly to the right, so that her back was to Daniel.

"Oh, you look so beautiful," she said loudly, pulling Helen into another hug. While her face was close to Helen's left ear, she whispered, "Rob is outside; he's waiting for you. He said to give you this. Call him when you are ready."

Helen felt something heavy drop into the pocket of her dress. She had so many things she wanted to say to Julia but no time. And Daniel was watching them closely.

"Yes, I truly cannot wait," she said, and then more quietly, "he came for me?"

"He did, he is a good man, and he has good friends." Julia smiled at Daniel again. He smiled back, his stupid round face grinning broadly.

Helen pulled Julia towards her again. "I need some time; I can't get away."

"Leave that to me, child."

"That's enough now," Daniel interrupted. "Get back to the Lodge or I will call for back up."

"Yes, dear," Julia said quietly, "although I am not quite sure what back up you would need to deal with an old lady like me."

And with that she made her way back up the corridor.

"Julia, wait . . ." Helen didn't want to see her leave again, but she couldn't find the right words to thank the woman who had not only saved her as a teenager but was doing so again. "Would you join us on the journey?" She hoped this was cryptic enough for Daniel, who was now staring at her intently.

"No, my sweet Martha; my place is here, with Helen."

As Julia left, Helen turned back to Daniel. His face was dark. "What did she say to you?"

"Oh, nothing, my love, just the ramblings of a crazy woman."

"I don't believe you. What did she give you?"

Helen weighed up the options in an instant. He knew. There was no doubt about that, and he was angry. But she would not give up her chance of seeing Rob again.

"Oh, nothing, just a trinket for the wedding. I knew her when I was younger, you see."

"Show me."

"That would be bad luck, and we need every blessing with us now."

"Show me now. I command you."

Something Helen had not seen before flashed across Daniel's face. *Rage.* The righteous anger of someone who believes he has a right to be obeyed. Her hand reached instinctively to cover her pocket. He grabbed her wrist and twisted her arm painfully away from her side. With his free hand he then reached into the pocket and took out a phone.

"What is this?" He was shouting now, his face so close to hers that she could feel the warmth of his breath on her cheek.

"I don't know. She gave it to me. It's mine now. Please give it back."

She reached out with her free hand to take it from him, but he pushed her away and she fell heavily into the wall.

"Daniel, please, it's mine."

"You know this is forbidden. This is the temptation. We knew we would face it and that you would be weak. You must be strong now, Martha, and I must lead you to be strong. The Great Lord will come to me tonight and I expect to be with the Great Mother when he appears. Now, you must wait in the car; I will be back in a few minutes. The Great Mother's instructions are very clear to me now. I expect you to be ready when I reach the car, this is very important."

"Yes, Daniel." It hurt to know that Rob was so close. Without the phone it meant nothing. She realised she must get the car and follow her own plan. "Can I have the keys?"

A cruel laugh emitted from Daniel's mouth. "The keys? Of course not. Wait by the car and I will be there when I am ready."

And with no further words he set off down the corridor holding the two cans of fuel and the phone.

CHAPTER 47

Rob had listened to the exchange taking place in the heart of the Community with growing rage.

"Who the hell is that? Who the hell does he think he is talking to?" Daniel had spoken to his wife like she was a naughty child. "Command! He commands her, does he? We'll see about that!"

The eruptions kept coming with every sentence he heard. Saric listened hard, calculating all the time. There were risks with going in. Big risks. Sense Check had provided him with a full schematic of the site, including the layout of the building. He had memorised it. But even that had built-in risks. The data they had access to was three decades old, from when the hotel's connection to the town's electricity grid had been upgraded. The layout could have been altered; it probably had been. But two very promising facts had been set out in the exchange they had just heard. Firstly, Helen was currently with Ollie. Secondly, Helen was heading for the parking area. Saric had considered the door to the building from the parking area one of his possible entrance points. He could not have asked for more.

There was simply no way of being sure of where the occupants would be, or how quickly they could mobilise a response if they knew they had an intruder. He could cover the ground between the main building and the Lodge in less than three minutes, but he estimated an eight-year-old might take twice that time. He had executed far more dangerous missions than this, but failure never seemed to carry much by way of consequence in those days. His life, perhaps, but Saric had never been intimidated by death.

"I don't like this, Saric. This bastard has got the phone. Something's going on."

"He told her to go to a car," Saric noted. "If she is about to leave the compound, it would be cleaner to extract her then."

"What about Ollie? What if they do come out and he's not with them?"

Saric tapped the screen of his tablet. The transcript of the exchange they had just heard was inconclusive as to whether Helen had been ordered to the car on her own or not.

"We're wasting time. This arsehole has got your phone. This is all going to get out soon. We have to go in, now!"

Mick, who until now had been silent, suddenly spoke up. "The boy's got a point."

Saric thought for a moment, as Rob and Mick stared at him. As he reached a conclusion, Mick recognised the look and knew the answer before it came. Rob felt a wave of fear, but not for himself. He wasn't sure if he recognised the man in front of him at all, but he hadn't felt closer to seeing his wife and son since the day they were taken.

"Fine. He clicked the screen of his tablet a few times. If this goes the wrong way, follow the instructions I have just sent you exactly. Turn the phone on and let me know if anything develops. Go to radio comms."

"I'll be up there," Mick added. "I can't take anyone out for you. But I'll make a noise if that helps."

"Thanks, Mick."

"Rob, you have three minutes to execute."

With that, Saric grabbed the fence where it was already torn and pulled it back with such force that one of the posts came out of the floor. He squeezed his massive frame through the gap, raced across the gardens of the Lodge and disappeared.

As soon as Saric was out of sight, Rob exchanged a look with Mick, and they too shot off. They had discussed and agreed the distraction that might help buy Saric some time or cover. Mick led the way through the rocky terrain, with Texas at his side. Rob followed.

The schematic that Sense Check had uncovered for the hotel showed where it had been connected to the town's electricity network. The cable had been buried in some places, but most of it had been housed in a protective casing. Mick took Rob straight to a stretch of cable that he knew was easily accessible. There were access panels at various points along the casing.

Rob smashed the panel open with the back of an axe. He reached into the access panel and confirmed the cable was there. If he'd had more time, Saric would have considered a more sophisticated way of cutting the cable. As it was, the solution was unsubtle. Mick passed Rob a shotgun and stood well back. Rob wrapped a leather belt around his hand, positioned the gun against the cable and twisted himself out of the way, expecting the shot to rebound out of the box. When he pulled the trigger, the sound of the gun echoed up and down the cable housing. Rob's hand was untouched. The faint hum of activity coming from the Lodge stopped and was replaced by confused voices.

"Done," said Rob.

367

"Good work, boy," replied Mick and headed off into the rocks, with Rob following in his footsteps. Texas, who hadn't flinched at all at the sound of the gun, bounded off after her master.

As they ran, Rob had his radio earpiece in one ear waiting for Saric to make contact. In the other ear, he had the feed from Saric's phone.

"Approaching main building," came Saric's voice in Rob's ear.

"OK," said Rob in reply. He knew not to waste words.

Until now, Saric's phone had picked up nothing but rustling and the occasional grunt. It was like listening to a voicemail from someone who has pocket-dialled you. Then came the voice.

"Great Lord, I am ready to hear you. I am ready!"

The man that had stolen Saric's phone from Helen was speaking. His voice sounded frantic. Volatile.

"I am yours, and I will be your vessel. The truth will be revealed. This travesty will burn to the ground, and I shall rebuild it."

Following this introductory statement, his voice dropped to a conspiratorial tone. "Oh, Lord, it is in you that I know this must be done . . . I will be your servant and they will be servants to your voice. In the flames this will be healed . . . when you come to me, oh Great Lord, bless me with the final truth and reveal to me how I shall raise your voice from the ashes." The voice paused. There was more rustling.

"As I give this place to the fire of the Great Lord, bless me. And bless my new wife, Helen. And my new son, Oliver. Let them learn to take their rightful place at my side. Let our union come together today and bless her with the strength to give me all of herself. Even her son will be mine. Bless us all, Great Lord!"

Rob stumbled as he heard the voice. As something took hold of him, he was briefly aware of the sound of the gush of flames bursting into life. A satisfied grunt came from the voice.

Over the years since he had lost his wife and son, Rob had become accustomed to being overwhelmed by emotion. Until now, he had always stepped into the feeling and allowed himself to disintegrate. He had learned not to fight it. The same feeling of being overwhelmed grew in him now. There was too much emotion to be able to feel anything at all. For the first time, though, since Helen and Ollie had been taken from him, his body did not react in defeat. Not this time. From somewhere deep inside, a pure form of power engulfed him. His wife and son needed him. *Right now*. No sense of defeat could have possibly prepared him for the feeling of absolute power that now flowed through every cell of his body. Every sense was heightened but also fell away. His body seemed to disappear around him, until he was just a floating energy.

He became aware of where he was and where he needed to be. He covered the ground between him and Mick in three steps. Texas looked at him as if noticing him for the first time.

Just as Rob was about to accelerate away from the older man, the voice returned.

"Oh, my goodness, what have you done? You're crazy! What are you doing?"

Rob recognised Julia's voice.

"Mick, it's Julia," he said. His voice sounded distant. He pulled out the tablet, flicked on the audio and gave it to Mick. "Help her if you can," he said, before sprinting off at a pace Mick had no chance of keeping up with.

As he raced off, Rob heard Julia's voice. "No, stay away from me. What are you doing? No! Ahhh!"

A loud thud concluded the exchange. Rob thought he heard Mick accelerate behind him, but he couldn't be sure. He found his way to the gap in the fence Saric had used. He dipped through it without missing a step.

I'm coming Ollie. I'm coming Helen.

As he came around the Lodge, he absorbed everything before him in an instant. The foreign landscape, which until now had set him slightly off balance, seemed entirely his. There were people moving towards where he had broken the electrical cable. They were focused and not a threat. The women of the Lodge were confused, and harmlessly wandering around. Some men had come out of the main building and were heading to an outbuilding. They might see him, but he didn't care. Three unarmed men. It might as well have been three small children. If they saw him, he would destroy them in seconds. The one thing that seemed completely out of place was the small jet of smoke pouring out of the roof. Just as Rob processed how strange this seemed, another man appeared at the main entrance. Some sort of exchange took place with the outbuilding group, and they broke into a sprint towards their destination.

Rob stopped for a moment and took a deep breath to absorb everything. He touched his earpiece.

"Saric, the main building is on fire. I heard him start it. Julia's in the building. I'm coming."

371

Saric did not answer.

CHAPTER 48

Saric walked quickly and purposefully towards the main building. He did not run; that would waste energy and attract attention, but he kept his stride long and even. He considered the direct route across the lawns but decided it would be better to follow the tree line as far as possible. While it would add at least two minutes to the time it took to reach his destination, it was probably simpler to avoid Community members if he could.

When he reached a point directly opposite the front entrance to the house, he stopped for a moment and observed the scene. To reach the car park, he needed to cross the principal driveway, which led to the entrance to the main building. That would leave him exposed for perhaps twenty seconds. He watched and waited as three women slowly left the building and turned right along the path towards one of the outer cabins.

Once the women were safely on the other side of the building, their backs to him, he slipped quietly out of the tree line, across the dirt path and into the trees opposite. From there he travelled north until he was directly facing the car park.

In front of him were the same two battered trucks he and Rob had seen on their first visit. Sense Check's map had shown no other road entrances or parking areas. If Helen was heading for a car, she would be coming here.

There were two ways that Helen might reach the car park from the corridor where she had been. The first was a side door that led directly from the building that Saric was now facing. In all probability, this was the way she would come.

Less likely, but not impossible, was that she would leave through the main door that Saric had just seen the three women use. From where he now stood, he had a line of sight to this door, and he was pleased with his location; it triangulated the two exits well. But really, he was covering the main door only because Sense Check had suggested he did so, with both routes from the corridor being approximately the same distance. Helen would use the side door; she did not want to be seen.

Saric had spent much of his adult life sitting or standing in uncomfortable locations waiting an indeterminate amount of time for an event or an action that would require him to act. He had learned to be patient – to keep his mind alert while also keeping it relaxed. He did that now. He didn't know how long it would take for Rob to execute the plan.

A short while later, a strange silence passed over the property, as the air conditioning that had been humming unnoticed in the background stopped.

Well done, Rob, Saric thought to himself. Now he just needed the Community members to follow the expected steps. He ran through the timings in his mind.

It would take a few seconds for people to notice the power had failed and to look around them sighing or groaning, then another few seconds for them to wait for the power to come back on. When it failed to do so, right at the time Saric expected, people began to emerge from the buildings, glancing between them and checking whether all parts of the property were affected.

Once they had established that there was no power anywhere, a couple of men wandered along the line of the exposed cable, exchanging a few words as they walked. Another group made their way towards the generator room.

Power cuts in an area this remote would be quite a common occurrence, so they didn't look too concerned, but equally these people had very little excitement in their lives. It was the latter fact that would make the plan work. People liked excitement, and in a place like this a power cut might be the most interesting thing to happen all week.

As the men reached the smashed panel, a look passed between them and they called over a few other men, while pointing at the box in front of them. Soon they were joined by more men and, finally, the women and children. Within a minute or two, a group of Community members were standing in front of the damaged power cable, pointing in various directions and discussing what might have happened.

There was activity in the main house, too.

The front door opened slowly, a pair of eyes glanced hesitantly through the gap and, when no one was visible outside, the door opened fully and a woman and child stepped out and made their way across the gravel towards the vehicles.

He had never met her before, but Saric would have recognised her anywhere. She was five years older than she was in the photo that he had stared at every day since she had disappeared, but it was her. Despite her obvious anxiety, her green eyes shone as she tucked her untidy light brown hair behind her ear. Her other hand held onto a young boy who could be no one other than Rob's son. Saric knew that familial resemblance in offspring was often overstated by the assessment of friends and family members, but this wasn't the case here. A younger version of Rob's face looked out over the car park.

Helen pulled Ollie between the two vans and looked around anxiously. Saric didn't know how long he had before the man who'd taken her phone arrived, so he wasted no time. He covered the wide space between the tree line and the vans in a dozen long strides.

Helen spun around and pulled Ollie closer to her. She looked like a trapped animal, ready to fight for its life.

He spoke before she could. "Helen, my name is Saric, I am here with Rob. I need you to come with me."

She looked back at him; he could not read her expression. "How do I know that's true?"

"The phone that Julia gave to you earlier belongs to me. We met her yesterday and know how she helped you to escape before. Rob is waiting outside the perimeter for you."

"I'm not going with you; anyone could know that. How do I know you aren't part of their plan to keep me here? I am getting out of here on my own."

"Helen, I am a detective. Rob employed me to find you and we have spent the last five years looking for you. I have been in your house, and

I've seen the photo of the three of you at the zoo on your mantelpiece by Rob's armchair, and the toy dinosaurs on Ollie's windowsill."

She paused, looking at him deeply.

He met her gaze. "Helen, we have very little time. I need you to come with me, please."

She took a deep breath and pulled Ollie even closer to her. The boy was clearly terrified, but he did not hide. Instead, he was standing up straight and holding his mother's hand protectively. *Rob would be proud.*

"OK, we'll come," said Helen bravely, and then, as if now determined to see this new plan through, she added, "Daniel is at the chapel over there. If he finds us, he'll . . ."

"Let me worry about that," Saric interrupted. "Just follow me."

Saric glanced at Ollie, wondering whether he would be open to being carried. It would be faster but only if he did not struggle. Before he reached a conclusion, two things happened simultaneously; a pair of figures stepped out of the side door and a woman's scream arose from outside the chapel.

•

Helen instinctively pulled Ollie closer to the van, but it was too late. Her parents had seen her.

"Martha! What do you think you are doing out here? Oliver should be with me in the activity room. You know it is our time with him after lunch. Why have you brought him out here?"

Helen didn't know what to say. Causing a fuss now would be counterproductive, but she needed to get away. "Sorry, I lost track of the time. We were just talking about how well Ollie has been doing in his lessons."

"He is a very bright boy," her mother agreed, "but this isn't the time. You will see him this evening when Daniel is with you. You'd like to see Daniel, wouldn't you, Oliver?"

Ollie grunted and scuffed the floor with the back of his shoe.

"I'm very sorry, but Ollie and I are busy," Helen tried again, taking Ollie's hand firmly and moving to walk past her parents and back towards the building.

Her father stepped out in front of her. He was a tall man with a large frame, and he towered over Helen as he blocked her path.

"Martha, that's enough. Give Ollie to your mother. You are supposed to be working; you will be able to visit him later, as agreed."

Something in Helen snapped. Ollie was her son, not theirs. They had lost any right they may have had to be his grandparents many years before he was born. They were cruel and dishonest people who covered their behaviour with a veil of respectability through their status as elders in a community that knew no better than to accept them.

For years, she had tolerated this to keep Ollie safe, but no more. One way or another, she was leaving today.

"That's it, I'm not playing your games anymore. We're leaving." There was anger in her voice now, but she managed to keep it low, conscious that Ollie wouldn't understand what was happening or why she was arguing with his grandparents like this.

"You can't do that. I forbid it!"

"Do you know what? Once upon a time that might have scared me, but not anymore. You can't forbid me from doing anything. You are a weak man who hides behind an illusion to maintain the most tenuous grip on a shred of power in a small corner of an unimportant place. You think you are important? You are nothing."

She pushed past her father, her right shoulder hitting the right side of his torso. He was large but weak and being caught off guard caused him to stumble backwards. He was also quick. He reached his long arm behind him, and Helen felt a huge hand grip around her upper arm. It hurt.

Unable to free herself, she put herself between her father and Ollie as much as she could.

He was shouting now, his grip on her arm tightening, his fingertips biting into her flesh. "You think I am nothing? But you cannot leave unless I let you. How do you propose to get away now?"

From the corner of her eye, Helen saw a figure step out from behind the closest van.

"I suggest you might like to discuss that matter with me," Saric said calmly, as he stepped closer to Helen's father.

"What . . . who . . . who are you?"

"It is my belief that Helen and Ollie want to go home," said Saric, ignoring the question. He looked at Helen. She nodded.

"This is their home!" her father blasted. "This has always been their home. This *will* always be their home." He paused, suddenly unsure why he was arguing this point with a total stranger.

Saric broke the momentary silence. "You are no longer of any consequence." As he spoke, his earpiece sprang to life again. There were three pieces of information: the main building was on fire; someone was coming for Helen and Ollie, and Julia was in the building.

"Young lady, you are coming with me," Helen's father announced. Before he could pull her away, Saric slid in between them. He felt Helen's energy rise behind him. She was going to go for this man. *This could get messy*, he thought. *And time consuming.*

Helen's father took hold of Saric by the arms and twisted his body, as if to throw him out of his way. A look of shock filled the old man's eyes, as his effort had no effect whatsoever. Saric stood completely unmoved.

We don't have time for this, he thought. He pushed the old man backwards, hoping the impossible odds would become clear.

Helen's father stumbled back a few paces before regaining his balance. There was a wild look in his eyes. "You will not keep me from my daughter. I command you to get out of my way. This is my community. You must obey me." He looked around the parking area for something to take the stranger on with. He grabbed a wrench from a workbench.

Too much time here, thought Saric. *I must end this right now.*

Saric glanced at Helen. She returned his look with an expression that he took to mean he had her permission. The old man lurched towards him, the wrench held high in the air. Saric stepped inside the attack and powered his huge fist straight through the man's face. His neck snapped backwards as he fell to the floor.

For the briefest moment, the world seemed to fall silent, before the man's agonising cry echoed around the parking area. His nose was clearly broken. Teeth were missing. Ollie looked away, terrified. The old man's legs shook, and he kicked them as he held his hands to his face.

"No!" screamed Helen's mother. "What have you done? The Great Lord strike him down!"

Saric was unsure whether that was an instruction; in any case, he was not struck down. The old woman slumped to the floor next to her husband, who spat blood and let out a stream of noises that did not quite amount to any words. Clutching at her crucifix, she started praying under her breath.

"Time to go," said Saric to Helen.

Before Helen could move, her mother turned towards her son. "Ollie, you cannot leave me, I am your grandmother!"

Ollie pulled his shoulders back, wiped the tears of fear from his eyes and stepped between his mother and the misshapen ball of anger and despair on its knees in the dirt. "So what?" he spat, before stepping back firmly into his mother's grasp.

"Love beats biology," Saric commented. Then to Helen, he added, "this way."

The three of them sprinted back the way Saric had come.

CHAPTER 49

As they ran, Saric weighed up their options. The new information he had received from Rob changed things. It shouldn't, but it had.

It shouldn't change things because they had a plan and nothing that he had heard should affect the execution of it. But it would change things, because people don't follow plans when the people they love are in danger.

Helen was faster than he had expected but Ollie was struggling to match their pace. Saric tried to encourage him along, but he was holding them up. To his right, he could see smoke streaming from the windows of the western side of the building. The fire was large. *Too large*, he thought.

People were streaming towards the blaze. A few of them were trying to fight it using hoses that had been brought up from the grounds, but they were no match for the flames. More people were gathered around whispering excitedly.

People are strange, Saric thought.

He paused to give Ollie time to catch up. "Rob, I've got them," he said into his microphone. "Meet me by the fence."

As he said it, Mick came round the corner of the outbuilding they had been heading towards and ran straight into them. He looked terrified. Despite the fact he was breathing heavily, his face was deathly pale. He struggled to catch his breath and bent double, placing his hands on the fronts of his thighs. Texas bounced around beside him. "It's Julia . . . I can't find her . . . I think she's in there with him. Please, Saric, help me." He was pleading now. Texas barked.

Saric looked at Mick and then at Helen; if it came to a choice, he knew his priority. But he owed Mick, and he hated owing people. "Where's Rob?" he asked the older man.

"Isn't he with you? He was way ahead of me."

"No, we haven't seen him." Saric felt his stomach fall; he was losing control of the situation.

Mick started to speak but Saric silenced him with an outstretched palm. "Rob . . . Rob . . . where are you? Rob, I have them. I need you here to get them out."

A few moments later, a voice came through the earpiece. "Saric, the fire. There are kids in there. I can see them at the windows."

"Where are you?" he said. Mick and Helen looked at him questioningly, unable to hear the other side of the conversation.

"The guy who took your phone. He was after Helen. He hurt Julia. I followed the phone into the building. The fire started in the chapel. It's bad, Saric. They are trapped upstairs. I'm pretty sure I saw Julia up there, too."

Saric was surprised when it was Helen who interrupted the silence. "Whatever it is, we need to help."

"I came here for you, not them," Saric said, honestly.

"You don't understand. I made him start the fire. It was supposed to be a small distraction. I . . . he . . . it wasn't supposed to go like this. I pushed him too far."

She was so certain, and Saric knew that arguing with her would be futile and would only waste time. He also saw precisely why Rob had spent the last five years of his life looking for this woman.

"OK, but you and Ollie can't be anywhere near there. Wait behind here and we'll be as quick as we can." He gestured for Helen and Ollie to tuck in behind the outbuilding. It wasn't a perfect cover, but it sat far enough back into the tree line that it was unlikely anyone would notice them there. In any case, all eyes were on the fire.

Helen started to argue but the look in Saric's eyes made her think twice. She nodded silently and took Ollie by the hand. He was still staring at Saric but followed her quietly.

Mick and Saric stood for a moment to assess the situation. They could see shapes moving at the windows. The fire was moving from the west side, but it had also swept across the whole back of the building. Saric processed the map of the hotel he had memorised. If his data was up to date, there should have been a way out from the second floor. Something must have trapped them.

A group of Community men had gone in through the front door, but they were only inside for a few seconds before coming back out again, while frantically pointing and shouting.

"They need to come out of the window," Mick concluded out loud. The second-floor window was several metres up. It would be a dangerous distance to jump.

"Why don't they bring a ladder round?" Saric asked.

"That's the storeroom," Mick said, pointing to it. A group of men were at the door trying to kick it in. "I'm going to help them get in there," he added, before running off.

Saric had no intention of joining the Community people, even if they were fighting a fire. He had seen the anger and fear in the old couple's faces. Despite all that was going on, his help would not be welcome here. In any case, he needed Rob secure before taking any other steps.

He tapped his earpiece. "Rob, get the hell out of there. Helen and Ollie are here with me. We need to join up, now."

Rob's voice was hushed as he came back into Saric's ear. "I'm stuck for a moment. People all over the place."

"When you can move, go to the parking area exit. Then come to the outbuilding southwest from there. If you get into trouble, call me. Otherwise, I'll stay out of the way."

"OK. Got to go."

Saric's mind was whirring. Keep Helen and the boy safe. Cover Rob's exit. Do something to get people out of the building. This was exactly why he had wanted to do this alone.

In the moments that Saric was processing his next step, the loud mechanical clunk of heavy machinery coming to life sounded from the outbuilding. A splutter of black smoke came from the chimney before the engine that had just started up found its rhythm and started whirring.

The door swung open, and three men filed out.

Another problem, thought Saric. He didn't know how long Rob would be and he didn't want his location to be known. These men could go nowhere for now. They looked at him, astonished. Saric surveyed them with cold, dark eyes.

They could see the rifle slung across his shoulder. "Who are you?" one of them asked.

"Get back in that room until I give you permission to leave."

"Screw you." The youngest of the men, who was somewhere in his mid-twenties, hadn't taken his eyes off the rifle. He lunged for it. The other two lurched instinctively into action.

Saric grabbed the younger man and swung him under his arm, as if he were a toy. With his right hand, he pulled out one of Mick's borrowed hunting knives and rested the cold steel on the man's neck. He froze in terror, pleading only with his eyes for the other two to beg for mercy on his behalf.

Saric became aware that Helen had emerged from her hiding place and was watching. She had a look of disbelief on her face.

"Please, please," started one of the other men. "We need to help with the fire. There are people trapped. Come on, man. You can't do this. We need to help."

Saric's expression did not change. He felt a tear from the trapped man's eyes trickle onto his hand.

"Stop it," shouted Helen. "If you're here for me, you mustn't. Rob would never send you on these terms. Please. Let them help."

Saric let the man in his arms go. He stumbled to the floor before his friends lifted him back up again. They looked at Saric with an expression he could not place and sprinted off towards the main building.

CHAPTER 50

The generator they had started up had brought electricity back to the Community and sparked a wave of activity. The door Mick had gone off to help break through was suddenly opened, and ladders brought to the windows.

"Rob, Rob, are you there?"

Saric got no reply.

Can't stay here now, he thought.

"I need to talk to Rob," said Helen.

"There's no time. We've just told them where we are."

"Ollie and I are going nowhere with you until I have spoken to Rob."

"We have radio connection, but he's unable to come in right now."

"Now, you listen to me. I need to get out of here right away. But I'm not going with you. You are insane. I already have a plan. If Rob's not here, I'll take my chances without you."

No more time, thought Saric.

But it was too late. He heard a gunshot ring out. The bullet smashed into the front of the outbuilding. Saric and Helen ran behind the building, where Ollie was still crouching in the spot where his mum had left him.

"Here," said Saric, and he took his earpiece out and passed it to Helen. "Press here to speak. Rob's on the other end. Keep checking for him. Tell him we've gone to the Lodge if he comes in. And tell me."

Saric knew there was too much open space to make a move under fire. He took the rifle from his shoulder; it was a good piece of kit. He had used the Eastern European equivalent as a child with his father. It wasn't quick to reload, but as long as Mick had kept it properly targeted, it was still a useful weapon.

He crouched and peered around the side of the building. His attacker must have been positioned dead in front of them. It wasn't until he had moved more than halfway along the building that he caught sight of the man. Helen's father was standing next to him, holding what looked like a towel to his face, while the flames pouring from the centre of the Community building rose above him. He had his back to the men and women struggling to free their loved ones from the second floor. Saric was pretty sure the gun was in the hands of one of the men he had allowed to run back to help with the fire.

It was an easy enough target, but as Saric brought the gun to his shoulder, another shot rang out from a second gunman. The angle was different, and the marksman more skilled. The shot hit the wall only a few feet from Saric. He sprinted to the back of the building to regroup.

Two gunmen posed a problem. It was a question of angles, reaction times and how good he thought his two attackers were with their weapons. The first shot had been way off target, and he was fairly sure that given a second chance, the gunman would miss again. Even so, he couldn't be relied upon to miss. In fact, in Saric's opinion, the chances were that his next shot would hit its target. This wasn't certain, but there was a better than fifty per cent chance. And he certainly couldn't let the second man have another shot.

Saric reasoned that he could shoot gunman number two easily enough; he wouldn't miss – in fact, he could still make the shot at three times the distance.

Practice until you can't fail had been his father's mantra, and he had practised a lot, both at home and in combat.

But to shoot gunman number two, he would have to expose himself to gunman number one, which is where the angles came in. Could Saric fire at the second man, rebalance himself, move his gun to aim at the first one and shoot before he could land a shot on him in return? It was simple trigonometry really, with a bit of physics thrown in, but there were too many variables to be sure of an outcome.

In his favour was the gunman's poor technique; it might take him many attempts to hit Saric, but probability doesn't always work out how it should. Even if there was a ten per cent chance of hitting his target with an individual shot, he could still hit Saric with his first shot in ten.

He took a deep breath, wishing Rob was here, or even Mick. But he was alone, and he needed to protect Helen. He looked back at her. "If this goes wrong, you need to get to the Lodge. This will buy you enough time, but make sure you get there. You have the radio, so hide there and wait until Rob finds you."

Helen looked at him suspiciously. Saric realised there was a lot going on behind her eyes, more than he had expected from the photos he had stared at for hours on end.

She nodded and he nodded back. He prepared his gun and stepped out to take his chances.

He crept slowly round the side of the building, keeping himself as close as possible to the wall and making the target he created for anyone who might notice him and take a shot at him as small as possible. He reassessed the location of the men. They hadn't moved. The angle hadn't changed. He stepped back a pace. Now out of sight, he closed his eyes and rehearsed the movement, preparing his body to act. Then he breathed deeply and stepped out into the open, his gun raised towards gunman number two.

But they didn't notice him. Instead, they were staring at a young woman who was pulling at gunman number one's arm and pleading with him to follow her. "We need your help! The children are trapped! What are you doing here? You should all be over there!"

Helen's father mumbled something. He sounded angry but his speech was slurred. He waved the young woman away, but she was insistent, pointing towards the main building with tears in her eyes.

Saric reassessed the situation. Collateral damage would be a problem. He could not take the shot.

•

Helen tried several times to contact Rob using the strange man's earpiece. She pressed the button and called his name but there was no response at all. Was it possible that this was all staged somehow? Had her parents found out about the plan and set her up? It was the sort of test they might sanction to prove a point about faith, or loyalty, or some other vague construct.

But the damage to her father's face had been real, and the strange man had known things about her real life that he could only have found out from Rob. She had made the decision to trust him in the car park, and she intended to do so, but not at the expense of common sense. Right now, his plan to help her escape worked in her favour. She would follow him while keeping the situation under review. Her trust in him could not be blind.

What he had said about things going wrong bothered her. There were two men shooting at him. He seemed competent, more than competent in fact, and she hadn't met anyone in the Community who was any good with a firearm, but still, it didn't seem like a fair fight.

She needed to level the odds.

Ollie was trembling in her arms. She hadn't intended for things to go this way. Their escape was supposed to be calm, and she was supposed to be in control. This was chaos, and the best way to help Ollie was to get him out as quickly as possible.

She pulled him closer towards her and buried her face in his hair; then she held him in front of her. "Ollie, I need you to stay here for just a minute. I'll be back soon, but while I am away, I need you to stay very still and very quiet. Do you understand?"

He nodded but said nothing. He looked so small.

She looked around for something of use and found a large piece of brick that had fallen from the corner of the building. It was a little too large for her hand, but she managed to keep hold of it, and it was heavy enough that it might work. She crept around the other side of the building, the way Saric had gone. It was important not to be seen. She inched her way between the trees, keeping her eyes fixed on the scene in front of her. As she moved, the earpiece clicked slightly, and she heard a voice.

"Helen, Helen, are you there?" For a moment, her heart stopped, and the world fell silent. In the entire universe, there was only her and that voice. Silently, she reaffirmed her love for him. She wished she could speak and let him know that she and Ollie were OK, but she was too close now. To her left, her father was standing uselessly next to one of the young men who aspired to follow in his footsteps one day. In front of her, perhaps thirty metres away, was an older man. He was one of her father's friends. Then, from nowhere, another figure entered the scene, begging them to help with the fire.

It was just the distraction she needed. Sweet, innocent Jessica, who had been overlooked her whole life, had found just the right moment to act. There was a determination in her eyes that Helen had never seen before.

While all eyes were on Jessica, Helen crept silently from the tree line and circled behind the older gun man. She had never done anything like this before. How hard did it need to be? She wished she knew, but she never thought she'd have to do this, so there was no frame of reference. She was close now but still no one had seen her. For a moment, she wondered if she was invisible to them, or whether they just didn't see her as a threat.

All at once she was close enough. She raised the brick high above her head and with both hands swung it down against the back of his head. He crumpled to the ground silently. She had expected more impact, more noise, but he just melted away. As soon as contact had been made, she ran back towards the trees, holding her breath. A shot rang out close by and she waited for the impact, but none came.

CHAPTER 51

Rob had followed Saric's phone to the car park. As he pushed the door open, he saw a man a few years younger than him and an older couple walking out the front of the parking area. They seemed animated.

There was still no sign of Helen and Ollie. The original hit of adrenaline had seeped away a little, but he kept an otherworldly sense of focus. He felt no fear but remained cautious. He did not want an unnecessary confrontation to distract him from what he was doing.

He walked out into the space in front of him, between the vans. Satisfied there really was no one here, he decided to keep following the phone's signal. He pulled out the tablet, but the signal was gone. Saric's phone had finally run out of battery.

Rob thought of the younger man who had just headed towards the front entrance of the main building. *That must have been him*, he decided.

Before he could move, a loud group of men swung open the parking area's main doors. They shouted at each other to collect various things.

"Where's the rope? Get that."

"What the hell do we need that for?"

"Hurry up, if they can't get into the workshop, we're going to need this."

Rob slid quietly onto one knee between the vans. Six men. He fancied his chances of being able to run through them without being stopped, but if they did get him, even this pumped up they might stop him getting to Helen and Ollie. It was too risky. He held his position, his heart thumping in his chest.

It seemed like ages whilst the men collected whatever they thought would be useful, all the time screaming at each other and offering different suggestions. From the discussion, it was clear that many of the women had been cut off in the building, along with some of the children. The focus seemed to be on getting them out the window.

Had the fire spread so fast? he thought, but even as he thought it, he realised it wasn't surprising. As he had run past it, the chapel had been a raging inferno.

As he crouched out of sight, Helen's voice appeared in his head. He was completely unprepared for it. At some level, he knew, of course, that she was here and that he was hoping, expecting even, to see her again for the first time in five years. But to hear her actual voice right now seemed utterly bizarre. His mind finally caught up enough to realise that she was with Saric. She must be.

I can't make a sound right now, Helen, he silently told her.

Finally, after what seemed like an age, the men left the parking area.

Rob tapped his earpiece. "Helen, Helen, are you there? Helen? Saric? Is anyone there?"

There was no reply.

He ran to the exit. The men had taken what they had gathered to the east side of the main entrance, where another group had just set up a ladder and started helping the women and children out of the window and down to safety. Mick was with them, with Texas by his side.

If Helen was with Saric, she must be safe. Whoever the voice on the phone was, Rob was certain they would not pose a threat to his friend. He needed to get back to the Lodge. Despite the chaos, Rob would still prefer not to be seen. He plotted a route in his mind: across the courtyard, behind the outbuilding, through the trees and off by the side of the lake.

As he processed his thoughts, he noticed Mick had peeled away from the main group crowded around the burning building. The evacuation seemed to be working. It was slow with only one ladder, but people were getting out. But something had caught Mick's attention a few windows further down, in Rob's direction. He was gesturing to someone. Texas was barking now, reflecting the growing panic in his master.

Rob figured that before making his exit, he could get to Mick and let him know it was over without any real chance of being noticed. He paced towards him. As he got closer, it became clear that Mick was trying to communicate with someone.

"Mick, we're done. Saric's got Helen."

Mick did not appear to hear Rob's words. He remained focused on the second-floor window in front of him. Rob looked up.

"She was checking the other rooms and now she's trapped. I have to get up there."

Rob looked up. Julia was at the window, a look of panic and terror in her face. She was trying to explain something with hand gestures and even smiled to try and reassure Mick, but it didn't work. Suddenly, she turned around and disappeared.

Texas was jumping and barking furiously, desperate to do something.

"I have to get up there," Mick repeated. "Help me."

The situation hit Rob. He could feel the heat from the fire. He could see flames in the rooms below, where they were still getting people out. Smoke was leaking from the window Julia had just left.

"You can't go in there, Mick."

Mick looked at Rob as if he was completely insane. Julia reappeared at the window. She was coughing. She shook her head in a gesture that let them both know there was no way out.

"I'm sorry," she mouthed to Mick.

"No! No! No!" Mick launched himself towards the building. There was an old metal downpipe running down the wall next to where Julia was stuck. Mick tossed the gun he was still carrying from his shoulder to the floor. With surprising agility, he leapt high up the wall, gaining purchase on the downpipe with both hands. He wedged a foot between the pipe and the wall and managed to get his right hand to the first-floor window ledge. He hung there for a moment, every muscle strained, and his face red with effort. Without thinking, Rob followed him. He pulled himself up the same drainpipe using just his arms. As he reached Mick's ankles, he clamped his feet around the pipe, grabbed hold of Mick's leg and shunted him upwards. Mick used the momentum to position himself on the first-floor window ledge.

Seeing Mick was close enough to hear him, Julia leaned out the open window, coughed and then called to him, "Mick, I can feel the heat. Mick, Mick. Hurry, please."

Mick did not need Rob anymore. He raced up the remaining pipe like a wild animal, reached a hand across to Julia's ledge and pulled himself up into the room. Rob fell back to the floor and took a step backwards. The heat from the building was strong now. He looked up, desperate to see Mick coming back out with Julia. But they had disappeared from view.

Find a way out, Mick, come on.

To his left, the activity of the crowd seemed to have ended. The people were moving away from the building. Rob thought he heard a gunshot echo through the noise.

Come on Mick, Julia. Where are you? There is no more time.

The timbers of the lower floor were starting to give way. Flames jumped and swirled as they found new paths to consume the building.

Too late, Mick. Where are you?

Texas jumped up against the wall where he had watched his friend and master disappear. He barked frantically, begging Mick to return.

Just as Rob was about to lose hope, Mick appeared again with Julia in his arms. She looked like a doll. Mick's eyes were wide and there were flames behind him, around him. He looked down at Julia and with his large, rough hands touched her face with the soft tenderness of a man who has come to know love.

An enormous cracking noise filled the air as the timbers that had held the Community's building up for decades finally conceded to the destructive power of the fire. Rob watched as Mick and Julia fell from sight into the flames below. The whole side of the building collapsed.

A blast of intense heat hit Rob. Somewhere deep inside he realised this was going to hurt. But right now, he just turned and ran. Texas, escaping from the heat too, found herself at Rob's heel.

CHAPTER 52

While everyone else kept their eyes peeled on the woman pleading with the first gunman to join the evacuation party, Saric watched Helen slip quietly from the other side of the building carrying a brick. She raised her arms and brought the weight down against the back of a man's head. Saric was impressed by her bravery more than her style, but she was resourceful, and he admired that. More, though, he admired the determination on her face as she carried out her task. Even in all of this, which must have seemed so odd and chaotic to everyone else, she was thinking clearly.

It took the other men a full three seconds to notice what had happened and a further four staring at each other before they acted. It was sloppy; that kind of hesitation costs lives.

By the time gunman number one started to move across the scene towards the crumpled body of the man on the floor, Helen was almost back at the outbuilding. Saric tracked the gunman's movements with his weapon. Once he was safely away from the woman, he gently squeezed the trigger. A loud bang echoed across the courtyard and the running man fell to the ground, grasping his right shoulder.

Saric was satisfied. He was incapacitated for the purposes of the current scenario but would ultimately be fine.

Helen's father stared at him with confusion in his eyes. Saric's mind was clear. He aimed the gun squarely at the older man's chest and held it there. Even from ninety metres away, he could see the fear now. He waited. Eventually, the man shook his head slightly and turned away, walking slowly back to the main building, his head hanging low.

Saric looked behind him and found Helen staring at him. "Nice work," she said.

"Thanks, but it's me who should be thanking you. That could have ended badly."

She shrugged. "What now?"

"We get to the fence line. Rob will find us."

And so, the three figures made their way across the grounds and towards the Lodge. They walked quickly rather than ran and even risked a glance behind them from time to time.

At the fence line, Helen stood facing the property and took it all in. She had done this once before, walked out in the certain knowledge that she would never see this place again. And yet here she was. This time was different, though. This time she had her husband and a mad man on her side.

●

Rob kept running. He didn't know what else to do. All he knew was that he had to find Helen and Ollie and get as far away from here as possible.

He ran hard, wondering if he could outrun what he had just seen while deep down knowing that he could not.

●

Helen watched a figure running across the ground towards them. He was moving quickly and purposefully. Could this be the moment when five years of hope became reality?

But something wasn't right in the way the man was moving, or perhaps it was his shape. Helen wasn't sure. Maybe she wouldn't recognise him. Could he have changed that much? And what would he think of her? Instinctively, she moved her hand to her hair and tried to make it right. This wasn't how she had pictured this scene.

As the figure got closer, she realised her mistake; the man was shorter than Rob, and his hair was darker.

Daniel.

"It's him," she whispered to Saric.

Saric reached for his gun. Helen put her hand on his arm to stop him. He flinched slightly as she touched him but hesitated.

Daniel was out of breath, and by the time he arrived his face was redder and puffier than usual.

"I did it, my love, the Great Lord is pleased. He is waiting for us."

"Get away," Saric growled.

Daniel looked at the man in confusion, but without fear. Helen thought how this was all her fault. She had broken him. She had known what she was doing, and what it might do to him, and she had long ago reconciled this in her mind. But standing here in front of him, seeing what she had done to Daniel and all those other Community members now dragging loved ones from the flames, it felt different to how she had imagined it.

Daniel still hadn't moved.

Even though he was two feet away from her, Helen felt the tension in Saric's body. He was ready to strike. And she knew that Daniel would be dead.

She couldn't allow that. She had to keep talking. Maybe she could send Daniel on a path to recovery.

"Daniel, listen to me, the Great Mother who has brought you this far, must now leave you. You have done well. Now it is time to rebuild."

She paused, letting this idea sink in. She wanted to take his mind back to before they met. "The fire will allow you to emerge anew. As if this were all a dream, you will wake up now. Go back to be before the Great Mother."

He looked at her and she was reminded of how young he was. A child really. He hadn't stood a chance.

Slowly, she took his hands in hers. "Daniel, it is time for you to go now. To *wake up*."

Wordlessly, he turned and walked towards the lake. When he was halfway there, he fell to his knees and raised his face to the sky. He was too far away for Helen to hear the words, but she could see his lips moving. She hoped he was praying.

Another figure was running towards them now. This time she had no doubt. As he approached, she felt her heart beating hard in her chest. He was fast but it felt like he was moving in slow motion. When he was perhaps twenty metres away, he paused. He was bigger than she remembered, and he looked fitter, but his eyes were the same, and so was his smile.

He stared at her for what seemed like an eternity. She took in every part of him. And then he was running again and she was in his arms. He held her tight, and she buried her face in his chest. Tears flooded into her eyes. Neither of them could find any words. He kissed the top of her head, nestled his face in her hair and breathed deeply. She pulled him in even tighter.

Slowly they broke apart. He wasn't just here for her. Keeping one arm wrapped around her, he turned towards Ollie. The small boy was holding tightly onto Saric's hand and staring at Rob like he was a stranger.

CHAPTER 53

Anticipating a successful mission, Saric had worked through their return to the UK. The journey had been uneventful, albeit expensive. Rob and Helen had been inseparable the whole time.

Ollie found it harder.

Soon after getting out of the Community, he had looked up at his dad from under the safety of his mother's arms. Rob looked back, his eyes full of love.

"Isn't Daniel going to be my dad anymore?"

Helen looked at Rob. She asked for his trust with her eyes. "Daniel was never really going to be anything to us, Ollie. It was all pretend."

"Oh," Ollie replied. "Is this my real dad?"

"Yes, sweetheart, this is your real dad. He didn't know where we went, but he found us. That's because he always loved us – loved you."

Ollie turned his attention to the man in front of him. He didn't know this man's voice, but it was still soothing, still reassuring, as if it had always been with him.

413

"Daniel said he would look after me and mum. He is a very important man. Are you sure you can look after mum like he would have done?"

Rob leaned forward and took hold of Ollie's small hand. "Yes, my son, I am."

•

On the way down from Scotland, where they had landed on a private airstrip, Rob called his dad. "I'm sorry I've not been in touch for a while. I've been away with Saric."

"Are you alright, boy?"

"Yes, Dad, I'm alright. We all are."

"What do you mean? Who's we?"

"Dad, we found them. We found Helen and Ollie."

He heard his dad sit down and take a deep breath.

"Where are they now?" he asked.

"Dad, they are here with me, right now. We are coming home. With Saric. And a dog. Her name is Texas."

At the sound of her name, Texas, who was sitting upright in the front passenger seat, looked round at Rob, Helen and Ollie in the back.

"Son, can I talk to her, please?"

Rob passed the phone to his wife.

"Hello, Geoff."

"Helen, is that really you? Are you alright? Is Ollie with you?"

"Oh, Geoff, yes, we are here." She could not think of anything else to say. Hearing another voice from this life hit her hard. She really was back.

•

The path to the old cottage was more overgrown than Helen remembered, and the bright red door seemed somehow smaller. She had imagined this moment many times over the last five years; stepping back into their home, to be welcomed back with open arms by old friends and family. She had also imagined carrying on with her old job and working with her colleagues from the same office. She had not imagined feeling nervous, but as she walked up the gravel drive from the taxi, she realised she was apprehensive. She wasn't quite sure why; it was just some vague feeling that she could not quite name or place.

They had been apart for so long. She had changed, she knew that. She had done things that she wasn't sure she would ever be able to talk to Rob about, and she had hurt people and destroyed their lives. She could not tell Rob, but how could she keep it from him? How could she reconcile keeping another secret from him when even after the lies she had already told, he had travelled halfway across the world to save her?

She was comforted by Ollie at her side. He had been through this with her, and while he could not possibly understand all of it, it helped her to know that he was here. She worried about him, too, about the damage that had been done from his time in the Community. How could she ever make up for that? After everything he had experienced, would he ever be able to lead a normal life?

The sun was shining in the hallway, and she could see the dust floating idly in its rays. The door closed behind her, and she turned to Rob. He looked nervous too.

"Would you like tea?" He was already in the kitchen as he said it. There was no need to answer, she was back in England. Of course there would be tea. "Please, sit down, you must be tired."

He was making her feel like a guest in her own home. Maybe she was.

"You must be, too. It's been a long week." It didn't sound like enough. How should she thank him for what he had done? How could they even begin to discuss it? But how could they avoid it when it was present in their every word and thought?

"I'll go to the shop in a bit, I don't really have much in, and I'll need to get some stuff for Ollie, too. I'm sorry, I don't have much for kids."

"It's fine, there's plenty of time. Let's just have some . . ." She looked around and panic raced through her. Where was Ollie?

A moment later, she heard a muffled noise coming from the next room. She ran through full of fear that they were here again to take them. She burst through the open door, with Rob close behind her, and immediately stopped.

In front of them, Ollie was curled up on Rob's armchair. He was fast asleep, with a shaggy grey dog by his side.

EPILOGUE

To say thank you for resolving her situation, Hannah had invited Saric, Grace, Rob and Helen to dinner at her place. She was now the full legal owner of the lease on her shop and home. Seeing as he was tidying up that point, Lord Chandlerton had instructed his solicitors to regularise the historic planning position, too. For the first time, Hannah had all the right paperwork in place. She had never really worried about any of it before, but since it had been brought to her attention in such a threatening way, it was a great relief to be settled again.

Saric and Grace had arrived early on purpose; they wanted some advice.

Hannah was better at puddings than main meals, so Rose busied herself in the kitchen whilst Hannah, Grace and Saric sat around the dining table. Saric and Grace had missed each other more than either of them had expected. They sat close to each other and embraced the feeling of being looked after. Grace popped a lemon and basil marinaded olive into her mouth, as Saric explained what was on their mind.

"Overall, Hannah, we would have to say Rob's case has been resolved successfully," Saric began. Grace rolled her eyes and Hannah allowed

418

herself a little smile. Saric carried on. "I have to draw a case together before I can sign it off as complete. It's how Sense Check learns. You know it churns through a lot of data on any case, but on this one it's astronomical. Five years I've been turning this case over. Sense Check needs to reconcile what was and wasn't useful. Anyway, this only normally takes a couple of days at the most; Sense Check does a lot of it automatically. On this case, I've been at it solidly for a week."

Hannah interrupted him. "Have you not seen them since you got back?" She seemed concerned.

"Well, yes, I've popped round a couple of times just to look in on them."

"He's been round every day," Grace clarified.

"Good," said Hannah.

"The point is, I've not been doing any work other than this. On the way to finding Helen in this last phase, I've put a lot of information to one side and shelved anything that wasn't directly relevant. But now that the immediate danger has passed and I am looking back at all the information together, there are points of interest that I didn't notice before."

Saric took a deep breath through his nose. He looked solemn. "The thing is, Hannah, we're not really sure what Rob should know, what he needs to know, or what I should tell him."

Hannah said nothing for a moment. "Can't you just tell him the truth?"

"I'm not suggesting I lie to him, I just don't know how much truth to tell him."

"OK," said Hannah, "tell me what you are worried about."

Saric had already explained the events of the last few weeks to Hannah, so she knew how they had pieced it together, and about Julia and Mick and how they had helped them get to Helen.

"When we included every possible explanation for Helen's disappearance in the scope of the enquiry, I set up Sense Check to focus on questions about who was involved and where they might be. With those questions answered, I pointed it at the question of why then. Why come after Helen fourteen years after she had escaped? Sense Check has possibly the most efficient system in the world for finding people, and according to it, given that Helen kept off social media and they had the whole world to search and any possible name, the odds of finding Helen before she died were extremely small, maybe fewer than one per cent. This would obviously be influenced by how much money the Community could spend on detective services, but, well, you get the point. The more likely conclusion is that they knew where she went. Given what Helen has told us about the Community's arrangement with the town, much of which we had already determined, it seems Julia's postcard told them where she was within weeks of her escape.

"If they didn't come for her straightaway, we have to ask ourselves what changed. What sparked their interest in her? Helen has already told us that the Community was more interested in Ollie than in her. Sense Check has recreated a search based on the public online material available at that point in time. Rob and Helen were careful with social media, but you can't avoid leaving a trace altogether. If they had kept a track on her from the beginning, they would have known what name she was using, where she worked, where she had bought a house and when she got married. But none of that seems likely to be a trigger for their renewed interest."

Saric's face grew more serious. "Given they needed to take Helen and Ollie overseas, I estimate it would take somewhere between six months to a year to plan the extraction. Sense Check looked at that time point."

Saric took his phone out of his pocket and flicked open a picture. He showed it to Hannah. It was a photograph of Rob's dad sat on his sofa with small children around him. In his arms was baby Ollie, who was clutching Squashy Dog and gazing up at his granddad. It was a screenshot from an old Facebook post. The caption read 'Proud Grandad'. Standing behind the sofa was Rob, his brother, and his cousin. They were with their wives, including Helen. Everyone was smiling.

"I thought they didn't use social media," said Hannah.

"They didn't, and their family kept them off theirs, at least normally. This is the one that slipped through." Saric sighed. "Rob's dad, Geoff, posted it. It's the only one Sense Check found. He probably just had the settings wrong for a while. He doesn't even have a Facebook account anymore."

"And you are wondering whether to tell Rob that his father is most likely responsible for letting Helen's parents know they had a grandson?" Hannah said, setting down her wine glass carefully on the table in front of her.

"Yes, I think he should know, but Grace reckons he won't want to."

Hannah exchanged another look with Grace, smiling slightly as she did so. "Saric, the truth is important, we all know that, but it's not everything. What possible benefit could come from Rob knowing all of that? And what about Geoff? If you tell Rob, would you also tell his father? Would you have him know that he triggered the abduction of his own grandson? Or, if not, would you expect Rob to know but keep that from his own father?

"No, it might be the truth, but it's not necessary for him to know, and it's not kind to anyone to tell them."

Saric looked at Hannah for a long time. Grace had made arguments so similar that for a moment he wondered if they had discussed them in advance, but in the end, he knew that they hadn't. He also knew that he had to trust someone, and if he couldn't trust the two women sitting at the table with him now, then he didn't know who else he would turn to.

"There's something else, Hannah."

"Good grief, Saric. Go on."

"You know how Helen explained that she was right on the cusp of making her own escape when we got there. She told us that she had manipulated this man, Daniel, to help her. She didn't go into much detail.

"Well, Sense Check has reviewed the whole transcript of what was said into my phone after we gave it to Julia. The program is all over the place with some of what Helen said. Read this."

Saric pressed some buttons on his phone and passed it back to Hannah again.

It read: *"You know this is forbidden. This is the temptation. We knew we would face it and that you would be weak. You must be strong now, Martha, and I must lead you to be strong. The Great Lord will come to me tonight and I expect to be with the Great Mother when he appears. Now, you must wait in the car; I will be back in a few minutes. The Great Mother's instructions are very clear to me now. I expect you to be ready when I reach the car, this is very important."*

Saric explained: "Sense Check flagged this as a potentially verifiable assertion regarding the location of the Great Mother. You know how it can be overly literal at times. We know from Helen that in their religion – if that's what it is – the Great Mother is a sort of pseudo-Mary from the Christian Bible, blurred with other spiritual motherhood figures. So, why would he need to tell Helen about expecting her there, as if she's something she mustn't forget to pack? I think we maybe get the answer in this section. It was the last thing she said to him."

Saric flicked the screen onto another section of text: *"Daniel, listen to me, the Great Mother who has brought you this far, must now leave you. You have done well. Now it is time to rebuild. The fire will allow you to emerge anew. As if this were all a dream, you will wake up now. Go*

back to be before the Great Mother. Daniel, it is time for you to go now.
To wake up."

"Now, you know that Sense Check has to make certain grammatical assumptions when it translates spoken word," Saric said. "Well, if those grammar options could give different meanings, it flags it. Add one comma to that opening sentence and see what happens."

Saric scrolled down to the alternative sentence.

"Daniel, listen to me, the Great Mother, who has brought you this far, must now leave you."

Hannah looked unsure. "Are you saying that Helen was the Great Mother to this man?"

"Yes, that's exactly what I'm saying. I've been looking into hypnotic language. I think she has got right into this guy's mind. Look at that sentence: 'As if this were all a dream, you will wake up now.' The tense doesn't work. It's an instruction. They call it a post-hypnotic suggestion. She's telling him to wake up from some sort of trance she's put him in. Look, she repeats it. And here, 'Go back to be before the Great Mother.' When you first read that, you think she's telling him to go back to the Community, where he will find the Great Mother. But I don't think that's it at all. I think she wants him to go back in time, to before she became the Great Mother for him."

Saric paused to let Hannah take it in.

"I saw this man," he eventually continued. "He was a wreck. He set the place on fire because she told him too. I think she's probably destroyed him."

"I see," said Hannah. "Tell me, what would you have done if you were in that situation?"

"I would have walked out of the front door and dealt with anyone who tried to stop me in the way that they deserved."

Hannah nodded. "What about if you were a woman, without your considerable height and weight advantages, alone but for a toddler whom you had to protect? And what if instead of having the combat skills you had learned in the military, you understood how people's brains work? I mean really understood, and that you had spent your career learning how to influence that thinking, to reshape it? What would you have done then?"

Saric didn't respond.

"Saric, I don't know Helen well, so I can't tell you what to do here. If you believe there's a chance she might do something similar to Rob, or to Ollie, or that she is a danger to those around her, then you must tell him. There is no question of that.

"But if you think she did what she did as an act of survival, to protect herself and her child, then no, don't tell him. He doesn't need to know. Maybe one day Helen will share it with him, or perhaps she won't, but that should be her choice. She has had so little control over what has happened to her for such a long time. If you trust in her love for Rob, then don't presume to know what is best for them. They will find their own way through this."

A bell rang, and Hannah's big dog bounded towards the door. "I'll go," said Grace. She motioned to Hannah to stay in her seat and stepped towards the stairs to the ground floor of the shop.

"Thank you, Hannah, for everything," said Saric.

Hannah returned his smile. "It's me who should be thanking you, for all of this—" she gestured towards the house. "It's such a weight off my mind to know that we are safe."

"That's what I do, I was happy to help. What I meant was, thank you for showing me what matters. Sometimes I get so caught up in the case that I miss the things that you see."

Before Hannah could reply, Grace returned to the room, followed by a nervous looking Helen and a worried looking Rob. Hannah quickly stood up and greeted the new guests.

"Helen! How are you?" She hugged her, and they exchanged kisses as if they were old friends.

"I'm well, thank you, Hannah. Sorry we are late. Ollie got a bit upset at bedtime."

"Not at all, you are right on time, and—" her attention switched to Rob, who was standing as if he was Helen's shadow, "—it's so good to see you. Now, come in and get yourselves settled. What would you like to drink?"

A few minutes later, the five friends were sitting around the dining table. They had each offered Rose assistance in the kitchen, all of which had been politely declined with a: "You're here to enjoy yourselves, leave it to me."

After the opening pleasantries subsided, they all felt a brief sense of awkwardness as a silence took hold for a moment too long. They needed someone to think of somewhere to take the conversation.

"OK, Hannah, what's the best book in this bookshop?" asked Rob.

Hannah wrinkled up her nose, before giving a detailed and reasoned argument for how such a question could not possibly have any true meaning. And everyone at the table had a view to share. The evening had begun.

Printed in Great Britain
by Amazon